THE HONORABLE HAVELOCKE JAMES APPEARED TO HAVE EVERYTHING

He had a fortune beyond counting and a family name beyond reproach.

He had flawless good looks that were irresistibly complemented by the exquisite handiwork of the most elegant tailors in the realm.

He had as a fiancée the belle of society, Lady Antonia Burke, and as amorous amusement, the most captivating Cyprians in the city.

He had strength and skill that no man could best, and a heart that no woman could melt.

In short, he had so much as to leave Miss Phila Ainsley with very little reason for hope.

But when was love ever wise. . . ?

THE NONPAREIL

THE NONPAREIL

Dawn Lindsey

A SIGNET BOOK

NEW AMERICAN LIBRARY

NAL BOOKS ARE AVAILABLE AT QUANTITY DISCOUNTS WHEN USED
TO PROMOTE PRODUCTS OR SERVICES. FOR INFORMATION PLEASE
WRITE TO PREMIUM MARKETING DIVISION, NEW AMERICAN LIBRARY,
1633 BROADWAY, NEW YORK, NEW YORK 10019.

SIGNET TRADEMARK REG. U.S. PAT. OFF. AND FOREIGN COUNTRIES
REGISTERED TRADEMARK—MARCA REGISTRADA
HECHO EN CHICAGO, U.S.A.

SIGNET, SIGNET CLASSIC, MENTOR, PLUME, MERIDIAN AND NAL BOOKS
are published by New American Library,
1633 Broadway, New York, New York 10019

First Printing, February, 1986

1 2 3 4 5 6 7 8 9

PRINTED IN THE UNITED STATES OF AMERICA

1

The shabby house in Hanford Square was located in a far from fashionable district of London, a fact its occupants had belatedly discovered soon after their arrival from Somerset. It had been let sight unseen for six months, based upon the assurances of the house agents employed that it was exactly what the client was looking for, and indeed only available so late into the Season due to an unfortunate bereavement suffered in the family of the previous tenant.

This last fact, at least, might have been true, as they discovered for themselves when they tried hastily to make other arrangements. At that late date it seemed impossible to find anything not located in an even worse neighborhood, or, as Mrs. Coates said with unaccustomed bitterness, fit to house her cattle in at home.

"For if you ask me, if the previous tenant suffered a bereavement it was caused by someone looking under the dining room rug, as I did this morning. I nearly had a spasm myself. And as for remembering what this place cost your uncle, first to last, which is a thing I try not to do more than once or twice a day, since it only serves to make me remember how criminally we was taken in, well, all I can say is that it ought to have been located next to St. James Palace. Not that ordinarily we would begrudge the expense, as I hope you know, my dear. But when it comes to finding on top of everything else, as I did yesterday, that nobody remains in London past May—which I'm sure doesn't surprise me, for a nastier, dirtier place I've yet to see—then I don't mind admitting I'm thinking of packing it in and admitting defeat."

Since the trip had only been undertaken, at much expense and inconvenience, to provide her daughters a much-longed-for Season in London, her listener knew that this was an idle threat. Mrs. Coates was an indulgent mama, and possessed of

5

a far weaker will than either of her two eldest daughters, and in the end she was easily persuaded to vent her spleen by writing a long and extremely frank letter to the firm of Abley and Moffat, House Agents, concerning her intention of informing all her friends never to utilize such an unreliable and deceitful firm again.

It might be supposed that, having got their way, the eldest Misses Coates would have been content. But anyone supposing that did not know them very well. They had long ago gotten into the habit of speaking their minds without hesitation, and managed to quarrel just as bitterly in London as at home.

They were doing so over the breakfast table that morning. The eldest Miss Coates, an ethereal blond dressed that morning in celestial (and expensive) shades of blue, was saying in furious accents at jarring odds with her lovely face, "I declare, if it weren't for the dress having been ruined, I could almost *die* laughing at the thought of you in pink with your hair! Lord, I don't know where you get your awful taste from!"

Her sister, a lively red-head not her equal in beauty, but who looked to be rather more good-natured, ignored that and merely remarked placidly, "As a matter of fact, Mr. Terrell said I looked like an angel in it."

"Mr. Terrell!" repeated Lydia in accents of loathing. "I don't know why you even bothered to come to London! If that's all you were interested in, you might have stayed at home."

"Why, so I'm beginning to think," retorted Lettice. "If you ask me, we might all of us have remained at home, for all the good it's going to do us. At least I mean to enjoy myself while we're here."

"Take care you don't enjoy yourself too much! Even Mama would balk at bringing home too embarrassing a souvenir of your visit to London."

"Now girls!" objected their mama half-heartedly. "I won't have talk like that at the breakfast table. And I'm sure I've told you time out of mind not to go borrowing of each other's things. Not that it don't seem to me that sisters oughtn't to be able to share but so it is."

"Never mind the dress, Mama. Phila can mend it in a

trice," said Letty carelessly, "and anyway, that's not what she's mad about. She's just jealous because I went out last night and had a good time while she stayed at home."

"With Mr. Terrell and those awful Begleys of yours? Don't make me laugh! I'd sooner have stayed at home, than be reduced to meeting no one but exactly the same sort we might have met there."

Since the argument showed every sign of heating up again, Mrs. Coates could only be grateful for a diversion from an unexpected quarter. The fourth member of the breakfast party, who had taken no part in the conversation thus far, said in her calm way, "Oh yes! It's only the slightest of tears, as Lettice says, Aunt Chloe. I'm sure it will hardly show once it's been mended."

She was a shy-looking child, with a mop of unruly black curls and a pair of large, expressive gray eyes. She did not much resemble either of the other two young ladies, but since she was in fact no more than a distant relation it was not very surprising. Certainly in the company of her more beautiful and forceful cousins she had a habit of fading into the background.

Aunt Chloe's eyes softened as they rested upon her. "That's like you, Phila-love," she said kindly. "But it's not your place to be mending Lydia's gowns for her, and so I've told you."

"No it isn't!" muttered the fifth and final member of the party, with a fierce glare at her eldest sister. "Let her mend it herself if it's so important to her."

It was at that inopportune moment that a morning visitor was announced. Miss Prudence Coates blushed hotly and resumed her contemplation of her plate, and Phila could not quite manage to hide the glow that came into her eyes at the unexpected arrival of her brother. But since Mr. Derrick Ainsley, while a good-looking youth, betrayed no signs of admiring either of his cousins' charms, and was, unfortunately, quite as poor as his sister, neither of those young ladies showed any embarrassment at having been caught behaving in a manner that might have been thought beneath them.

It was left to Mrs. Coates, a hospitable and kindly woman, to beam fondly upon the newcomer and immediately dispatch the maid for a clean plate. "Well, isn't this pleasant?" she asked. "And I know one who'll think the sun has suddenly come out, I daresay!" As Phila blushed she added truthfully, "Not that I'd just as soon not have your brother find us behaving like fishwives, which I'm sure he must think! But then I daresay he must know what families are like."

Mr. Derrick Ainsley didn't, if it meant quarreling at the drop of a hat and making a real effort to do one's siblings an ill turn; but he obligingly took a chair and accepted a cup of tea, if not the enormous breakfast his hostess kindly urged on him, since she was convinced he could not be adequately fed in the lodgings he had taken.

It might have been thought that when his own mama had died some three years before a better solution could have been found than leaving his sister with distant relations until then wholly unknown to them. Derry did think it, for however kind, Mrs. Coates and her jovial husband had not the slightest pretensions to gentility, and though their fortune was considerable, it had been earned by Uncle Jos's going cheerfully everyday to his manufactory in Somerset.

To do her justice, Aunt Chloe had recognized the unsuitability herself when she had first proffered the invitation. "For Lord knows we're not quality, nor ever will be, despite of our being distantly related. But the thing is," she added in her usual blunt way, "I hope you know we'll be kind to her, and I don't know what else is to become of her, poor little thing."

Nor did Derry. Still at Cambridge himself, and overcome with both grief and horror at finding himself, unexpectedly, in sole charge of a sixteen-year-old girl, he had seemed to have no choice but to agree to the arrangement. None of their other relations had shown the slightest inclination to take on the care of a gently-bred and quite penniless orphan; and Derry had been wise enough to realize that nothing would be accomplished by quitting university, as had been his first intention, and trying to find employment that would support them both.

Fortunately, a small legacy left him by his maternal grandmother had enabled him to finish his education, and with the help of Uncle Jos he had been able to find a position in a solicitor's office that enabled him to remain close to his sister.

Since his ambition was to follow in his father's footsteps and embrace a military career, this could hardly be viewed as a wholly unmixed blessing. In fact, he had soon found the work tedious beyond compare, and could envision the years stretching out before him, each as depressing as the last.

It was then that fortune had at last taken a positive hand in his affairs. His eldest cousin had long had her sights set on a London Season, since she viewed it as the only proper venue for her beauty, and had at last succeeded in persuading her indulgent papa to give in to the scheme. At the same time, Derry himself came into an unexpected windfall in the guise of an inheritance left him by a forgotten great aunt. It was hardly a fortune, but it was enough to give him new hope that he might not waste the rest of his life searching out deeds and bills of sale in a dusty law office.

Naturally, Phila had been included in the proposed visit to London, for as Aunt Chloe confided to Derry in her frank way, "I won't disguise from you that we had her in mind as much as our own girls when we was at last brought to consent to the scheme. To my mind it don't do to wrap things up in clean linen, so I'll tell you to your head we've been troubled as what's to become of her. Aside from the fact she don't seem to shine in my girls' company, I'm sure neither of us would be happy to see her married to anyone she's likely to meet in Somerset. Now, you needn't blush and disclaim, my dear! I'm sure I'm not ashamed to admit to what I am, which is good yeoman stock, whatever may be Lydia's ambitions! And so, the long and the short of it is, we've made up our minds to go to London, and if you're agreeable, take Phila with us, for it's certain she's never likely to meet anyone suitable around here."

Derry might indeed be embarrassed by this outspokennesses, but it was impossible for him to deny the truth of what she said. It came as rather a shock to him to realize that Phila was old enough to be thinking of marriage, for he still thought of her as a child. But it took no reflection at all to realize that he had no desire for her to wed anyone within the Coateses' circle. He was therefore easily brought to consent to the scheme, and with little more difficulty to take a leave of absence from his solicitor's office to accompany them.

He had kindly been invited to make one of their lively household, but he had preferred to set himself up in modest bachelor lodgings where he could enjoy himself, and yet be close enough, he fondly imagined, to keep a close eye on his sister.

After that promising beginning, however, things had gone rapidly downhill. The house that had been let was found to be wholly unsuitable; and even worse, the acquaintance in Somerset who had boasted of her fashionable London relations was discovered to have been guilty of the grossest of exaggerations. Her sister might indeed reside on the fringes of the fashionable world, but she had so far shown herself wholly unwilling to foster the ambitions of ones she considered to be her social inferiors, especially since she had three daughters of her own to dispose of. In fact, it now had begun to look as if the whole journey had been made for nothing.

Aunt Chloe was kindly questioning Derry about his stay in London, but Lydia, bored with the turn the conversation had taken, interrupted her to say, "Never mind that, Mama! I need to know when Phila can mend my dress. I want to wear it this afternoon."

"Well, it's nothing to do with me," interjected Letty, "but Phila had far better come with me and Lizzie to go shopping. She can help me choose the ribbons for my new straw."

Priddy scowled once more, but Phila said hurriedly, "Oh, no, thank you! I promised Priddy I would take her to the Royal Academy this morning. But I can easily mend Lydia's gown before we go."

"Well, love, if you're sure," said her harried aunt. "Though I'm sure you'd enjoy yourself more going with Letty and her friend than trailing Priddy around some stuffy museum."

"Well, rather her than me," said Letty truthfully, jumping up. "I must run. I promised to meet Lizzie half an hour ago. And I daresay Phila would like a word with her brother without all of us around."

At this hint, Aunt Chloe hauled her own bulk to her feet, saying cheerfully that she must have a word with the cook anyway. But she lingered in the doorway after the others had gone. "In fact I'm wishful of having a word with your brother myself, now that Letty puts me in mind of it, my dear. I was wishing I had someone to advise me, for when it comes to learning, on top of everything else, that no one remains in London in the summer but Cits and mushrooms, which I'm sure is nothing to be surprised at, then I don't mind admitting I'm stumped. As Lettie says, we might as well have remained at home, which I'm beginning to wish we had done. And so I made up my mind to ask your brother's advice when next he should favor us with a visit.''

Derry had flushed and said uncomfortably, "Good Lord, ma'am, I'm the last one to advise you on such a subject!''

"Aye, but you're bound to know more than me. Letty told me she once saw you in the Park with what she termed a real Corinthian, whatever that may be, and I'm sure some of your fine friends must know. What I wish to find out is, whether we've thrown away our money and may just as well go home now as later, which I don't mind admitting I'm tempted to do, whatever the fuss Lydia kicks up.''

Derry's cheeks were by now very red, but he promised to make some inquiries. Aunt Chloe seemed satisfied with that, for she soon took herself off, again inviting Derry to take his potluck with them whenever he cared to, and kindly telling Phila that she was not to feel obliged to go with Priddy if her brother should be so kind as to invite her to go anywhere with him. "For Priddy can stay home for once, or I daresay I could take her, though I can't imagine what you find there to occupy yourself with, my dear, with nothing but a bunch of old paintings to stare at,'' she said frankly.

As Derry at last returned from holding the door for her he exclaimed involuntarily, "Good God, Phila, I don't know how you bear it! Are they always like that?''

Phila blushed a little. "Yes, but they don't mean anything by it.''

"I'll tell you something else, too,'' he added strongly. "If you ask me, Aunt Chloe has absolutely no control over any of you! That Lydia is a complete shrew, and Lettice seems to me to be as wild as bedamned. And as for the way they have you fetching and carrying for them . . .! 'No, Aunt Chloe, I like to mend Lydia's dress!' '' he mimicked unkindly. " 'Please let me take my cousin Priddy to the museum.' You let them impose upon you far too much!''

2

Derry's outburst had been instinctive, born as much out of his own guilt as his dislike of seeing his sister waiting on those he considered infinitely her inferior; but he regretted it almost as soon as the words were out of his mouth.

But Phila had stiffened, her usually gentle face taking on what he described as one of her mulish expressions. Generally she was the most biddable girl in the world, but she also had what he considered an absurdly tender heart, and could change in a flash when she saw what she perceived as ingratitude or injustice.

"And what am I supposed to do?" she asked irrefutably. "Refuse to do anything to help Aunt Chloe, when she has given me a home and treated me as one of her own daughters?"

Derry reddened. "No, but I won't have you behaving as an unpaid servant in the house either! Anyway, you know this arrangement is only a temporary one, until I—until I can get settled myself."

After a moment Phila agreed to it, if without enthusiasm, since she hated to quarrel. "Yes, never mind! Do you think Aunt Chloe has wasted her money in bringing the girls to London?"

She had gone automatically to begin stacking the breakfast dishes and he watched her in resentment, having to forcibly remind himself that in their own home she had frequently helped with the domestic chores. "Good God, *I* don't know! I'm not so sure it was a good idea anyway, after seeing this house, and the way our precious cousins carry on in London. And don't pretend to me you care whether Lydia succeeds or not in her ambitions, after the way she treats you."

Phila reddened, but said truthfully, after a moment. "No, but Aunt Chloe and Uncle Jos care, and after all the money they've spent it would be dreadful to see them disappointed."

"I tell you what it is, Phila," Derry said roundly. "You've

far too soft a heart for your own good! Next you'll be telling me you feel sorry for Priddy as well!''

"No, for Priddy doesn't need—at least—" She stopped as he burst out laughing. "Well, but how could I help but care, when they have been so kind to me?"

The memory of the reason for his own visit that morning made Derry's smile fade, and he said off-handedly, after a moment. "At any rate, I didn't come to argue with you. Do you know—I was wondering if Uncle Jos was planning on coming to Town anytime soon. He spoke of it before we left.''

"Uncle Jos?" she repeated in surprise. "I don't know. I rather think he's had to put off his visit for a few weeks. Why? Is something wrong?"

"No, of course not. I just wondered—" Abruptly his mask deserted him. "Oh God, Phila!" he said raggedly, "I had no right ripping up at you, especially when I've—and if Uncle Jos isn't coming, I don't know what I'll do!"

She was by now thoroughly alarmed, the dishes forgotten. "Derry! Oh Derry, what is it?"

He made an effort to pull himself together. "I didn't mean to tell you, except that if I can't come up with two hundred pounds in the next week or so, you'll have found out soon enough. The truth is, I'm ruined! Rolled up!"

"Derry!"

"I'm sorry," he said roughly. "I shouldn't have told you. Only—now that Mama's dead, we have to stick together."

"But how could you come to owe *two hundred pounds*?"

He tried to laugh, and failed miserably. "I've discovered it's fatally easy in London, my dear! If you must know, I lost it at faro. And you needn't look like that! I think it must have been the most miserable hour I've ever spent, so if I ever get out of this, I'm not likely to do it again anytime soon. There were men there that lost ten times that much that night. We'd gone to—well, never mind, but a hell someone knew of.'' He drew a ragged breath. "I know I shouldn't have gone, but I'd never seen one before, and I—I guess I was curious. After that, it seemed impossible not to play. You can imagine my shock when I discovered the minimum wager was fifty pounds. Before I knew it I'd lost the whole two hundred pounds. After that, I managed to mutter something about making banking arrangements out of town, and slunk away. I've never felt such a fool."

"But Derry, you can't ask Uncle Jos to lend you two hundred pounds!" She cried in dismay. "Not after all he's already done for us."

He flushed up again defensively. "Do you think I don't know that? But it's either that or debtors' prison." As he saw her face, he said more calmly, "I'm sorry, Phila, but you just don't understand! I don't like it any more than you do, especially—especially since it means the end of all hope that I'll ever escape from old Ligget's office. For of course I must pay Uncle Jos back, every penny, if it takes me the rest of my life. And it probably will," he ended gloomily.

"Oh, Derry." It seemed to her incredible that he could have risked his entire future for a few minutes' play at some hell, but she was wise enough to know that men looked at these things differently. But to ask Uncle Jos to pay Derry's gambling debts, on top of everything else, was wholly repugnant to her. "Your—your legacy?" she asked hesitantly.

"Spent! At least this quarter's. And they made it clear there would be no breaking the trust. Phila, I tell you, if Uncle Jos can't lend me the money I may as well put an end to my existence at once! Or else take the King's shilling, which I might as well do since there's now no hope of my ever being able to buy my commission," he ended, sunk in gloom once more.

She was deeply troubled, for of all his wild threats she thought it the most likely. She had dreaded for years learning that he had given up all hope and run away to enlist rather than spend another hour in the solicitor's office. But she still could not believe he meant to ruin his life for the sake of a mere gambling debt, and said so. "But surely if you just went to the man and explained . . . ?"

He laughed again, though hollowly. "I can just see myself going to Havelocke James and telling him I can't afford to pay him. Phila, he's one of the richest and most influential men in London! I might as well enlist if ever that story got around, for no regiment would have me."

"But if he's so rich . . . !"

"Phila, no! I keep telling you, you just don't understand. A man's gambling debts are—well, sacred. No matter what happens, I shall have to pay him. If Uncle Jos can't lend me the money—but that doesn't bear thinking of. And you needn't worry, for I'll pay him back, I promise you."

She thought that she would by far prefer to confront a dozen strangers rather than have to ask Uncle Jos for the money. It was not that he would begrudge it, though he would be disappointed to think Derry could have been so irresponsible. But she could not bear to have him think them grasping or ungrateful, after everything he had done for them.

But then she was aware that Derry, however he might chafe sometimes at the obligation they were under to the Coateses, had not been obliged, as she had, to live for three years on another person's charity. Knowing that the roof over her head, every bite of food she ate, and even the clothes on her back were due to someone else's kindness, had made her morbidly sensitive on the subject, she knew; to the point it sometimes seemed she must choke under the heavy sense of obligation she was under. It was why she leapt at any chance to be useful, since it made her feel in some small way that she was earning her keep; and why she accepted without complaint the spite of her older cousins, however often she might have cried herself to sleep in that first year.

But then no one, with the possible exception of Priddy, the only member of the Coates family she was at ease with, had any notion how she felt. Not even Derry. In the beginning it would only have made him feel more guilty, since he could not support her himself. And now, though it angered her sometimes to hear him object to her fetching and carrying for her cousins, it would serve no purpose for him to know how unhappy she was, since as far as she could tell there was no hope of any change.

But it made her persist now, in the face of Derry's obvious irritation, "But Derry, if he's as rich as you say, surely he would not wish you to ruin yourself over a mere gambling debt!"

"Mere! Phila, you don't understand, and it does no good to talk of it. I tell you, if such a tale were to get around I'd be ruined anyway. A man may welsh on his tailor sooner than a debt of honor. And the hell we went to was not an ordinary one. It's run by a few of the big men—Alvanley, James and the like—none of your riffraff, and no house holding the bank! James is one of the leaders of the ton. They even call him the Nonpareil, because he's a top-sawyer, and first at all manner of sport and—oh, you wouldn't understand, but you may take it from me I'd sooner go to the Jews than ask him to let me pay it out. I shall have to go to him, of course, to explain about the delay, and that will be hard enough, God knows!''

She did not begin to understand a masculine code that said gambling debts had precedence over one's legitimate bills, and one might borrow money from a man who had been too generous already, but not from a perfect stranger, but she was wise enough to say no more. Nor did Derry remain much longer, saying he must go and write to Uncle Jos, and hope that the post would reach him by the end of the week, though it would be dashed awkward. If Uncle Jos—but there was no point in talking about that, after all. In the meantime, she was not to worry.

This last request was, of course, impossible for her to obey. Nor could she resist asking, when alone with Priddy later, ''If—if someone you loved were in trouble, and you *knew* what ought to be done, only he—they!—won't listen to you, what should you do?''

Priddy was sprawled inelegantly on her bed, her nose buried in a book, but she looked up at that with interest. She was a serious, awkward child, with none of her sisters' promise of beauty. Nor did she have any patience for polite fiction. ''Why?'' she asked bluntly. ''Is your brother in trouble?''

''Yes—no! I can't tell you! Oh, but Priddy, I *know* what ought to be done!''

''Well, if it was one of my sisters, I wouldn't lift a finger to help them,'' said Priddy frankly. ''It makes me sick the way they order you about.''

''Yes, but I could have kicked you this morning for springing to my defense! In the first place, I don't mind mending Lydia's gown, and in the second, it only makes matters worse and you know I can't abide quarreling!''

''Then you shouldn't be living here,'' said Priddy with mordant humor. ''If you'd only stand up to them once in a while they wouldn't act that way.''

''No, if I stood up to them it would only make Aunt Chloe

uncomfortable," said Phila inarguably. "And I don't mind helping. It—it makes me feel a little as if I'm earning my keep."

When Priddy made a disgusted noise at that, Phila added, with unexpected humor, "Anyway, my brother says the same thing about you. And if it comes to it, I'd far rather mend Lydia's dress than spend hours waiting for you in some stuffy museum. That I find even more boring, since you tend to forget my presence for whole hours at a time, and cause me to be in disgrace with Aunt Chloe by refusing to come away until your sketch is finished and we're late for dinner."

When Priddy merely grinned and returned to her book, Phila said, reverting to her main worry, "If one wants to know where a—where a gentleman lives, how does one find out?"

Priddy glanced up again curiously. "I don't know. There's a book, I suppose. What are you going to do?"

"I can't sit around and let Derry ruin his life all because of—of some absurd rules! If one wanted such a book, where would one find it?"

"There may be one in the library downstairs, though it looks as if no one's been in there in years. Is your brother about to ruin his life?"

"Yes—no! Oh, Priddy, don't ask," said Phila guiltily. "Let's go and look at once."

Priddy looked even more curious, but obediently got up and led the way downstairs. "If you mean really a gentleman, I know there's a book, for Papa showed it to me one time." She said helpfully, "It has all the nobility and people like that in it."

"Well, he doesn't have a title, but Derry said he was very important, so I daresay he'd be in it. Oh, hurry! I still have to mend Lydia's gown."

After some time Priddy managed to unearth a dusty copy of *The Peerage*, stuck carelessly on the top shelf between someone's travel journals. She clapped the covers together energetically, while Phila rose from her cramped position on the floor where she had been sorting through a hopeless mishmash of sporting tomes and old periodicals, coughing and begging Priddy not to stir up any more dust.

Priddy proudly bore her prize to the scarred table and

began to inspect it with some interest. "Listen to this, Phila! It tells you all about how to address the King, and what to wear to Court. I should show this to Lydia." Abruptly, she began to giggle. "Oh, but wouldn't I like to see her rigged out like that!"

Phila came to look at an engraving showing a fashionably willowy lady decked out in side hoops and tight lacing, with strings of huge pearls and knots of ribbon covering every inch of her low décolletage, and at least a dozen waving plumes in her high-dressed hair. "Yes, but perhaps it's out of date," she suggested doubtfully. "I can't believe they dress like that, even to go to Court."

"If you ask me, it's no sillier than any other fashion. Let's see if the man you want is in here. What's his name?"

"James. Yes, I'm sure that's it. Havelocke James."

She peered over Priddy's shoulder while she thumbed through the pages. "Jackson—Jaffrey—James! Here it is! The Honorable Havelocke James, brother to—never mind that! Principal seat at Jameson Priory located in Kent, a mansion of some antiquity—never mind that either!—also has estates in Yorkshire, Devonshire, and Sussex. Known for his philanthropic interests . . . Once owned the fabled race horse Gypsy that won the Derby four times running . . . Member of White's, Brook's, etc., etc., attended Eton and Oxford—oh, here it is at last! Has his Town residence at Number 20 South Audley Street."

"Number 20 South Audley Street," repeated Phila, committing it to memory. "Oh, thank goodness!"

"Yes, but what are you going to do? If you ask me, he sounds awfully grand. And it says that he was born in 1750, which makes him well over sixty."

"Yes, but that isn't old," pointed out Phila. "And I can't help thinking it will make it—easier if he is older and—and fatherly."

"It probably only means he suffers from the gout and is ill-tempered. You're not going to go see him, are you?"

Phila flushed a little guiltily. "Yes. I can't explain—at least not now—but I told you I knew what ought to be done. I don't like to ask you to lie to Aunt Chloe for me, but I can go and come back while you're sketching. It won't take very long—at least I hope not—and I'll be back to escort you home, I promise."

"That's all right, silly. I can get home by myself, and Mama doesn't matter. But I can't help thinking it's a mistake. You don't know anything about this man, after all."

"I'm sure he must be respectable. Derry said he was a leader of the 'ton'." Then her small face grew unexpectedly determined. "And anyway, it doesn't matter! The most he can do is refuse to see me. And I *can't* let Derry ruin his future or—or ask anything more of Uncle Jos without at least attempting to prevent it."

3

Priddy looked a little impressed, despite herself, and said no more. She did, however, after looking Phila over critically, voice an unexpected objection. "Are you going to wear that dress?"

Phila looked down a little self-consciously at her serviceable muslin. "Yes. Why?"

"Because if he is as old as you say, you'll stand a better chance wearing your prettiest dress. You know how all Papa's friends make fools of themselves hanging over Lydia and Lettice, and pinching their cheeks and calling them their pretty pusses. It's disgusting, but you might as well take advantage of it."

"Yes, but I'm not nearly pretty enough," pointed out Phila, blushing.

"Yes, you are. If you ask me, you're far prettier than either of my sisters. You just don't make enough of yourself."

Phila blushed again, but had to laugh. "And I like your looks far better than Lydia's pink and white prettiness." But she obediently went up to change her gown, followed by her self-appointed advisor.

Priddy looked her few dresses over critically and voted in favor of a soft yellow muslin Aunt Chloe had insisted on

bestowing upon Phila for their trip to London. While Phila
pulled off the old one and struggled with hooks, Priddy added
in the voice of one resigned, "And whatever you do, don't
let him frighten you. You will, though. You never stand up to
anyone."

"Yes, I do!" objected Phila from the folds of her dress. "I
just don't like—brangling."

"No, you don't. But then perhaps he'll be out of town, and
nothing will come of it," said Priddy pessimistically.

The Honorable Havelocke James was not out of town,
though he had spent the previous week at Newmarket, and
certainly planned to attend the Derby later in the month, as he
did every year.

He was, in fact, dressing for the day, having been out
particularly late the night before, and only risen at an hour
that would have made Priddy stare. He was not one of those
men who never emerge from their bedchambers before noon,
or spend several hours over the arrangement of their neckcloth; but the results he achieved were invariably elegant, and
merited the high wage he paid to his valet.

He might have been shocked to discover that that same
valet would have settled for far less in order to remain in the
employ of one who, aside from having been blessed with
birth and fortune and a figure that required no artifice to pad
out a narrow shoulder or an inadequate thigh, and a handsome, if remote countenance dominated by a pair of sometimes overly-shrewd gray eyes, was possessed as well of that
even rarer attribute: a pleasant manner toward his servants.
He might, on occasion, dress an errant dependent down in a
manner icy enough to make the miscreant tremble in his
shoes, but for the most part his temper was even, his de-
mands not unreasonable, and though he expected a high level
of service, he was willing to pay accordingly and never failed
to reward one with his absent smile. Add to that the fact that
he rarely kept his servants up to all hours of the night waiting
for him, or returned in a state that required him to be put to
bed by the boots and his valet, and it was perhaps understand-
able why, in the opinion of most of his staff, he came close to
being the ideal employer.

Nims, patiently handing him his neckcloth and waiting to

hand him into his coat, observed his handsome profile and could not help thinking his master was looking preoccupied over something. It was nothing you could put your finger on, but of late he had seemed more absent than usual, a faint, dissatisfied frown between his brows when he thought no one was looking, and a certain weariness in his manner. But since it did not affect his usual manner in dealing with his servants, and he went about his engagements as always, Nims dismissed it as being none of his business.

Mr. James's secretary, Mr. Charles Shelby, had also noticed the change, but was able to put his finger more nearly on the cause. In fact, he suspected his employer was merely bored. At thirty-one courted, flattered, and with enough money to indulge his every whim, there was very little Mr. James could not have if he desired it. His life was well ordered, he did exactly what he pleased, with enough good friends to provide him companionship when he wished it, without being thrust into unwanted intimacy when he didn't. Nor did he lack for feminine companionship. Over the years Mr. Shelby had been aware of at least two high-flyers in his employer's keeping, and he was a prize catch on the Marriage Mart, with half the most beautiful young ladies every Season setting their caps at him.

That he did not pick up any of these, Charles knew, was generally attributed to the fact that he had never gotten over his first, tragic love. But his secretary was unable to detect in him any signs of a broken heart. Charles even wondered sometimes, guiltily, if his employer possessed a heart at all. He contributed to a great many charities, as his father had done before him, but out of a sense of duty rather than any genuine love for his fellow men. He possessed a great many friends and a mother and sister who both adored him, in their own, widely different ways; but Charles had yet to see anyone break past that faint, impeccably-mannered screen his employer put up around himself. It was as if nothing ever quite touched him, neither joy nor sorrow nor great anger or great happiness, or any completely human emotion.

Havelocke James, though he would have been a little startled by this unexpectedly acute assessment, would not have disagreed with it. He was indeed bored, though he could not have said why, or when he had been first aware of a feeling of vague discontent.

He was aware it was popularly believed his heart was in the grave, but even Caroline's tragic death had not affected him as it should have. Theirs had been a storybook romance. She had been the Toast of London, and he a prize catch. Whatever had been his mother's feelings on the subject of their engagement, and these were almost always obscure, the world had been thrown into raptures.

Nothing, it had seemed, stood in the way of a perfect fictional ending, except that the beauty was not only tempestuous but willful and spoiled, and he had been far too young to handle her. They had quarreled, almost incessantly. Twice the engagement was called off, and then resumed in a flood of tears. If it had occurred to either of them that this was scarcely a felicitous prelude to wedded bliss, they had succeeded in ignoring such unpleasant reality.

Then only a month before the wedding they had quarreled one last time, over a new pair of matched bays he had just purchased. He had then been in his first heady—and mistaken— conceit that he was awake on every suit, quite top of the trees, and the pair were ugly brutes, still only half broken and wholly unsuitable for a lady to handle. He had made the mistake of telling Caroline so, probably in superior terms. She had cajoled, then threatened, and ended by taking them out without his permission and breaking her neck.

He had sold the pair for a ridiculous sum and dismissed the groom who had had them poled up for her without his permission, but even in his first grief and guilt he had been aware of a curious relief. Nor could he have the animals destroyed, as his critics said he should have. The fault had lain rather with him and her, and with the indulgent parents who had petted and spoiled her from the hour of her birth. Instead, he had shut up his town house and gone abroad.

He had returned with a new cynicism, and a determination never again to risk his own and someone else's happiness by indulging in such high flights of passion. If the world believed his heart buried in the grave with Caroline, he was cynically aware that it had not taken many months before he had trouble even in conjuring up her face, and that his grief had more to do with shock and guilt than a broken heart.

However that might be, the world continued to believe what it chose, particularly when he showed no signs of settling on any of the young beauties paraded for his notice year after year. It began to be said that he might never marry, or, when he did, it would be for convenience this time, unlike the first. The most popular candidate was the somewhat scandalous Lady Antonia Burke. They had known each other all their lives, it would be an excellent match for both, and neither were obviously looking for high romance.

The Nonpareil was certainly aware of these rumors, and was in no hurry to dispel them, since they afforded him a measure of protection. Nor was he in any hurry to fulfill them. He was aware Tony would make him an excellent wife, but such a marriage would be perilously close to admitting that life held no surprises for him any longer. And he was not quite ready to admit that yet.

And so he went on, his vague dissatisfaction not enough to make him contemplate altering his present pleasant life, but enough to make him wonder if something were not missing, and that there should be more, somehow.

In fact, life held so few surprises for him that when he was interrupted by his secretary, he said merely, in some amusement, "Come in, Charles, and stop looking so guilty! Unless, of course, you have come to put me in mind of an unpleasant duty I have forgotten, in which case I should warn you that I am in no mood for duty today."

Charles Shelby, a pleasant-faced young man with a rather shy smile, laughed at that. "No, sir. At least, I hope you won't think it unpleasant. I'm sorry to disturb you, but the thing is, there's a young lady below who wishes to speak with you."

"A young *lady*, did you say?" repeated his employer in astonishment. "And wipe that smirk off your face, Nims! I can assure you, any sowing of wild oats of mine was a very long time ago. Unless, of course, she is a *very* young lady?"

Charles blushed, but shook his head. "No, of course not, sir! That is, I daresay she is very young, but I hope you know if I had any suspicion it was anything like that I would never have troubled you."

The valet, who had ignored the unjust aspersion on his character, calmly handed his employer into his coat. "I'm relieved to hear it," remarked the latter, adjusting a cuff and removing a minute speck from one sleeve. He regarded himself in the mirror for a moment, then nodded. "Thank you, Nims. That will be all. How, by the way, Charles, is it that you come to be employed in announcing visitors to me? I certainly was under the impression I had a butler and far too many footmen who might have been better suited to the task."

Nims had removed the unused cravats and bowed himself out. The secretary hesitated, obviously in some embarrassment. "Yes, sir. Only I happened to be passing, and West asked me to speak with the young lady. I don't think he knew quite what to do with her."

"You alarm me! Ten to one she *is* dirty linen, or else has come to persuade me to subscribe my name for a set of novels, handsomely bound in marbleboard. And to think that only recently I was lamenting that nothing out of the ordinary ever happened to me."

Charles laughed. "I don't think it's either one of those, sir."

"Ah," said his employer, regarding him with amusement. "*Very* pretty! Clearly I must lose no time in meeting this vision for myself. What's her name, by the way?"

There was a moment of stunned silence. "Oh, Lord!" said Mr. Shelby ruefully. "I forgot to ask her!"

"Good God, let us waste no more time in going down to see this Circe of yours."

If he was amused at his usually reliable secretary's uncharacteristic lapse, he was certainly unprepared, when he had made his leisurely way downstairs to find waiting for him in his bookroom not the sophisticated beauty he had been expecting but a shy girl with a mop of unruly curls sitting nervously on the edge of a chair.

She looked around as he came in and her eyes, her most expressive feature, grew round with astonishment. "Oh, are you—that is, you can't be—"

She broke off then in embarrassment. The Nonpareil was amused despite himself, but he thought he must certainly have a word with Charles after this. If he had not suspected dirty linen, and though the child was obviously gently-bred, there was no trace of any escort, which strongly suggested she had come out without permission, he was certainly aware that very young ladies ranked high on his employer's list of those to be avoided.

But since there was no help for it, he advanced into the room and said politely, "Yes? You wished to speak with me, I believe?"

"Oh, *no!*" she blurted. Sudden doubt made her add, "That is—surely *you* cannot be Mr. Havelocke James!"

He was even more amused. "I'm afraid so," he said sympathetically.

"But—but you're not sixty!"

His lips twitched. "Ah, at a guess, I would say you are confusing me with my father, whose name I share. Unfortunately I hope you haven't come to see him, since he has been dead for many years."

She digested this. "Oh, dear! I'm not—I'm not making a very good beginning, I'm afraid. The thing is—we looked you up in a book before I came. But I daresay it was a very *old* book, for I thought the dress out of date."

"Very likely." He came and sat down. He was still aware of the impropriety, but he had never been able to resist the ridiculous, and this absurd child rather amused him. "But now that we have straightened that out, you still have the advantage of me, you know. You know my name, but I don't yet know yours, since my secretary rather unaccountably forgot to get it from you."

Phila blushed. Her determination had sustained her through the act of hailing a cab and being driven to what even she recognized as a very fashionable neighborhood, and even through confronting a forbidding-looking butler who had listened to her stammered business with every indication of disapproval and contempt. Fortunately, she had then been rescued by a kindly young man who had promised to speak to his employer for her. But the subsequent discovery that in place of the fatherly figure she had been expecting, Mr. Havelocke James was a much younger gentleman with a cool, handsome countenance and an undoubtedly fashionable air put her errand in a very different light, even in her own eyes.

But it was too late to withdraw now, so she said a little defiantly, "It's—it's Phila—that is, Philadelphia Ainsley!

And I didn't give it to your secretary, for fear you wouldn't see me.''

"Then you were mistaken, for I've never known anyone called Philadelphia before. Is your father a Quaker?''

"No. Oh, no. No, of course not!'' She had expected him to recognize the name but he gave no sign of it. "He was a soldier.''

"Then he certainly could not have been a Quaker,'' he agreed. "How did you come by such an unusual name?''

"My father had a sister who lived in Philadelphia. In America, you know. She sent such a handsome christening gift that Papa said—said that I should have to be named Philadelphia. He was always joking that way, but mostly I don't mind it, and everyone calls me Phila. But that's not why I didn't give your secretary my name,'' she added, burning her boats. "I'm afraid my—my brother owes you two hundred pounds!''

His brows rose and she thought he stiffened a little, but after a moment he said merely, "I see. Am I to understand he asked you to come and see me?''

"No! Oh, no!'' she cried in sudden horror. "He doesn't even know I'm here! But it seemed to me preferable to—to risk coming and trying to explain to you than borrowing the money from Uncle Jos, after all he's already done for us, and taking the rest of Derry's life to repay a sum that very likely you would never even notice!''

His expression thawed slightly. "Very likely,'' he agreed ruefully. "But I don't usually make it a habit to win large sums off impecunious youths. I'm afraid you have had a wasted journey, for I never intended to hold your brother to his debt.''

She stared at him, relief overcoming the last of her embarrassment. "You didn't? Oh—oh I *knew* it could not be right for him to ruin his life for the sake of a mere gambling debt! Oh, how *thankful* I am I plucked up the courage to come here!''

He smiled, aware he ought to bring this unconventional interview to an end before he was embroiled in exactly the sort of entanglement he most deplored. Instead he asked sympathetically, "Was your brother likely to ruin himself over two hundred pounds?''

"Yes! That is, he meant to ask Uncle Jos for the money, which I couldn't bear, and it would have put an end to his military ambitions, for it would have taken him *years* to pay him back from his wages in Mr. Ligget's office. And I've been so afraid that if he really got desperate enough, he would take the King's shilling after all, despite what he says."

"No, he mustn't be allowed to do that. Who is Uncle Jos, by the way?"

"Josiah Coates. I've lived with him and Aunt Chloe ever since my mother died three years ago." She blushed a little painfully. "They're not really my aunt and uncle, but they were kind enough to offer me a home."

"And does—er—Derry also make his home with them?"

"Oh, no. He was up at Cambridge at first, and then when he came down, Uncle Jos found him the position in a solicitor's office. It was very kind of him, but Derry hates it; which is what made it so very hard for him to think he would never escape now, and all for a mere gambling debt."

"Yes, if he means to be a soldier it would be hard to be stuck in a solicitor's office," agreed the Nonpareil. "Do I take it Papa is no longer living either?"

"No. He died at Talavera," she said with some difficulty. "And whatever people may say, he was a hero and it doesn't matter if he died before he could make—make proper provisions for us."

"You must be very proud of him," he said gently. "If it is any comfort to you, I and a great many others have long thought it criminal the way our government has abandoned the families of its heroes."

"Yes," she said practically. "But it doesn't help much when you are forced to live on another person's charity, however kindly given."

He read far more into what she didn't say than what she did and said sympathetically, "In fact, it would be easier to bear if it were not so kindly given, for then you might be justified in resenting your benefactor instead of being obliged to be forever grateful."

"Oh yes! How did you know? In fact it sometimes seems as if I cannot *bear* to be grateful any longer!"

"My dear, just because I have never been unfortunate

enough to be poor does not mean I cannot place myself in your position, and strongly sympathize with you. And I have been long aware that gratitude is the very devil.''

"Yes, for however much you try you cannot always be grateful,'' she admitted gloomily. "I sometimes find myself almost *resenting* their kindness. And it seems as if I shall never manage to get out from it, but shall be weighted down with it for the rest of my life!''

"You poor child! I take it Derry does not understand?''

She flushed. "No, but then he has never been forced to live with it, as I have,'' she said truthfully. "I can't blame him. Anyway, I know I refine too much upon it, and generally I try to be sensible.''

He thought that was one of the saddest things he had ever heard. He did not have to be poor himself to imagine the slights she must have to endure, real or otherwise, and the humiliation of knowing herself the poor relation, welcome only out of duty and as long as she remained pleasant and useful.

He remembered her brother as an extremely callow youth and imagined she would not get much help from that quarter. He had recognized at a glance that he was out of his depth, and would have had him ejected if it had been possible without fatally wounding his and his youthful companions' pride. As it was, he had never had any intentions of accepting his money, as he had meant to tell him when he came to redeem his vouchers.

He said gently now, "I think you *do* refine too much upon it, my dear, but you have my sympathy. You—''

He was interrupted. There was a knock at the door and his butler came in, stiff with disapproval. "I beg your pardon, sir, but I thought I ought to remind you that you were due at Sir Adrian's fifteen minutes ago.''

Mr. James was annoyed, but he saw at a glance that his absurd young guest's confidences were at an end. She had flushed up self-consciously and begun to pull on her gloves, saying nervously, "Yes, I must go! Priddy will be wondering what has become of me!''

"Very well, West, thank you. Ask Mr. Shelby to join us if he is still in the house. I would like him to escort Miss—er—

Ainsley home. And have one of my carriages sent around. You may go now."

After the butler had disapprovingly bowed himself out, she said quickly, "That won't be necessary! I came in a cab, and I have to meet my youngest cousin at the Royal Academy. I never thanked you either, and I do! You can't know how much."

"You have nothing to thank me for, Miss Ainsley," he said truthfully. "I told you I never had any intention of accepting your brother's money. But I'm afraid that brings us to an unpleasant subject. I may not be my own father, but I regret that I am almost old enough to be your father, and as such I must tell you that what you did today may have been well-intentioned, but it was very dangerous. After all, you knew nothing about me before you came. The risk you ran was far more dangerous than your brother's losing two hundred pounds he could not afford to repay."

She hung her curly head so abjectly that he had to make an effort to maintain a straight face, aware of the incongruity of his preaching propriety. "Needless to say, no one shall learn of your visit from me or my staff, but at the very least you risked your reputation by coming here, and that was very foolish. Now we will say no more about it. Send your brother to me and perhaps I can make him understand that more than his own happiness was at stake by his actions. He has a very loving sister who depends upon him more than he knows. I hope, by the way, that he is properly appreciative of that fact, but human nature being what it is, I take leave to doubt it."

"Yes," she managed, scarlet by now. "And you are not old enough to be my father, for I'm nineteen, though I don't look it."

He was surprised, for she did indeed look younger. But there was time for no more. Charles came in then, with his shy smile, and expressed delight at the opportunity of escorting Miss Ainsley home.

The Nonpareil himself escorted her out to his waiting carriage, and put her in it. "Good-bye, Miss Ainsley. Don't forget to send your brother to me, and try to remember that however desirable a warm heart may be, it is best tempered with a little wisdom."

She managed a shy reply, the door was shut, and he turned

to find the critical eye of his butler on him, still waiting on the step. "That will be all, West. I shall walk. I need hardly remind you, I'm sure, that the young lady's visit is not to be spoken of."

"No, sir," said the butler disapprovingly.

"I shall doubtless shortly be receiving a visit from the young lady's brother. You will admit him, and may be as starched up as you please, since I am desirous of teaching him a lesson. In the meantime, you may relieve me of your Friday-face, since I have no intention of limiting my visitors to suit my butler. I shall probably be out late."

The butler bowed frigidly and withdrew.

Much later that same evening, Mr. Shelby was sitting before a small fire in the bookroom reading, when his employer strolled in.

"Still up, Charles?" he inquired pleasantly, going to pour himself a glass of brandy. "Did you escort Miss Ainsley home safely?"

Charles put down his book. "No, sir. That is, she wouldn't let me. Apparently her young cousin was waiting for her at the Royal Academy. I naturally offered to go in and find her cousin, but she—Miss Ainsley—seemed to think her aunt would become suspicious if they came home in a strange carriage."

He was extremely curious as to what his employer had made of Miss Ainsley, and aware that he had erred in allowing chivalry to overcome his usual sense of duty. He added, a little self-consciously, "I am sorry if you did not quite like it, sir, but she was so very determined, and at the same time so—so—"

"You needn't say anything more!" said his employer. "No more than you did I find myself able to snub the youthful Miss Ainsley. I hope I shall not come to regret it. But in fact I already do, since I collect I am shortly to receive a visit from her equally youthful brother."

"Her brother, sir? Is that what she came about?"

"Yes, it appears he owes me two hundred pounds, though I must confess the matter had slipped my mind. She informed me that she saw no reason why her brother should ruin himself over a sum that very likely I wouldn't even notice, which is why she steeled herself to come here.''

Mr. Shelby struggled with himself. "G-good Lord! I mean—I mean, of course she shouldn't have done it, but—well, it required a good deal of courage.''

"On the contrary,'' said his employer. "She also informed me that she thought it far preferable to brave me in my den than be required to borrow such a sum from the uncle who has already been so kind to them.''

Mr. Shelby lost the unequal struggle. "I'm sorry, sir! But it *is* funny. You must know most people are terrified of you!''

"Yes, but she thought I was my father, which must account for it.'' He yawned and finished his brandy. "In fact, I gathered the distinct impression Miss Ainsley counts no sacrifice too great in defense of her brother. It is now my unpleasant duty, clearly, to try to bring him to a sense of his responsibilities. And to think that only this morning I was complaining that my life had become drearily predictable.''

4

Phila may not have wanted to alert Aunt Chloe to her afternoon's activities, but the main reason she had refused Mr. Shelby's escort was that she was anxious to go at once and tell Derry the news before he could write to Uncle Jos.

But when she dragged Priddy to her brother's lodgings in Duke Street, it was to find that he was out, and his landlady had no idea when he was returning.

In the end, she had no choice but to dash off a quick note under the landlady's unfriendly eye, nibbling her pen and at last contenting herself with saying that it was *urgent* (underlined) that she see him immediately. She would be at home the rest of the day and in the morning. In the meantime, he was *not* (even more heavily underlined) to write to Uncle Jos until he had spoken with her.

She waited on pins and needles all evening to hear his knock on the door, but either his landlady had not condescended to give him her note as she had promised, or he had not come home before going out for the evening, for by bedtime he had not come.

She feared any delay made it more likely that he would already have written to Uncle Jos, but she was obliged to bide her soul in patience. It had occurred to her, belatedly, that Derry was likely to be very angry with her, for while he had not actually forbidden her to go see Mr. James, he had made it very clear he considered it out of the question to go see him himself. She only hoped his relief at having the debt out from over his head would outweigh that. And even if it did not, she would far prefer having Derry a little angry with her than knowing he had asked Uncle Jos for the money, or done one of the other dreadful things he had threatened.

By ten o'clock the next morning he still had not come, and Phila was faced with a quandary. One of the few things Aunt Chloe had found to enjoy in London was to be gently driven around the Park at the fashionable hour in the smart new laundalet Uncle Jos had purchased for their use in London. She knew almost no one in Town, but she liked to look at all the fine gowns and carriages, keeping up a running and frequently highly audible commentary on whatever caught her eye, and causing those close enough to overhear her remarks to glare or put up their glasses in frigid disapproval.

Phila could have refused to accompany her that morning on the grounds she was expecting her brother, particularly since she found such excursions highly embarrassing due to Aunt Chloe's comments and Letty's habit of catching the eyes of any dashing young gallant they might meet. But she knew that Aunt Chloe would be disappointed, and so contented herself with leaving a message to tell Derry where she had gone.

Since he was not a particularly early riser, she did not really expect to see him. She was therefore pleasantly surprised, shortly after they arrived in the Park, to see him riding toward them astride a showy hired hack, and accompanied by another gentleman.

Aunt Chloe had spotted him at the same moment, and immediately ordered her coachman to pull up, greeting them cheerfully. "Well, isn't this nice! They tell me this is the fashionable hour, and I'm sure it must be true, for I swear I've never seen so many fine peacocks. I was just telling the girls it's far better than any play. Did you ever see so many plumes as on that woman over there? She looks like a hearse, if you ask me."

"Mama!" hissed Lydia, scarlet with mortification.

"Lordy, they come to be stared at." But she obediently withdrew her gaze from a stout matron who was pointedly trying to appear unconscious of her regard. "And she as stout as I am, too! At least I hope I know better than to make such a cake of myself as to rig myself out like that! But here am I rambling on as usual. And this must be one of your friends?"

Derry made stilted introductions, but Phila was too preoccupied to hear them. It seemed to her Derry was looking alarmingly stiff and unlike himself. She could only think that something dreadful must have happened since he had talked to her yesterday, and could scarcely contain herself until there was a lull in the conversation and she could say, "Oh, very happy to meet you, I'm sure. Derry! I must talk to you. We're going home almost immediately, I think."

"Aye," broke in Aunt Chloe happily. "Come and take your nuncheon with us, if you've a mind to. Your young friend here as well, if he don't mind potluck."

Mr. Naseby, acutely uncomfortable, murmured some polite excuse, but Derry cut him short. "Thank you, but we—have another engagement. Phila, I'll be by at two. See that you're there!"

Phila was almost overcome with fear. She had never seen Derry look quite like that before, and could only stammer, "Yes—oh, yes!"

Mr. Naseby looked curiously from brother to sister, but murmured politely, "Very happy to have met you."

As they drove away, Aunt Chloe said happily, "That Mr. Naseby seemed quite nice, I thought. I'm sure I hope your brother may bring him home some time."

"So do I," remarked Letty thoughtfully, looking back to where Mr. Naseby had returned his hat to his head and was turning away.

"And that shows just how much either of you know!" retorted Lydia in some contempt. "If you ask me, he's every bit as poor as—'' Even she had the grace to blush, but then finished defiantly, ''Well, I don't care! It's true, after all. I daresay he's as poor as her brother, and that's not what I'm looking for, I thank you!''

Phila flushed scarlet, and Aunt Chloe protested half-heartedly, ''Now, Lydia-love, I won't have you being unkind!''

''She doesn't know how to be anything else!'' put in Priddy furiously. ''She's just jealous because Phila's a lady and she's not!''

Lydia laughed. ''Oh, yes. Phila's such a fine lady she's had to come and live on Papa's charity! You may believe I mean to do a great deal better for myself!''

''Beast! Your nose is just put out of joint because that Mr. Naseby wasn't taken in by your famous beauty, and neither is Phila's brother.''

''Do you think I want every stray Tom, Dick, and Harry staring at me like Lettice does?''

Lettice yawned. ''At least I don't scare all the men away with my conceited airs.''

''I didn't notice he was particularly taken by you, either.''

''No,'' said Priddy, coming out with one of her disastrous truths. ''If you ask me, the only one he did admire was Phila, and that's what this is all about.''

It took a moment for the truth of this to sink in, and then all eyes swiveled to an aghast Phila. ''Well, bless me!'' exclaimed Aunt Chloe. ''Priddy's right. And none more deserving, neither, for I've yet to hear Phila enter into such nasty name-calling. I daresay both your noses should be put out of joint if she should catch a husband first.''

Nothing seemed more certain, for Lydia was looking furious, and even Lettice a little stunned, as if she had never considered Phila in the light of a possible rival.

''And what's more,'' pursued Aunt Chloe with unaccustomed sternness, ''if she did, you can be sure she wouldn't forget her cousins in her good fortune, which is more than either of you deserve. So let's just hear no more of charity!''

''Do you think I want *Phila* to find me a husband?'' demanded Lydia scornfully.

''More unlikely things have happened, and so I warn you. If you ask me, it was the best thing I ever did, inviting Phila to come live with us. She's the only one among you that ain't spoiled rotten, more's the pity, or can condescend to lift a finger around the house, instead of believing she was born with a silver spoon in her mouth, which none of my girls weren't, I can promise you. Now let me hear you apologize. Both of you!''

"No—oh, no, Aunt Chloe!" begged Phila, very near to tears. "Oh, please . . . !''

After a moment Aunt Chloe relented. "Aye, well, I don't mean to make you uncomfortable, my dear. And it's like you to be so generous, but your Uncle Jos was right, I'm afraid. You're worth two of my own daughters, however much it might pain me to say it. And I won't stand for cruelty.''

Phila averted her face. Taking in her obvious distress, Aunt Chloe added more tolerantly, "Well, we'll say no more. But if your Mr. Naseby should happen to call, you may be sure he'll be welcome.''

"Well, I hope he may call," said Letty thoughtfully. "I thought he was nice.''

Once home, and alone in Priddy's bedchamber, Phila said distractedly, "Oh, Priddy, how dare you stir up such a fuss?''

"I don't care!" retorted Priddy mutinously. "They make me sick! And if you ask me, he *was* looking at you. In fact, he could scarcely take his eyes off you.''

"Probably because he didn't know where else to look! Oh Priddy, I'm so afraid—oh, I should have waited for Derry yesterday until he came back!''

By the time Derry at last came, she was in a considerable state. She had taken the precaution of stationing herself in the front hall to wait for his knock, and so was able to let him in herself and take him into a small room at the back of the house that was seldom used, where they were unlikely to be disturbed.

But Derry's first words were not what she had expected. "Why the devil does Priddy always glare at me like that?" he demanded irritably.

"Priddy?''

"I met her out front and she looked at me as if I were a bluebeard, or something even worse.''

"Oh, she glares like that at everybody. It doesn't mean anything. She doesn't much like men, you know. Derry—''

"Good God! What the devil does she know about it anyway?"

"Perhaps nothing, but somehow I think she may never marry. She means to be an artist, you know." She hesitated, and added a little defiantly, "I—we mean to set up house-keeping together when she is a little older."

He stared at her, his face set. "What nonsense! Of course you will do no such thing!"

"It's not nonsense. And I must do something, you know. I can't remain forever on Aunt Chloe's hands."

"You know this was never meant to be anything more than a temporary arrangement. Set up housekeeping with Priddy! I've never heard anything more ridiculous. In fact, if you must know, that's what I came to talk to you about. You can't stay with the Coateses any longer, Phila."

It was the very last thing she had expected. "Can't stay with the Coateses?" she repeated dazedly. "Derry, what is it? Oh, what has happened? You haven't *quarreled* with Uncle Jos, have you?"

He looked away, biting his lip. "No, of course not. How could I, since I haven't seen him in three weeks? Nothing's the matter—or at least, everything is, but it's nothing to do with Uncle Jos. I just—I just don't think it's wise for you to remain with them any longer."

She could only gape at him. "Not remain? But why? And where would I go?"

"Can't you just accept my word for it that it will no longer do?" he cried irritably. "I should never have left you with them in the first place. I knew—well, it does no good talking about it, and there was no other choice at the time. But when I saw you in the Park today I realized what a fool I had been."

"Saw me in the Park?" She felt as if she had stumbled into a nightmare. "None of this makes any sense! Everyone goes to the Park."

He had taken a few steps away, but now he turned back impatiently. "I might have known you would only make things more difficult than they are already," he said bitterly. "I have no intention of discussing it, but you may take my word for it that it won't do! If you must know, no one would mistake our cousins for anything but what they are, and I won't have my sister seen in such company!"

5

Phila gasped, but recovered quickly. She could only think that, like her, Derry had been embarrassed by the attention they attracted. Even so, his reaction seemed all out of proportion to the event.

"I know," she said, blushing a little. "It embarrasses me as well. But she enjoys it so, and no one knows us! If they stare a little, what does it matter?"

"Stare a little!" he repeated with an unkind laugh. "I don't wonder people stare when they see you. I did myself! To be blunt, you looked like—well, never mind! But our aunt is a vulgar old busybody and our cousins obviously before the hammer to the best bidder! Even Priddy is a misanthrope at twelve! I should have seen for myself long ago how they must appear to the world—well, I did see, but I closed my eyes to it."

"Is *that* why Mr. Naseby was staring at me?" asked Phila, flushing.

"Very likely! I tell you, everyone will mistake you for the same as long as you're seen in such company. I should never have let you come to London with them. At least in Somerset you lived mostly retired."

Phila had flushed up hotly with shame, a little sick to think that that was why Mr. Naseby had stared at her so, and why others stared and whispered as they passed. But it did not take long for her quick loyalty to surface, and she grew a little angry as well. "Then I think that's horrid!" she said. "And I think you're no better than anyone else if you mean to allow such malicious opinions to weigh with you. You, of all people, know how very much reason we have to be grateful to the Coateses."

He was nearly as red as she was. "Do you think I don't know that? It's damned awkward, I know."

"And anyway," she broke in hotly, "what would we tell

them? That after having lived on their charity for three years, I'm too good to be seen with them? I won't do it! I can't!''

"I might have known you would only make things even more difficult! I don't like it any better than you do—in fact, I feel damned ungrateful. But I tell you, it won't do. Even Aunt Chloe saw it herself, when you first came to live with them! Leaving everything else aside, she has absolutely no control over you girls. I had to endure a damned officious lecture from my landlady this morning, because she didn't believe that you were my sister. In case you don't know it, nice girls don't have the freedom that you and our precious cousins have. In fact, Corny tells me they don't go anywhere without their mamas or a maid to accompany them, at least in Town. If you ask me, you're well on the way to becoming as big a hoyden as either of our cousins.''

Her own gentle temper aroused by now, Phila was on the brink of some very hasty words, which she would almost certainly have regretted later, when memory of her own recent actions made her close her mouth again abruptly. If Derry could carry on so over a relatively harmless visit to her own brother's lodgings, when she had been accompanied by Priddy, how much worse would he take the news that she had called on a complete stranger for the purpose of asking him to forgive her brother's gambling debt, and that without any escort at all?

What he had said still angered her, especially what she could only see as his ingratitude toward the Coateses; but she realized unhappily that her own escapade would only add fuel to Derry's argument, once he learned of it. The news she had been longing to tell him now took on all the appearances of a guilty secret, and prevented her from pursuing the argument as she would have liked. Nor did she dare yet confess to him what she had done.

"But Derry," she asked finally, "where would I go? Even if what you say is true, what else can I do?''

His anger seemed to evaporate as well. "I don't know," he said heavily. "For one thing, you can return to Somerset, for a start." As she paled visibly, he added bracingly, "You needn't worry. I'll find something to tell the Coateses. And as soon as I'm able, I'll make other arrangements. It may not be soon, though, because of this dashed gambling debt of mine. I certainly picked an excellent time to make a complete fool of myself, didn't I?''

She could no longer remain silent, and haltingly told him what she had done.

He stiffened rather alarmingly, but in the end took it better than she had come to fear. ''I—oh, God! It just proves what I've been saying. In fact, it's my fault for I should never have told you in the first place. It was unnecessary anyway, as it happens, for I'd already found the money myself.''

That surprised her as much as anything he had said to her that day. ''Found the money yourself?'' she repeated in astonishment. ''But—where—how? Oh, you haven't done anything foolish, have you?''

''No, I have not!'' he said irritably. ''If you must know, I won it, and you needn't look so disapproving! Even Papa gambled now and then, I happen to know, and anyway, I won, which is the important thing. I even managed to clear something over and above the two hundred, which means it may not be so long after all before I can purchase my commission. Or at least it did, before this. But I can't do anything now until I've figured out what's to be done with you.''

She was guiltily silent once more, and he added, his spirits lightening a little, ''A new friend of mine gave me a tip on the fourth race at Newmarket yesterday. As a matter of fact, I won nearly four hundred pounds! I could scarcely believe it myself, when only the day before I'd been desperate to put my hands on two hundred. And he says he can put me onto other sure things from time to time. I wish you could meet him, Phila,'' he added boyishly. ''He's—well, everything I hope to be myself one day! He's a captain himself, although in the Light Bobs. He says the rest of the army calls the Life Guard bandbox soldiers. I know I've always had my heart set on them, because Papa was a Life Guard, but he says these days I'll enjoy the Light Bobs much more. You should hear some of his stories! He's seen a good deal of action, and says if the war doesn't end before I get a chance to get in it, he'll put in a word for me with his colonel.''

He flushed and added impulsively, ''You don't know what this means to me, Phila, after so long thinking—well, that I would never escape old Ligget's office. Jack's still recovering from a wound, and on light duty for the moment. There's a good chance I could go with him when he returns to his regiment. They're billeted in Spain at the moment, but he says he expects any day to hear they've advanced into France itself. But in the meantime he says it won't do me any harm to get a little Town polish, and anyway, the real fighting's still before us, when Wellington meets Napoleon himself at last.''

He looked very young suddenly, and excited, and she had to restrain the sudden chill she felt. The thought of Derry, thousands of miles away and possibly in danger, made her blood run cold, but she had lived too long in a military family to let him see that. She had always known that was his ambition, but had allowed her fears to be lulled a little when it had seemed still far in the future. And it would be far worse if she could not even remain with the Coateses, where she had established some sort of a life for herself.

Perhaps aware of her silence, or merely returning to earth from some pleasant dream, Derry flushed a little and added hurriedly, ''Of course, it won't be for several months yet, anyway. I must find something to do with you, and of course I must try to make my apologies to Mr. James. I only hope he'll understand that your actions sprang from complete innocence. It was my fault for ever having told you, and you didn't understand—well, never mind, but it will be deuced awkward, I can tell you. I only hope the story don't get about or we'll both of us be ruined.''

It galled her a little to think of Derry's making her apologies to Mr. James. She had not found him in the least unapproachable, and even more, he had understood, as no one had ever done before, the difficulties of her situation. But then, she obviously did not understand the sophisticated code governing fashionable behavior in London. Nor did she think she much cared for it, from all she had heard so far. ''Yes, please,'' she managed. ''He said you were to go and see him anyway.''

''I should rather think so! I must pay him what I owe anyway. I only hope he won't be too starched up.''

That brought her head up in surprise again. ''Pay him? But I told you he said—''

''Good God, Phila, do we have to go through all that

again? Of course I must pay him! So you see why what you did, apart from everything else, was totally unnecessary. I only hope you will remember it the next time you are tempted to meddle in my affairs!''

She thought that unfair, but let it pass. "And I don't have to leave London right away?''

He must have recognized the militant tilt to her chin, for he backed down a little. ''No. I daresay it would be too pointed an insult so shortly after arriving. I can only hope Aunt Chloe will decide to return home herself, after what she was saying the other day. In the meantime, try to stay close to home. And for God's sake, don't go calling on any more strange men!''

Derry might have been appalled at the news of what Phila had done, but by the time he had presented himself in South Audley Street, to be looked over dismissingly by as top-lofty an old butler as ever had been his misfortune to encounter, then left to cool his heels for more than twenty minutes waiting for Mr. James, he was developing a new respect for his sister's courage.

Unfortunately, there had been no kindly Mr. Shelby to intercede for him. By the time he was at last conducted up a pair of elegant stairs by the disapproving butler, and admitted to a small room at the back of the house that had every appearance of an office, for it was fitted out in a businesslike manner at variance with the rest of the house, he was ready to admit that his own heart was beating uncomfortably fast, and he was wishing himself almost anywhere else.

Inside, he found a pleasant-faced young man seated before a workmanlike desk, and the elegant figure of the Nonpareil perched on a corner of it, swinging a booted foot. Derry was to discover, during the uncomfortable interview that followed, a fascination with that particular foot and the highly-polished boot upon it, for he soon found himself with nowhere else to put his eyes.

It began by Mr. James's breaking off his conversation and looking around as Derry was announced. He did not rise from his casual posture on the desk but said merely, his brows slightly raised, "Ah, Mr. Ainsley. I have been wondering when you'd find time to call.''

Derry was immediately put upon the defensive, and resented the interview's being conducted in the presence of a stranger, but flushed and said stiffly, "Yes, sir! I came as soon as I—I came as soon as my sister told me what she had done. At least—I was coming anyway, as I told you I would as soon as I was able to make—to make arrangements to pay you the money I owe you."

The brows rose still further. "Do I understand you have made such—er—arrangements?"

"Yes, sir!" said Derry, even more stiffly.

"May I ask how you managed to obtain such a sum? As I understood it, only yesterday you were wholly unable to do so without resorting to borrowing from an uncle your sister was unwilling for you to approach."

Derry cursed Phila, seeing that the interview was going to be even more unpleasant than he had expected. "Yes, sir!" he ground out. "My sister had no business telling you such things. As for where I got the money, I fail to see how that is any of your business. Suffice it to say that I am prepared at this moment to pay my debt and that I did not—borrow it from my uncle!"

He found himself under the uncomfortable gaze of a pair of cool gray eyes, and flushed still more, but after a moment the Nonpareil said merely, "Your point is taken, Mr. Ainsley. But you may keep your money. As I told your sister, I am not in the habit of winning large sums from youths unable to afford it.."

A white line appeared around Derry's mouth, and he held on to his temper only with difficulty. "This is all Phila's doing!" he burst out. "If she had not come, you would neither know nor care whether or not I could afford it! As a gentleman, I request you to have the courtesy to overlook what should never have taken place. I am here to repay the money I owe you. Sir!"

The Nonpareil was slightly amused but since it played no part in his plans to mollify the stiff-necked youth before him, said merely, "I am quite willing to overlook your sister's visit, Mr. Ainsley. But you are mistaken in thinking I neither knew nor cared whether you could afford the sum you lost the other night. As I said, I seldom make it a habit to win large sums off youths young enough to be my son, and I am not prepared to make an exception in your case, whatever your pride. Let us rather discuss your sister, since you have brought the subject up. I hope I need hardly assure you that no one will ever learn of her—er—ill-advised visit from me or anyone on my staff.''

''No, sir! I mean, yes, sir, thank you, sir! I can only assure you it will not happen again! She did not understand—she has no conception—''

The Nonpareil was no longer inclined to be amused. ''I require no apology for your sister's conduct, since I found her wholly delightful, even if her devotion to you seems somewhat unjustified. But however delightful, I need hardly remind you that her behavior in coming here was as improper as it was dangerous.''

Derry colored furiously. ''No, sir! I am aware—I have recently come to the conclusion that the present arrangement is—is unsatisfactory. I intend to remove her from the Coateses as soon as I can make other arrangements.''

''You relieve my mind. I hope in future you will contrive to remember that you have the responsibility for a very loving sister, and at least refrain from telling her if you must commit some indiscretion. Yes, I know it is none of my affair and you are longing to cram my impertinent words down my throat! Console yourself with the fact I did not have you thrown out of Watier's the other night, as was my first inclination. You would have found that far more humiliating, believe me. Good day, Mr. Ainsley. I trust it will not be necessary for us to meet again.''

Derry was left with no choice but to bow and withdraw with what remnants of his pride he could manage.

After he had gone, Mr. Shelby said sympathetically, ''Poor boy. You were a little hard on him, weren't you, sir?''

''I would like to have been even harder on him yet. Damned young fool! I wonder where he did get the money from?''

''Won it, most likely. I must confess, I couldn't help feeling a little sorry for him. It can't have been easy for him, especially with a young sister depending upon him.''

''I can easily refrain from feeling sorry for him,'' retorted his employer cynically. ''It is his sister who has had to bear the brunt of their misfortunes to date, and will continue to do so, I suspect.''

Then he shrugged. "Let us hope I was able to do some good. A novel experience for me. I wonder why I suspect I have not heard the last of the Ainsleys?''

6

Phila heard no more from Derry for several days, especially not the outcome of his interview with Mr. James. Then to her surprise she saw Mr. James again, while she was waiting for Priddy in the Royal Academy.

Priddy could disappear for hours, such considerations as meals or the time Aunt Chloe expected them back forgotten, while she attempted to capture some particular artist's trick of shading or expression, only to return with her dress torn and her face smudged. Phila was resigned to the inadequacies of her cousin as a companion, and filled in the time reading, or watching the museum-goers.

She was engaged in that pastime when she caught sight of Mr. James, engaged in deep conversation with a distinguished looking elderly gentleman.

She was surprised, since she had no way of knowing he was a notable collector, and since Derry's construction of her visit, a little embarrassed as well. But he must have caught sight of her, for after a moment he excused himself to his companion and came toward her, no evidence either of shock or loathing on his elegant features.

"Well, Miss Ainsley, we do seem to meet in the oddest places!'' he remarked. "Are you a serious student of the arts, or merely seeking a quiet place to rest your feet between shopping expeditions?''

She blushed, but laughed as well. "Neither, I'm afraid. I am waiting for my cousin.''

He sat down on the bench beside her. "I am relieved to know you are not wholly without escort.'' As she blushed again, he added, "Not that she seems to be doing you much good at the moment. Where is she?"

"I have been afraid to go and look," said Phila frankly. "She is a serious student of art, you see, and will spend hours capturing someone's way of drawing hands, or—or the effects of the sun through a glass bowl. But more often than not she has also managed to put a foot through her hem or tear a flounce, and is totally oblivious to the fact we were due home for lunch half an hour ago."

"Does Aunt Chloe mind a torn flounce in the interests of art?" he asked, sounding amused.

"Oh no, in general she is very good. But I fear she doesn't really understand the artistic temperament. Neither do I, I suppose, but I do understand that it must be boring to have to worry about things like lunch and hems when you are engrossed in your work."

"I sympathize with you, and hope your cousin properly appreciates you, in that case. My mother is also an artist—in her case a poetess—and so I know that living with one can be a trial. Does your cousin forget things you told her half an hour ago, and require to be spoken to at least a dozen times when in pursuit of her muse?"

Phila had looked surprised at this news, but said readily, "Yes, and forgets such mundane things as appointments and duties she promised to perform. But then, in justice, it must be difficult to be called away just at a delicate moment, only to eat, and it must seem to them that the things that the rest of us worry about are so nonsensical. Like the weather and purchasing new curtains for the drawing room and whether or not the cook has quit."

"Yes, no doubt you're right," he agreed. "Is she any good, your cousin?"

A little characteristic frown he was beginning to recognize appeared between Phila's dark brows. "I think so, but I must admit I am no judge," she said seriously. "But it often seems to me she is too hard on herself. She tears up most of what she does, and refuses to let anyone see it, even my aunt. And she gets so frustrated, even though she is only twelve." She looked up at him a little shyly. "Is that also part of the artistic temperament?"

"Undoubtedly. Do you always throw yourself so wholeheartedly into other people's affairs, Miss Ainsley?"

"No. But I think I would be unnatural if I did not care about those closest to me."

"Do you?" he looked a little struck by that. "I sometimes think there are very few people I care anything about, if the truth be known. You are a strange child, Miss Ainsley. At any rate, your cousin should have a teacher, no doubt."

It was no more than a careless suggestion, for in truth he was not very interested in her unknown cousin, but he was a little startled at the response he invoked. Her small face lit up and she cried, "Oh, why didn't I think of that? Oh, of course she must! In Somerset, you know, there was never anyone qualified, or whom she didn't wholly despise. But in London there must be any number of—of—impecunious artists who would be willing to give her lessons. And who might be able to make her see, as none of us can, that things are not as hopeless as she believes."

"Well, not any number," he corrected dryly. "But it should not be too difficult to find what you're looking for." If he was not very interested in the unknown cousin, he certainly had no intention of being drawn into the Ainsleys' affairs any further than he already was. He might find this absurd child refreshing, but he had far too much experience to allow himself to become involved because of transitory sympathy.

He was therefore a little surprised to hear himself offering, after a moment, to keep his eyes open in case he came across a likely candidate.

He might have offered her a diamond bracelet. He watched in some amusement as she flushed up with pleasure and gave him her heartfelt thanks.

"For in truth, Priddy didn't much wish to come with us to London," she confided. "Naturally, she has no interest in balls and things, and she didn't wish to leave Uncle Jos, besides not liking to shop and hating the crowds and the heat almost as much as Aunt Chloe does. Only the museums have reconciled her so far, because of course we have nothing so fine in Somerset. But it would change everything if she were to be able to take lessons as well."

He smiled faintly, wondering what could have possessed

him. "Then we must by no means disappoint her. Is that where you make your home? Somerset? Are you here for the Season?"

She blushed for some reason. "Yes, only—only things are not quite working out as planned. But you can't wish to hear about that. And you must not think you must keep me company. I am quite used to waiting for Priddy."

He was aware of a flicker of unease, aware that he was behaving uncharacteristically. But no more than the other evening did he find himself capable of snubbing the confiding and oddly touching Miss Ainsley.

So out tumbled the story of Aunt Chloe and her cousins, Lydia and Lettice, and the perfidy of the house agents and Mrs. Boyles, whose vaunted relations had so far proven less than useful. He was amused, but since he inferred quite as much from what she left out as what she said, more than a little appalled by the unwitting picture she drew. He had felt a stirring of pity the other day since his unusual guest obviously felt too keenly her position as poor relation, but he had supposed, if he had stopped to give the matter much thought, that her relations were the same class and wholly respectable. After hearing about Uncle Jos's manufactory and her Cousin Lydia's ambitions, he decided the situation was obviously much worse than he had thought. He was not particularly shocked, for he had seen far too many such invasions by young ladies desirous of bartering their beauty and Papa's money for a title. Some were even successful, though it was a great deal more difficult to be accepted by the ton. But it was obviously not the place for a gently bred girl of more than usual sensitivity and only an irresponsible brother to look after her.

He still had no intention of becoming involved, of course. But he found himself wishing he had been even harder on her brother, and hoping he indeed intended to remove her from such an aunt's charge, as he had said.

It had also occurred to him that Miss Ainsley was perfectly capable of asking him to further the ambitions of her worldly cousins, in which case it would have been impossible to avoid giving her a snub. Fortunately she did not, but whether this was because she had thought better of it, or because as he suspected, they were interrupted before she could do so, he had no way of knowing.

Looking up, he found himself under the scrutiny of a decidedly plain child with sandy hair and freckles, and a pair of disconcertingly direct eyes. At the moment they were regarding him with more than a little skepticism, and he had no trouble in recognizing in their owner the missing artist.

He said as much, and Phila broke off to look around immediately, saying, "Priddy! Oh, thank heavens you have not torn off your flounce again, or got charcoal all over your dress. Are you ready to go now?"

Her charge was decidedly grubby, and one stocking had fallen down, but these were evidently considered matters of no moment. Priddy acknowledged her cousin's rather flustered introduction by studying him even more thoroughly and objecting, "But you're not old!"

Phila blushed and he said in some amusement, "I fear you flatter me. Miss Ainsley tells me you're an artist, Miss Coates."

Priddy glared at Phila and said baldly, "No, I'm not, and I don't think I ever will be either. I can't seem to get anything *right!*"

He recognized all the perfectionist tendencies of the true artist and said calmly, "Certainly not if you mean to let every little setback discourage you. May I see?"

Before she could prevent him he had taken her sketchblock and was thumbing through it.

"Some of these are very good," he said in some surprise after a moment. "You should certainly have a teacher. Your eye for line is excellent, but you could use help with perspective."

Priddy turned a painful scarlet, forgetting her resentment at his daring to look without her permission. "I know. However hard I try, I don't seem able to get anywhere."

"My dear child, it's not a matter of life and death, you know. An hour with a good teacher would give you the trick. Even I could help you, and I fear I am the rankest amateur."

Abruptly he sat down again and pulled a gold pencil from his pocket. "Here, let me show you. You have the face right—the features and the shading—but it looks flat because you haven't managed to put any depth into it. If you turn the same sketch a little, remembering that human heads are neither round nor oval, but somewhere in between . . .''

As he spoke, and both of them stared in astonishment, a fairly good copy of Priddy's original drawing was rapidly emerging beneath his slender fingers. "Now, then, divide the head into thirds, and remember that the face itself really takes up very little of the head, and there! I fear I'm shockingly rusty, but I think you can see what I mean.''

Priddy was eagerly hanging over his shoulder by then. "In thirds?'' she questioned. "But what if . . .''

She bombarded him with questions after that, at last sitting down beside him and impatiently taking his pencil into her own hands. He fielded all her questions, ruefully aware that his friends would be astonished if they could see him spending half an hour explaining perspective to a plain schoolgirl.

Once he met Phila's eyes over Priddy's head and smiled. "You're right, Miss Ainsley, she obviously needs a teacher. It shows just how hungry she is for knowledge that she can be grateful for such meager help as I can give her.''

"Oh, no!'' cried Phila warmly. "It seems to me that you are very good. Did you wish to be an artist as well?''

"I suspect I was seldom without a pencil and a scrap of paper when I was a boy. But if I meant to be a serious artist, lethargy and acceptance of the limitations of my talent long since dissuaded me.''

Priddy regained his attention then, until he at last held up a hand, laughing. "Enough, you insatiable child! You are rapidly taking me beyond my expertise, and your cousin is no doubt almost drooping with boredom by this time. She ought long ago to have reminded us both of our manners. I hope, by the way, you are properly appreciative of her sacrifices in the interest of your art.''

Priddy blushed unbecomingly. "Phila knows that I am,'' she said gruffly.

He smiled over her head once more at Phila, rising to shake hands with her. "I wonder why I doubt it! I really must go. I beg your pardon for having seemed to have forgotten you, Miss Ainsley, especially since I have not even the excuse of an artistic temperament.''

He cut short their attempt at thanks, saying with some truth, if surprise, "I enjoyed it. It has done me good to try my hand again. I will keep my eye open for a competent teacher. And when she is famous, I may look back and congratulate myself on having had some small part in developing her career."

Priddy flushed again, but after he had gone said surprisingly, "I don't suppose he really will find me a teacher, but I liked him."

Coming from Priddy, that was praise indeed. She then added, "I won't say anything to Mama about having met him, though. She'd probably expect him to help Lydia get accepted into the ton!"

After a moment Phila guiltily agreed. She had naturally said nothing about her earlier visit to Mr. James to Aunt Chloe, and that omission made it impossible to explain where she had come to meet such an influential person. And though it had indeed occurred to her to ask Mr. James for help in furthering her cousins' ambitions, Derry's recent remarks about the Coateses, and a vague recognition of Mr. James' obvious social standing, had kept her silent. While he had been very kind to her, and even to Priddy, she had a suspicion he could, if he chose, be far less kind to anyone he disliked, or whom he suspected of trying to get something out of him for their own ends.

Well, she had tried to get something out of him for her own ends, if it came to that, and he had still been extraordinarily kind to her. But then he had said that he had never had any intention of taking Derry's money, so that perhaps explained it. She only knew that something in his manner when she had been telling him of the Coateses and Lydia's ambitions had made her think that very likely he would disapprove of the Coateses even more than Derry did. She certainly could not imagine Mr. James and Aunt Chloe in the same room together, or hobnobbing about the trouble with London servants.

So however much she might dislike encouraging Priddy to lie to her mama, she too thought it best not to mention their afternoon's meeting.

It was a decision, however, she was to have cause to regret bitterly before very long.

7

Much to both Phila's and Priddy's surprise, Mr. James remembered his promise to find a teacher for Priddy, for within three days Aunt Chloe was the bewildered recipient of a call from a serious young gentleman by the name of Derwood McDermott who said that he understood she was looking for someone capable of giving art lessons.

Aunt Chloe nearly gaped at him. "I don't say I ain't," she said cautiously. "In fact, it's an excellent notion, now that I come to think of it. But how . . . ?"

Fortunately for both of them, Priddy had been near enough to overhear his arrival, and came hurriedly in to explain, a little redfaced, "He—I—a man I was talking to in the Royal Academy knew I might be interested in a teacher and said he might know of one. I—isn't that right?"

The serious young man evidently had a sense of humor, for his eyes twinkled, though he gravely agreed. "Your mother will naturally require more reference than that, however. If you would care to look at them, ma'am, I have a letter from the parents of my last pupil, a recommendation from the President of the Royal Academy, and, of course, a sample of my work."

Impressed, despite herself, Aunt Chloe disclaimed any desire to look at his references. "For in the end, it's my daughter you've to satisfy. If she wants you, which I don't scruple to tell you is by no means certain, for you're not the first teacher we've tried, and all of 'em failed to convince her they knew anything she didn't already— But, as I say, if you can manage to succeed where others have failed, I'm sure I've no objection. And since I don't know one end of a drawing from another, I'll leave you to discuss it with my daughter."

Aunt Chloe later explained this extraordinary tolerance to Phila by saying frankly, "I don't know why I didn't think of the notion myself, and if he can manage to satisfy her, which I warned him is by no means certain, I'll be very happy, whatever he should cost. I'm sure I don't need anyone else's reference to tell me when I'm meeting a nice young gentleman, though it hardly seems right he should be earning his keep giving drawing lessons to schoolgirls. But there, I daresay it takes all kinds in the world. Nor I don't mind admitting I've been feeling a little guilty for dragging Priddy all this way, especially since she didn't wish to come. Well, if it comes to that, I'd no wish to come myself, especially since it looks as if it will all have been wasted! But then I'm not one to beat a dead horse, as the saying is, and what's done is done. But what I mean to say is that very likely these lessons are the very thing, and I'm sure I don't begrudge the money, considering what I've laid out on the other two.''

Feeling guilty, Phila murmured agreement. But Aunt Chloe was never one to require much participation by anyone else in a conversation and went on frankly, ''Nor do I mind telling you that it will relieve my mind on another score if Priddy should happen to take to him. I never meant you to feel responsibility for keeping Priddy occupied in London, and so I've been meaning to tell you, my dear! It's like you, but you can't tell me you hadn't rather be going off with the others your age, and enjoying yourself, than escorting a schoolgirl about. I know you're fond of Priddy, but I also well know that she's less than an ideal companion once she gets a piece of chalk or a scrap of a pencil in her hand. Nor did I bring you to London to act as baby-sitter, as I hope you know, my dear!''

Phila was touched by this concern, but didn't dare tell her aunt that in fact she far preferred spending her time with Priddy, however unsatisfactory a companion she might be on occasion, than to trail along with Letty and her friend Lizzie shopping, or to stroll in the Park with Lydia. The former mostly ignored her, and took every opportunity to attract the attention of any passing male in a manner that embarrassed Phila terribly; and the latter maintained such a languorous pace and a condescending manner toward her younger cousin that the more energetic Phila was soon ready to scream with frustration.

However that might be, Mr. McDermott managed to satisfy Priddy and soon became a regular feature in their lives. As Priddy said in some awe after her initial interview with him, "He's really good, Phila! Far too good to be teaching a scrubby brat! It makes me feel guilty, especially for the small amount Mama's paying him."

If he agreed, however, he did not reveal it. He was a shy young man, diffident around any other member of the family, but evidently having no difficulty in dealing with the usually difficult Priddy. He came twice a week, when they closeted themselves in the small drawing room at the front of the house and usually had the floor littered with discarded drawings by the end of morning. And even Lettice noticed that almost immediately there was a discernable change in Priddy. Certainly she was less impatient, particularly with herself, and no longer convinced, except during rare lapses, that she would never succeed in becoming an artist.

Aunt Chloe was delighted to see her most difficult daughter drawn out of herself a little bit, particularly since Mr. McDermott also possessed seeming blinders where his pupil's older sisters were concerned. If he was impressed by Lydia's angelic fairness he did not reveal that either, but was always unfailingly polite and soon excused himself to go to Priddy. Phila was the only one he would sometimes stay a moment talking quietly to, but Aunt Chloe, recognizing a new danger, was soon able to relax. She did not doubt that no more than Uncle Jos would Derry welcome a possible alliance with a penniless art student, but she could detect no more than simple friendliness in either of them.

And she soon forgot the matter entirely in light of a new and most promising event. On one of her shopping expeditions Lydia had made the acquaintance of a fashionable young lady by the name of Miss Woodyard. A conversation had been struck up over a ribbon counter, and since they had both been going the same way, Miss Woodyard had obligingly offered Lydia a ride in her carriage.

For nearly a week nothing more came of this promising development. Then Lydia had the fortune to meet her again, in the Park, and was invited to come and visit her the next morning in Berkeley Square, while Miss Woodyard's mother would be visiting friends.

There could be no doubt that Miss Woodyard could greatly

further Lydia's ambitions if she had a mind to. Her address was excellent, her father a minor baronet, and she spoke with carelessness of Almack's and attending balls at Lady Jersey's and Venetian breakfasts at Lord Petersham's. She never went anywhere without being accompanied by either her mother or a maid, though she had been out for several Seasons.

Lydia returned from her visit able to talk of nothing else but the graciousness of the house in Berkeley Square, the size of Miss Woodyard's bedroom, where she had gone to put off her bonnet and shawl, the weight of the service with which they were served tea, and the excellence of every cake set before them. Miss Woodyard made no secret of the fact that Sir George Woodyard, her papa, was dreadfully poor, though it did not seem like it to Lydia's listeners, after hearing of the style and manner in which they lived. But Miss Woodyard was frank in her envy of Lydia's pin money, and gowns and jewels, and it did indeed seem as if a promising friendship were developing.

Phila was naturally happy on both fronts, though it left her with a great deal more time on her hands, since Priddy did not require her escort as much. But it made it more likely they would not be returning to Somerset any time soon, if Lydia's new friendship bore fruit, and that put Phila in some uncertainty. She had no intention, whatever Derry said, of abandoning Aunt Chloe as long as she might need her, and returning to Somerset. She could only hope that Derry had reconsidered, for she had heard nothing more from him since that last, unpleasant interview.

Derry had not reconsidered, and still intended to find some other arrangements for his sister as soon as possible; but if the truth be told his mind was not wholly on his sister's affairs at the moment. He had been shaken by his revelation in the Park, and his interview with Mr. James had been unpleasant enough to make him try to drown the memory in drinking blue ruin with his friend Corny. But after he had recovered from that episode, he was able to forget his worry for the most part in enjoying his new friends and his new-found wealth.

He had confided at least part of the affair to Corny that night, and found him sympathetic. "Aye, those great men are all the same. Be thankful you came out of it as well as you did. I don't mind admitting they scare me to death. You say your sister went to see him?'' He shook his head. ''Shouldn't have done it, of course, but—can't help admiring her! Got more courage than I have. And I daresay she may have softened the old boy up a little. Devilish high in the instep as a general rule, you know.''

''You wouldn't have thought she'd softened him up if you'd been there!'' said Derry with feeling. ''What she did was make me look a complete fool! I don't know how I managed to get out of there without slinking—or without planting the great Mr. James a facer, which I don't mind admitting I badly wanted to do!''

''Couldn't have,'' said the other simply. ''Devilish handy with his fives. Boxes with Jackson himself, you know.''

''I don't care!'' cried Derry impatiently. ''He had no business lecturing me like a—like a damned schoolboy.''

''Now that surprises me,'' observed Mr. Naseby. ''Don't know him myself, of course, but never heard he was inclined to be stuffy. No saint himself, the Nonpareil.''

''No, I know he isn't, which is what made it particularly galling. I am aware it was my fault that Phila went to him, but he needn't have made it look as if I am totally irresponsible and selfish where she is concerned!'' He flushed a little. ''Well, it is my fault! I had already realized that it would no longer do to leave her with the Coateses. I intend to make other arrangements as soon as I can. In fact, you might keep your eyes open in case you hear of some respectable woman willing to take charge of her for a fee.''

Mr. Naseby promised to keep his eyes open. He coughed and added uncomfortably, ''Naturally didn't like to say anything before, but—well, wouldn't like to see a sister of mine in such a household.'' He gave the matter some thought. ''Haven't got a sister,'' he amended conscientiously. ''But—well, there it is. Know what I mean.''

Since Derry found it impossible to defend himself, he resorted to anger once more. ''I told you I intended to, didn't I? At the very least I always meant to make some other arrangement before I went into the army.''

''Never thought I'd care for the army myself,'' commented

Mr. Naseby conversationally, grateful for a change of subject. "But then there's no accounting for tastes. It seems to me the soldiers I know are forever going off to some dashed unpleasant place. And what good does it do to look dashing in a uniform if no one ever gets to see you in it?"

"Oh—oh, be quiet! I'm sorry, but much you know about it."

"About what?" inquired a lazy voice behind them.

Derry turned quickly, his face lighting up. "Jack! Where did you spring from?"

Captain Kingsley hooked a chair with one booted foot and sat down. He was a handsome, stocky man some five or six years older than Derry, with a knowing face and the look of a man forever on the edge of some disreputable jest. That the jest was as frequently on him as anyone else made him a favorite of the younger officers, and impressionable youths like Derry. Mr. Naseby, not particularly impressionable, did not like him.

"What doesn't he know?" repeated Kingsley, a twinkle in his eyes.

"Oh, never mind. It's just that he doesn't understand why a fellow would rather be a soldier than anything else. He thinks it's nothing but drilling and discomfort."

"Well, I'll admit there's too much of both for my taste," said Captain Kingsley. "But the life has its compensations. Why? Is your friend here thinking of joining?"

"No, I ain't!" retorted Mr. Naseby shortly. "I ain't a Bartholomew Baby, at least!"

The captain laughed. Derry turned from Corny and said eagerly, "Are you finished for the day, Jack?"

"No, but I paid someone to sign me in. I'd had enough of playing soldier for one day. If I can't be where the action is, I'm damned if I'm going to trot myself around to headquarters every day and pretend to be useful."

Captain Kingsley was still recovering from his wounds, and was officially listed on half-duty, though his responsibilities did not seem to interfere with any of his pleasures. Derry was at first a little shocked to hear him speak so casually, but then his face cleared and he said, "Oh, Lord yes! You must be desperate to get back to the front."

"Not so desperate as all that. I don't mind, for London has

its compensations. You'll see what I mean tonight, if you care to join us. A couple of us are having a snug supper at the Red Lion, and then going on to see what the night holds. We'll probably look in at Covent Garden and ogle a few beauties, then find some sport later. I doubt we'll any of us see our beds much before morning, if I know my friends. What do you say?''

8.

There could be only one answer. Derry accepted eagerly, and after a moment, Mr. Naseby more reluctantly. He might not like Captain Kingsley, but his reasons were vague in the extreme. He had always distrusted easy, charming men, and he thought Captain Kingsley one of a careless breed of young officer always ripe for any spree, a great many of them either foolish or dangerous, and far too addicted to drinking and gambling.

On the other hand, Mr. Naseby liked young Ainsley. Himself having been on the Town for years, he recognized that, however much he might pretend otherwise, Derry was still not up to every rig and row in Town. He had therefore constituted himself in some part his protector, though he did not characterize it, even to himself, in exactly that way. But it was in that guise that he trailed after the other two, exactly, as he told himself bitterly, like a burr in a saddle.

If Mr. Naseby did not enjoy the subsequent evening, which included a lively attempt by one of their party to box the watch, and nearly ended in the roundhouse, Derry was still too new to London not to enjoy himself. He was a little shocked by the brush with the law, but even Corny, though disapproving, did not seem to think it out of the ordinary, so he swallowed his qualms.

It was indeed nearly dawn before they at last dropped Corny off at his lodgings. Jack had seemed to consume an enormou. amount of blue ruin, but seemed unaffected by it, and said cheerfully, as they reached Derry's lodgings, "By the way, I'm going up to Newmarket tomorrow. Care to come?"

Derry hesitated, for he had yet to solve the problem of Phila and felt a little guilty about going away on a pleasure jaunt while she remained in London. But after a moment the temptation grew too great and he eagerly accepted.

"Not too early, mind!" cautioned the captain, yawning. "I'll probably have the devil of a head in the morning."

If so, when Derry arrived a little after ten the next morning at the Albany, where Jack maintained rooms when he was in London, it did not seem to him that Jack was suffering from any aftereffects from the night before. He was admitted by the captain's batman and found Jack still dressing, but the remains of a substantial breakfast were still on the breakfast table, and Jack seemed as cheerful as ever.

When they reached Newmarket, Jack went almost immediately to find a rather greasy looking individual who wore a muffler wrapped around his throat despite the heat, and eyed Derry with obvious suspicion before going apart with Kingsley. After a short conference Jack came back and said cheerfully, "We're in luck. Stebbings says the favorite is likely to be scratched in the sixth. If we hurry, we can get our bets in before it's generally known, and get excellent odds."

From the looks of Stebbings, Derry suspected he might very well have had something to do with the favorite's being scratched, but when he said as much, Jack merely laughed. "Oh, no! You overrate him, I'm afraid. He merely slinks around, keeping his eyes and ears open, and bribing grooms for information. I've seldom known him to be wrong."

"Then why does he tell you?" persisted Derry.

"Because, my innocent, it's in his best interests to do so. I know the details of one or two of his little adventures which he naturally would prefer not be passed on, and as long as I'm careful not to abuse the privilege, he's willing to give me a tip now and then in exchange for my silence. Now let's go get our bets placed before it's too late."

Derry was a little shocked at that, though he tried not to be. And when, after the sixth race, he found himself with the incredible sum of five hundred pounds as winnings, it was even more difficult to remember his conscience. Certainly he had been aware for some weeks that the view of what was considered right and wrong in Somerset was very different from that prevailing in London, and he told himself he was merely being provincial. After all, Jack was an officer, and if he thought it right, then it must be.

"I—is this all there is to it?" he asked a little dazedly as he pocketed his winnings. "It seems impossible that only a week ago I was desperate to find even two hundred."

Jack grinned. "I'll admit it's not something they teach you at Eton. But then my motto has always been that the world was put here for my enjoyment, and to hell with the rules! Come on. I'm starved, and it just so happens I know a snug little house where the girls are clean and the owner's an old friend of mine. A very old friend. If she likes you, she'll give you supper and a rare old brandy she keeps for special occasions. If she doesn't, not even my recommendation will get you through the door. One of a kind, is Peg."

Peg evidently liked Derry. She was a pretty, rather hard-looking woman of something over thirty, wearing a very low-cut gown. She glanced quickly at Derry's fresh-faced good looks, but welcomed them both with every appearance of cordiality.

"Well, well, look who's here! I haven't seen you for months. Come in, the evening needed livening up."

To Derry's surprise, since his experience of such places was almost nonexistent, her "girls" proved to be generally both young and pretty. He was a little tongue-tied at first, but it proved impossible to remain so for very long. Peg indeed gave them a first-rate supper, where much champagne flowed and the spirits of the company were infectious. On top of his nearly sleepless night the champagne floated to his brain in pleasant waves, and he soon lost all shyness, feeling himself a complete man of the world at last.

After supper, while he was engaged in singing a duet with Lisette and Cora, two pretty blonds, and a young man whose name he had forgotten but who had promised to introduce him to his club, Peg jerked her head toward his direction and asked, "Who's the young Adonis, by the way? I didn't know you'd taken to robbing the cradle."

Jack merely laughed and put a hand around her waist. "There are a great many things you don't know about me. At any rate, he may prove useful."

She slapped his hand away. "I'm a respectable business-woman now. What are you up to?"

"There was a time when you weren't so particular. Nor so nosey, as I recall."

"I was always particular," she retorted. "I was just never in a position to exercise it before." She removed his arm again. "The trouble with you, Jack, is that you've come to believe in your own charm. That can always be dangerous, you know," she finished dryly, and walked away.

Derry rose the next morning to find himself back at the inn with no very clear recollection from the night before, and an oversized headache. Then his heart lurched as he remembered tales he had heard of such places and he scrambled out of bed to check his purse. His money was still there. In fact, it seemed to him he had never seen so much money in his life.

It meant the attainment of all his dreams. With one bet on a horse he had accomplished what years in old Ligget's office had failed to do. A week ago, as he had said, he had been desperate to find less than half the sum he now held in his hand. He felt elated, and a little guilty, for somehow it seemed to him it should not have been that easy. But Jack was right. The platitudes drilled into one at home and at school about hard work and sacrifice seemed to have no place in the real world.

Jack strolled in then, and they went down to breakfast. Derry had already learned the valuable lesson that while a gentleman might complain of being hungover, he never allowed it to affect his behavior the next day, or declined to engage in whatever was proposed, so he was able to put away nearly as large a breakfast as Jack. They were soon joined by Derry's singing acquaintance of the night before, whose name he still could not remember.

Sober, he proved to be a likeable young man with a friendly manner. Derry was surprised to discover, when he had an opportunity to ask Jack about him, that his father was the Earl of Barnstoke, a peer very high in the King's government.

However that might be, the Honorable Wallace (Cubby) Farnsworth showed no stiffness in his manner. By the time breakfast was over he had offered to drive back to London with them and take them to his club.

Cubby Farnsworth proved to be even more reckless a gambler than Jack; but while his luck seemed to be perpetually out, and he cheerfully scribbled voucher after voucher, content that his papa would bail him out, if necessary, Derry did not seem able to lose. Mindful of his last unpleasant experience he was at first hesitant in his bets, but when each one turned up a winner he soon lost his caution. Once or twice he went down heavily, and his heart would stop. But Jack assured him that the trick was to ride your luck, and so it proved. The next card invariably turned up a winner, and Derry, drunk on the excitement of winning far more than the burgundy he had drunk, was able to breathe again. The lesson he had so recently learned from Jack was true, if one only had the nerve to see it, and did not allow oneself to be weighed down by outmoded ideas. At the rate he was going he would soon have enough to settle his future, and Phila's as well, and never have to worry again about such mundane things as tradesmen's bills.

It was past four in the morning when he at last stumbled into bed, and slept the clock around. When he woke he did not know which day it was, and the faint headache he had experienced the morning before had become a raging torrent. But all he had to do was look in his purse to know that it had all been worth it. Toward the end of the evening, it was true, his luck had started to turn a little, but he still had emerged with a sum he would have considered a fortune only a week ago.

When he shyly told Corny about it that evening, when he dropped by to invite him to supper, Corny did not seem to be impressed. "Beginner's luck!" he said simply. "Seldom fails."

"I know that!" said Derry with some irritation. "I'm not as green as all that. But I mean to take advantage of it while it lasts."

Corny struggled between his conscience and his aversion to seeming to interfere. His conscience won. "Tell you what," he said awkwardly. "If I was you, I'd buy that pair of colors. What you said you always wanted, after all, and got the money now. Hate to see you lose it after all this."

"I'm not going to lose it! I told you I'm not such a fool as you obviously think. As soon as there's a hint that my luck has started to turn, I'll take what I have and run. But don't you see, this is my chance to change everything, and make a future for myself and my sister. All other considerations aside, it's not impossible I'll be killed, and then what would become of her? I've got to see she's taken care of before I can do anything else.''

Corny was obliged to acknowledge the force of this argument, but he also knew that the number of green young men who had successfully ridden their luck, instead of the other way around, was very small. He distrusted Captain Kingsley more than ever, for if he had not actually seen to it that Derry won in order to lure him into making still larger bets—which seemed impossible if they had been at someone else's club— his actions were still highly suspicious. Derry might be too inexperienced to realize it, but Mr. Naseby was perfectly aware that officers like Kingsley did not make it a habit to befriend impecunious younger men out of kindness. Not unless they had something to gain by it.

Even worse, from Corny's viewpoint, was Derry's latest friendship. Cubby Farnsworth was nearer to Derry's own age, and wholly without vice; but he was also wild to a fault, and unappreciative of the differences between a young man born, as he was, with a silver spoon in his mouth and an unlimited fortune at his disposal, and those less fortunate than he was. He would not willingly lead his newest friend into ruin, but the effect would be the same since he ran with a very fast crowd and thought nothing of losing a fortune at cards one night, then going cheerfully on to supper afterward.

All this Corny dutifully tried to point out to Derry, without much success. And since he ran the risk of alienating him completely, and at the best of times knew himself to be but a poor advocate, he soon gave it up.

9

Nor was Mr. Naseby the only one to be worried.

Phila had seen very little of her brother lately, but the impression that he was changing, and not wholly for the better, could not be dismissed from her mind. He naturally told her very little about his activities, but what little he did made her suspect that he had fallen in with a crowd that their mother would never have approved of.

It was nothing that she could quite put her finger on, for she lacked both Mr. Naseby's experience and his knowledge of Derry's actions. But it seemed to her that Derry had lost a little of his boyish good looks, when she saw him, and that he was different from the brother she remembered, harder and more cynical somehow. Though perhaps no one but she would have noticed.

She told herself that he was merely growing up. Certainly her last talk with Derry about gambling debts had made her see that her ideas were out of step with the rules governing masculine behavior, particularly in London. But like Mr. Naseby, she instinctively blamed Captain Kingsley, whom she had never met, for much of the change in her brother. She did not particularly suspect that he was deliberately leading her brother astray; but she was obliged to admit a prejudice against one who would encourage Derry to pay one gambling debt with the proceeds of another.

As it happened, Mr. Naseby was the one to inadvertently confirm Phila's suspicions.

Captain Kingsley had a friend, a Mr. Montague Drumm, that even Derry disliked. He was a big man, leaning to fat, and considerably older than Kingsley's usual companions, and possessed a coarse manner and the flashy habits that made Derry suspect he had come only lately, and probably unethically, into his money. But that he possessed a great deal of it there could be no doubt, for he dressed richly, was fond of flashing large diamonds on his fingers and tie pins, and waved large rolls of bills around.

He appeared mysteriously on the fringes of Society, and even men like Jack seemed to tolerate him, for no reason Derry could figure out. Once, when Derry asked him about it, Jack said carelessly, "Oh, Drumm's all right. As vulgar as bedamned, of course, but he has his uses. The worst I know of him is his taste, which I'll admit is execrable. But he amuses me. Doesn't he amuse you? You've become mighty high in the instep of late!"

Derry flushed, but persisted. "No, he don't amuse me, and if you ask me, he don't amuse you either. Why the devil do you let him hang around you?"

"I let all sorts of queer nabs hang around me if it comes to that." Then as Derry reluctantly laughed he added lazily, "Anyway, my spratling, I owe him money if you must know. He's not quick to press me for payment, and I'm not at all eager that he should. Now do you understand?"

As Derry looked startled Captain Kingley said in amusement, "Really, did you imagine I suffered the good Drumm for the sake of his conversation? I'll admit I'm careless of appearances, but not quite that careless. Unfortunately, we can't all be as devilish lucky as you are."

Derry flushed and said hesitantly, "If it's r-really a question of money, I c-could let you have a little."

"It is always a question of money, as I'm sure you will learn to your cost. But if he becomes too much of a nuisance, I'll merely rejoin my regiment. I have a scheme in mind for coming about again anyway. If it comes to anything, I'll let you in on it."

Derry thanked him and allowed the subject to drop. By now he had accumulated a considerable sum, one that he would have believed impossible six months ago. Only the fact that he was not yet certain what to do with Phila, and reluctant to leave London just yet, prevented him from fulfilling his dream. But he was not altogether disappointed to hear that Jack might be rejoining his regiment soon.

Unfortunately, he was walking with Mr. Naseby down Bond Street one day when they encountered Captain Kingsley standing in close conversation with Montague Drumm.

Derry would have avoided the encounter if possible, for his

opinion of Drumm had only lessened after learning why Jack tolerated him, but Jack looked up then and said cheerfully, "Ah, just the man I want! Tell Ainsley what you were just telling me, Drumm."

"Ah, well, in the general way I don't like to blabb of my information," said Mr. Drumm genially. "But seeing as how these is friends of yours, I don't mind putting them on to a good thing as well as you. And all I can say is that if you was looking for a tip in the Derby next month, you don't need to go no farther."

"Horse belong to you, does it?" inquired Mr. Naseby nastily.

But Drumm disclaimed any such pretensions. "Much above my touch, I can tell you! Owned by one of the real nabobs, and worth a king's ransom they say."

"In that case, how come we ain't heard of this famous animal?" asked Mr. Naseby.

"Because they're keeping him under wraps, and I can't say as I blame 'em," replied Drumm, unoffended. "I don't say it would do the odds any good if word of such a nag was to get around, but that ain't the real reason, I'll be bound. We all know there's plenty as wouldn't mind affecting the outcome by fair means or foul, and would think nothing of tampering with such an animal."

"How did you come to hear of it then?"

"Ah, now that would be telling, wouldn't it? All I can say is I have my sources, and they're usually reliable."

"Who owns the horse?" asked Kingsley interestedly.

"Well, now, for the moment that's my little secret, if you don't mind. But if my sources prove out, I'll be willing to let you in on it. I'll admit I wouldn't mind lessening the profits the owner means to make off it."

"An old enemy of yours, is it?"

"Let's just say I like to keep my books balanced, so to speak." But his attention had wandered, and he asked after a moment, "Who's the red-head trying to catch our eye?"

Derry glanced around, then stiffened. Lettice and his sister Phila were coming toward them, and there was no way to avoid a meeting.

Derry was newly sensitive about his ungenteel cousins, but to do him justice that was not the first thought that struck him. Jack was no snob, and he did not doubt for a moment that he would mistake Phila for anything but what she was. He might indeed attempt to set up a flirtation with Letty, which was hardly desirable, but there was nothing that could be done about that. But he would have given anything to have been able to avoid introducing the colorful Mr. Drumm to his sister.

It was not possible. Phila and his cousin had already reached them by then, and he had no choice but to make the necessary introductions.

Derry was not disappointed in Jack, who might be careless at times, but possessed excellent manners. And if he had given any thought to the matter, he would have said his reluctance to introduce Drumm to Phila was not out of any fear that Drumm might constitute a threat, but merely that he had no desire to expose his sister to such men. It certainly had never occurred to him that a man like Drumm might overlook the more obvious charms of his cousin Letty and take a fancy to Phila instead.

But that he did so was obvious even to the meanest intelligence. He exclaimed loudly against Derry for keeping two such charming relatives to himself, but it was to the blushing Phila that his eyes kept wandering, and who evoked his most extravagant compliments.

He insisted upon escorting them where they were going, despite Phila's stammered protest that it was only a step; and would have offered Phila his arm had not Jack forestalled him. He then fell into step beside them, ignoring Letty's claim to his attention, though for once Letty seemed untroubled at being outshone by her lesser cousin. She accepted Mr. Naseby's politely offered arm, secret amusement in her eyes.

When they reached the shop that was their destination, Mr. Drumm reluctantly stepped back, but promised to keep his eyes peeled, and said he would be surprised if they didn't meet again, indeed he would.

"My sister and her cousins live very much retired!" said Derry through clenched teeth.

Mr. Drumm merely chuckled. "No, no, the secret's out now! You can't expect to lock up two such treasures as these. Now, you wouldn't be as cruel as that, would you, Miss Ainsley?"

Phila almost shuddered, and drew the reluctant Letty away. Once they were out of earshot, however, she said unthinkingly, "Oh, where do you imagine my brother met such a man?"

"I don't know, and I can't say I cared much for Mr. Drumm myself," agreed Letty. "But he was certainly taken with you."

"Oh, don't!" begged Phila. "As for Captain Kingsley, I knew he was leading Derry into bad company, but I never suspected it would be as bad as that!"

Letty was looking unusually thoughtful. "Didn't you like the great Captain? He meant you to. I was beginning to think I had become invisible."

Phila shuddered again. "You might have them both with my blessing! At any rate, Mr. Naseby was kind to you, and if you ask me, he's far preferable to either of those."

"Yes," said Letty, brightening. "He is, isn't he? I'm almost sorry he never took Mama up on her invitation. I wonder if I can make him interested in me?"

Phila scarcely heard Letty's comment, for she was far too worried. Both times she had met Mr. Naseby she had been too preoccupied to pay him much attention, but he was not at all the usual type that appealed to Lettice. His appearance was unprepossessing, his manners, at least around women, shy almost to the point of awkwardness, and though she knew nothing against him, she was to the point of mistrusting all of Derry's new London acquaintances.

But she was soon to have cause to be extremely grateful to him, for he rescued them from the vulgar Mr. Drumm within a week of that first meeting.

Mr. Drumm must indeed have been keeping an eye out for them, for she and Letty were coming out of a linen draper's shop almost a week later when he accosted them. He came up and doffed his hat and said cheerfully, "Well, now! I warned you I'd be keeping my eyes out, and Montague Drumm ain't the man to give promises lightly! How do you do, Miss Ainsley? And your cousin, whose name I'm afraid I've forgotten."

"It's Coates," supplied Lettice willingly. "But I certainly haven't forgotten you."

He looked gratified. "No, I fancy most people don't forget

me," he said with simple pride. "My finger's in a great many pies, though you might not think it to look at me. Some that might surprise you, too."

"What exactly is your business, Mr. Drumm?" inquired the inquisitive Lettice.

But he refused to be pinned down on the point. "This and that, Miss! This and that, though as I said, some of it might surprise you. In fact, I think I ain't boasting when I say there's many a titled gentleman who has reasons to be grateful to me."

"And do you have business with Miss Ainsley's brother? Is that how you met him?"

But his expansive smile faded a little at that, and he said "Now, I don't carry no tales out of school, as it were. Nor it's not my intention to bore two such pretty young ladies with talk of business. You must allow me to escort you. I warned young Ainsley last time about allowing two such charming young ladies to go about without protection."

"The only one we need protecting from is you," muttered Lettice under her breath. But since it seemed she was likely to get no more out of him, and Phila was giving frantic appeals with her eyes to discourage him, she thanked him and assured him they were only going a step.

It is doubtful if any excuse save outright rudeness would have dissuaded their determined cavalier, but fortunately rescue arrived then in the form of Mr. Naseby's rather nondescript figure. He came up to them with none of his usual shyness, and said with a hard gleam in his pale blue eyes, "Good afternoon, Miss Ainsley! Miss Coates! Thought it was you. I will be happy to escort you wherever you're going. Shouldn't be out alone. Told Derr so the last time."

It looked for a moment as if Mr. Drumm meant to dispute the point, for his face grew a little red. But since it was plain by Mr. Naseby's bulldog attitude that he had no intention of leaving Mr. Drumm in possession of the field, and it did not suit his purpose to be obliged to include a chaperone, his good nature returned, and he bowed and soon took his leave, promising himself the treat of another meeting very soon.

Once he had gone Mr. Naseby said bluntly, "No wish to interfere, but if you take my advice, you'll avoid any such meeting. No wish to alarm you, but not the sort of fellow you ought to know. Told your brother so. In fact, be wise to tell him if the fellow pesters you at all again.''

"Oh, no!" agreed Phila in heartfelt tones. "I can never thank you enough for rescuing us."

When Mr. Naseby blushed and bowed again, she added, "In fact, I can't believe he's the sort *any* person of respectability ought to know. How on earth did my brother meet him?''

"Through the great captain," said Mr. Naseby bitterly, momentarily forgetting himself. "Hangs around him, though if you ask me he's up to no good. Tried to warn Derr, but he won't hear a word against his precious Jack.''

"Exactly what is Mr. Drumm's business?" asked Lettice curiously. "He wouldn't tell us.''

"I suspect Bow Street would like to know as well. I don't imagine much of his fortune was come by legally." Then, at Phila's horrified expression, he recalled his audience and blushed still more. "That is—forgot myself! Shouldn't have said so much. Beg you will forget it!''

"Nevertheless, I suspect it's true," said Lettice thoughtfully. "He reminds me of a man I once saw in Somerset. Papa said he was a regular leg, and as likely to end on the nubbing cheat as die safe at home in bed. Is that his lay?''

Mr. Naseby looked startled, but rather impressed as well, and since Phila obviously didn't understand a word of what had been said, answered frankly, "No. At least not that I know of. Gullgroping is more in his line. He likes to get people in debt to him, and then turn the knife. There's no fastener out on him—I checked. But that don't mean his activities would stand the light of day, for they wouldn't! In fact, thoroughly loose screw, if you ask me.''

Letty looked thoughtful, and even Phila understood enough to turn pale with worry.

10

If Mr. Naseby had given Phila more than enough to think about, and inadvertently confirmed her own worst fears, he was, unfortunately, nowhere in sight the next time Mr. Drumm accosted her.

She had accompanied Priddy to the Royal Portrait Gallery, and slipped out by herself to buy some black thread for Aunt Chloe, when Mr. Drumm drove by in a dashing tilbury.

Phila prayed he had not seen her, for she was without even Letty to deflect his overamorous nature. But he pulled up immediately, though not without some difficulty, for his horses jibbed a little and it was necessary for him to control them and then back up a few paces before he could speak to her.

"Well, well," he said, plainly delighted. "I told you we was likely to meet again one fine day, and this time without any of your usual watchdogs. Where's that cousin of yours? Not with you, eh?"

Phila was tempted to lie, but said instead, reluctantly, "No, not this time. But I have left another cousin in the museum, and must go back to her right away. I only stepped out for a moment, to—to buy some thread. My aunt does not like her to be left alone, for she's only twelve."

She could see the thought process in his face. "Now, now, no need to rush off, surely? She'll be safe enough. I've just had a capital notion! What if you was to climb up with me and we could take a turn about the Park, eh? Give us an opportunity to get to know each other better."

Phila had no desire to get to know him better. "No!" she blurted. "That is—I—I really must get back. Thank you, but—but another time, perhaps."

Mr. Drumm was not as stupid as he looked. He was perfectly aware she was afraid of him, but it only added to the piquancy as far as he was concerned. Nor was he imperceptive enough not to know she was worried about that brother of hers. He said, "That's too bad. And here was I thinking we might have a little chat about your brother."

Phila's eyes widened in alarm. "What about my brother?" she demanded, coming a little closer to his tilbury.

He smiled, satisfied that he was on the right track. "Now, I'm not one to go blabbing out of school! But I don't mind admitting that that brother of yours is getting in over his head. I just thought you might like to know."

Phila took this news in an unfortunately literal spirit. Her own suspicions, coupled with Mr. Naseby's unwise words, made her say sharply, "In over his head? How much does he owe you?"

Mr. Drumm was surprised, but not displeased at this turn of events, and by no means averse to taking advantage of it. "Now, that's not something we can discuss in the street. Get in. There may be a way you can help your brother."

Phila got in. Afterward she could only justify this folly by the fact that she was worried about Derry, and on a public street in an open carriage she did not think there could be much danger. In fact, she regretted the impulse almost as soon as it was born, and would have climbed out again if he had not set his horses in motion at just that moment.

She contented herself with saying quickly, "I should not have left my cousin! Please say what you have to say quickly, and then take me back."

But that he was not inclined to do. He chuckled and set his horses to going faster. "Now, not so fast, little lady! A turn around the Park won't do no harm, and it will give us privacy to discuss that brother of yours."

"No! I don't want to go to the Park with you!" cried Phila, losing all impulse toward politeness. "Oh, take me back at once!"

He showed no signs of obeying this behest. They were by now bowling down Piccadilly at a rapid rate, and she was terrified someone would see them, and even more terrified that he would collide with one of the numerous carriages and carts and pedestrians crowding the road. "Now, now, I'll take you back after we've had our little talk," he said cheerfully, oblivious of the traffic. "You're right, your brother owes me a pretty penny, but that's not to say I mightn't be persuaded to overlook the fact, if you was to be nice to me. You might say I've taken a real fancy to you, which is a thing that don't often happen, I can tell you.''

Phila gasped and turned even paler. She had mistrusted Mr. Drumm from the first, but she had had no idea he could be that wicked. She was not naive enough to misunderstand his meaning, and though her first impulse was to tell him precisely what she thought of him, concern for Derry made her swallow her first hasty words and say with difficulty, after a moment, ''I—I think you had better stop and let me down. If my brother owes you any money, he will repay it. Now please set me down!''

Again he showed no signs of obeying her. ''Not so fast, young lady. If you knew my plans for that brother of yours, you wouldn't be so standoffish. Not if you care about him, that is. But I could be persuaded to alter those plans, I don't doubt. If you was to make it worth my while, that is.''

Phila forgot her own fear for the moment. ''Oh, what are you planning? What have you done?'' she cried in horror.

He chuckled. ''I told you Montague Drumm ain't one to talk out of school. But if you wish to see that brother of yours live to join that regiment he's always talking about, you'll be mighty nice to me.''

Phila was by now really frightened, for she would put nothing past Mr. Drumm. Even Mr. Naseby had acknowledged that the authorities would probably be interested in his activities, and she did not doubt for a moment that he would hesitate to ruin her brother, or even worse, if it suited his purposes.

He apparently mistook her silence and her pale face for acquiescence, or at least thought he had her properly frightened, for he chuckled and attempted to put an arm around her. ''There, now, there's no need to look like that. You just be nice to me, as I said, and your brother will be all right. I knew from the first that you was a sensible young lady. And you won't find me ungenerous, that I can tell you. I ain't one to object to forking over the possibles when it suits my interest. How would a nice diamond necklace do for starters? Aye, I thought that would make you sit up!''

Phila had indeed sat up, but only to violently throw off his encroaching arm. ''I wouldn't accept a length of *thread* from you," she cried with loathing, "not even if it meant saving my brother from the gallows! Mr. Naseby was right to say the police are probably looking for you, for you are wholly despicable! And if they're not now, they will be after I go and tell them what you said to me. Now put me down at once at once—do you hear me—or else I'll scream."

His smile faded a little, for she had surprised him. He had not expected to have much difficulty with her, for he had used such ploys before with great success, and he had not had any reason to suppose her other than the shy child she seemed. A few threats, some easy tears, and they usually came around, particularly when he threw in the promise of some pretty bauble to distract them. Nor did he at all relish the idea of her going to the authorities. He did not think Bow Street really had anything they could pin on him, but it would make for a few awkward hours, and might result in the sort of attention he particularly wished to avoid at the moment.

Still, she was a tempting little morsel, and it would do his reputation no good if word should get around that he could be bested by a slip of a girl. He said, "Scream away, my dear. There's no one to hear you."

Phila looked around in alarm to discover that this was unfortunately true. While her attention had been occupied he had driven them, not to the Park as he said, but out on the road toward Kensington. At the moment there were no houses in sight, or even any other traffic. She was wholly alone with Mr. Drumm.

Worse, her folly had been such that no one had even seen her get up with him. Not even Priddy knew where she had gone. If Drumm chose to kidnap or murder her, it would be days before anyone thought to associate him with the event, or had any idea where to look for her.

By now she was really afraid; nevertheless the knowledge of her own folly in getting into this predicament stiffened her. She had been a fool to get up with him, but she would not let him see that he had succeeded in frightening her. She said, though her voice persisted in wobbling a little despite all she could do, "That may be so, but I have no intention of going another mile—another yard!—with you. I warn you. If you don't put me down at once, I shall jump."

"Don't be a little fool, my dear. You'd only succeed in

breaking your neck, and where would be the sense in that? Now, on the other hand, you just be a good little girl and remember that brother of yours, and there'll be no need for any unpleasantness. I've already said Montague Drumm ain't one to come down scaly, ain't I? What else would you like? A pretty new gown to go with the necklace, eh?''

Phila gave a sound that was half sob, half laugh. "I've already said I wouldn't accept a length of thread from you! And even if I succeed in breaking my neck, then you shall have some explaining to do, and so it will be worth it.''

"No, I won't," he explained reasonably. "For I won't be here, and there's no one to say I had anything to do with you.''

But she was no longer listening. With another breathless sob, she grabbed the reins below his inattentive hands and jerked them with all her strength.

The result was even better than she could have anticipated. She had already seen that he was a very bad driver, his control uneven on the reins and with a tendency to misjudge his speed or distances, so that he was forever having to haul his team up at the last moment, cursing and blaming them. The result was that his team was in a perpetual state of nerves, starting at the sound of his voice, and their mouths no doubt damaged by his constant sawing at the reins. Her heart had gone out to them from the beginning, but it served her purpose well at the moment. The sudden check threw them into complete confusion, as she had guessed it would, and they plunged and sidled, fighting the bit.

Even so, a competent whip could easily have brought them under control again. Montague Drumm, cursing violently, merely succeeded in completing the confusion. Phila was a little in awe of what she had caused, for the light tilbury was bucking and pitching alarmingly, and in danger of overturning. One of the horses had gotten over the traces, and both were by now terrified, but at least their speed had slowed considerably. She glanced again at Mr. Drumm and saw that he was by now alarmingly red in the face, all trace of his bonhomie gone. "You little bitch!" he cried. "By God, when I get my hands on you . . . !"

There was no danger of that at the moment, for it was all he could do to keep them from overturning. Phila gave another half hysterical laugh and said contemptuously, "What a despicable creature you are! I don't know how I could ever have been afraid of you for a moment."

He forgot his primary concern and reached for her, murder in his eye. Phila waited for no more, but closed her eyes and jumped.

Mr. Drumm's eyes started from his head, and he made a futile grab for her, but he was too late. And even if he had been inclined to go back and see if she was all right, it was beyond his power. Startled by that sudden lessening of weight on top of everything else, his team bolted with him, the reins now dangling uselessly free.

11

At almost the same moment, Havelocke James was making his leisurely way back to London in his curricle, having visited an old acquaintance outside Kensington Village. The afternoon was fine, he was in no particular hurry, and was chatting with his groom who had been with him for many years.

When he came upon an overturned tilbury in the ditch at the side of the road, he raised an eyebrow at Dimber and pulled up. But the horses had been removed from the shaft, and there was now nothing to see but the tilbury, its shaft broken and one wheel at an unnatural angle. So though Dimber jumped down to look around, he soon returned to remark that the owner must have led his horses to the nearest village. "If he weren't himself carried off on a plank. Can't have happened very long ago, though, for the traces are still warm."

As he climbed back into the curricle, his employer said callously, "He deserves it for overturning a tilbury. He is probably merely licking his wounds at the nearest tap, and hoping word of his mishap won't reach London. Let's go on."

Dimber leaned his shoulders back and crossed his arms over his chest. "Aye, there was a time, I disremember, when even you was known to overturn a tilbury."

The Nonpareil smiled. "When I was eleven, and showing off. And stop trying to take the wind out of my sails by enumerating to me the many instances of folly in my childhood, you old gullcatcher. It's been many years since I've needed rescuing."

Dimber grinned. "Aye, but you was a rare handful, you was. I remember Lady Annis didn't know each day whether you'd be brought home on a hurdle or in a box."

"I have no doubt she would have dealt with either eventuality with equal sangfroid."

Dimber's grin grew. He was perfectly aware that his employer's majestic mother had a considerable soft spot for both her children, but he had certainly never seen her thrown for a loss. Not even the time Mr. Locke had fallen off the stable roofs and broken his head open. She had merely ordered him carried upstairs, and herself cleaned the wound, remarking caustically that at least it was his head. He might have fallen on something else and really hurt himself. Nor had she spared a glance for the underlings gathered guiltily around, worried that they might understandably be held responsible for not preventing their master's only son from murdering himself.

The groom was still smiling at the memory when he heard the Nonpareil exclaim beside him, "Good God! That can't be our hapless coachman, surely?"

He looked up quickly to discover the bedraggled figure of a young girl trudging along the road before them.

The Nonpareil did not wait for an answer, but had already quickened their pace when the girl, evidently hearing their approach, turned a frightened face back to them.

The Nonpareil stiffened, and jerked his high-bred team to a stop in a manner that was highly injurious to their delicate mouths.

The girl had halted by now as well, and turned a pale and rather dirty face up to them. "I—oh!" she said unhappily, "I can't believe it is you. Please, will you take me back to London?"

Dimber glanced quickly at his master, but he seemed to have himself in hand now. Only his groom, who knew him so well, recognized the little tell-tale muscle that beat beside his cheek and alerted him to the fact that he was under the grip of some powerful emotion. "Certainly, Miss Ainsley," he said in a voice now devoid of all emotion. "Dimber, help her in, and then we shall have to leave you, I'm afraid. There should be an inn fairly close where you can hire a horse."

Dimber's face was even more impassive than his employer's, though his mind was rife with curiosity. Indeed, he was beginning to wonder if his master was too old to need rescuing after all. But he said merely, "Aye, sir, there's a small inn just a mile or so ahead, as I remember."

"Excellent. In that case you may go to the Rose and Crown."

The Rose and Crown was some distance behind them, and would entail a hot and dusty walk, but Dimber received his instructions without a blink. But the young lady said guiltily, "Oh, no! Don't make him walk on my account, please!"

"The walk will do him good," said the Nonpareil callously. "Help her up, Dimber. I will expect you when I see you."

She allowed herself to be helped up, looking both frightened and unhappy. She indeed looked as if she had been in a carriage accident, for her face was dirty, her bonnet hung down her back by its strings and her hair was coming down, and her dress was torn and dirty. Dimber stood back, wondering what the Nonpareil was letting himself in for.

Phila, in the meantime, was sitting unhappily beside Mr. James trying desperately to think of some excuse to give him. The truth obviously would not do, for she was deeply ashamed of her part in it, and for some reason could not bear to have Mr. James know about her connection with the vulgar Mr. Drumm. Derry had made her see that her previous escapade, in going to Mr. James's house, had been highly improper, and this even she could see was a hundred times worse.

She was still gripping her hands tightly in her lap, trying to steel herself to say something, or even look at him, when he spoke first beside her. "I am taking you to an inn where you may clean up, Miss Ainsley," he said in a rather harsh voice. "At the moment I wish only to know two things! Were you in the carriage that overturned, and are you—in any way hurt?"

She forgot her nervousness for a moment. "Oh, did he overturn?" she cried. "Oh, how *glad* I am!" Then she relieved her overwrought emotions by bursting into tears.

If it tested even the address of the Nonpareil to arrive at a strange inn with a young lady dissolved in tears and a great deal the worse for wear, he did not reveal it. As the landlady rushed out at the sound of a carriage, since they did not usually cater to the gentry, and most of their customers arrived on foot or in farm wagons, she gaped a little at sight of the bedraggled Phila beside so obviously elegant a gentleman. But so great was his air of assurance that she did not even question his explanation that his young relative had been in an accident, and required the use of a room to freshen up in.

She bobbed a hasty curtsy and set up a yell for her son to come and take the gentleman's horses, assuring him that she would see to the young lady herself, poor dearie. Some hot water and a nice cup of tea would soon set her to rights, and the gentleman could enjoy a heavy wet in the taproom in the meantime, which fortunately was devoid of company at that hour and he could have all to himself.

Her son ambled around a corner then, and gaped open-mouthed at the team standing in the modest yard. Then his eyes lit up with almost fanatic excitement when he understood he was actually expected to take charge of such high-bred uns and could only stammer his assurances that he would see to the gentleman's horses. Indeed he would!

His mother shook her head with affectionate despair, but assured his honor that young Ned, though he might look like a bobbing block, could be trusted to rub them down and bait his team proper. "For he's often called up to the local manor, when they're short a groom, and he seems to have a way with horses, though it's the only thing I've discovered he does have."

Such an encomium would undoubtedly have cast a chill into Dimber's soul. He invariably refused to let anyone but himself handle his master's much-sought-after grays, even at highly established posting houses. The thought of what was to become of the grays had already belatedly occurred to him, on his dusty walk, and made him regret the long years of training that had caused him to obey such a foolish order and abandon his master, and more to the point, his master's grays, to fend for themselves.

While it is doubtful that either the Nonpareil or his grays had ever graced such an humble establishment with their custom, Mr. James gave up the reins to the youth without another glance, and helped his shrinking passenger down and followed the landlady's stout figure inside.

Phila, escorted up the stairs to Mrs. Scaling's best bed-chamber, was not so impervious to their surroundings or the awkwardness of her situation. She was well aware the Nonpa-reil would never have patronized such a place but for her, and was afraid of what the landlady must be thinking. Then she caught a glimpse of herself in the slightly blotchy mirror the room boasted, and forgot everything else for the moment in horror at her appearance.

The landlady kindly supplied her with a comb and a brush, and hot water, and promised to have the kitchen girl leave off her preparations for dinner and see to Miss's gown the best she could, though it would never be the same, of course.

Phila, feeling some explanation was required of her, stam-mered some tale about having gone out without permission and overturned herself in a tilbury, and that seemed to satisfy the landlady, for she clicked her tongue and expressed the opinion that she was lucky it had been no worse. "But I daresay you needn't look so scared, Miss," she added kindly. "You may be in for a scold, but it's clear that uncle of yours is a real gentleman, and only concerned that you might have been seriously hurt. Now just you drink the tea the girl will bring up, and have a nice lie-down on the bed till your dress is ready. I'll bring it up myself and help you into it, so you needn't worry."

After some consideration Phila did as she was bid. She had, in truth, been more shaken than hurt in her jump from Mr. Drumm's carriage, but her legs seemed still to be shaky, and she was grateful for some moments of privacy before she was required to face Mr. James again.

She drank the tea that was brought to her, and by the time the landlady returned with her dress, having had the worst of the stains sponged out, and been mended and freshly ironed, she was more in command of herself. And since she had no more excuse to avoid it, she then followed the landlady back downstairs to the back of the house where Mr. James had been ensconced in the empty taproom.

She found him flicking over the pages of an old newspaper without much interest. He looked thoroughly bored and out of place, and she flushed guiltily. But he looked up then and rose, putting the newspaper aside. "Well, Miss Ainsley," he remarked evenly. "You look considerably better now. But I think it is time we had a talk, don't you?"

It was the last thing she wanted, but she was aware he was due some sort of explanation, and said with difficulty, "I—I have behaved very foolishly, I'm afraid. But no real harm has been done, after all. Can't we just leave it at that?"

His face hardened. He had been as shocked as one of his cynical nature could be by the sight of her trudging along the road in such a state. He had known her situation was a bad one, but he had allowed his disinclination to get involved, and her brother's assurances that he meant to do something about it, to reassure him.

Both, it seemed were at fault, nor could he lightly dismiss the matter any longer. He had little need to be told what had happened, and if he was man enough of the world to recognize that Miss Ainsley's somewhat disastrous naivity might encourage the more unscrupulous of his sex, it was clear her present situation invited disaster. He had no idea how she had managed to escape, or if she had really been in danger, but the mere contemplation of either made his blood run cold.

So he said, with more harshness than she had yet heard from him, "I cannot agree that no harm has been done, when I find you miles from London, alone and frightened. How did you manage to escape from the tilbury before it overturned?"

She hung her curly head, looking so absurdly youthful and guilty it was difficult for him to maintain his anger. "I—I'm afraid I was the one to cause it to overturn," she confessed.

There was a moment of silence, as he looked at her with suddenly keen interest. She had interested him before, primarily because of her unconventional behavior, and her obvious devotion to those near to her, but for the first time it began to occur to him that she was far from the simple child he had believed her. "*You* caused him to overturn?"

She flushed. "I—I grabbed at the reins. I never meant to

overturn him, only to slow us down enough that I could jump. Only he was such a bad whip that he lost control completely."

He had thought himself beyond being shocked at anything, but she had managed to shock him. "Good God! Do I take it you actually did jump from a moving vehicle?"

"Yes," she said defiantly, "for I warned him of what I should do if he didn't set me down at once! And I'm not sorry he overturned, for he was—he was—"

"I can imagine," he said dryly. "I only hope he may have broken his neck." He was at something of a loss, a rare experience for him, for though it was not his place to lecture her, clearly something must be done. "Miss Ainsley—"

"Yes, I know," she said. "I—I should never have gotten up with him in the first place. And I wouldn't have, because I already despised him, even before I knew he was such a coward, if only he had not said—"

She broke off, but he had no trouble in completing her sentence for her. "Something to do with your brother! I know!" he said grimly. As she flushed he added helplessly, "I believe I warned you once before of your habit of jumping to your brother's defense. You are by no means stupid, so you must know the danger you ran. Had your assailant been less of a coward, as you say, or you possessed of less wit and courage, you might not have escaped so easily."

"No, I know," she said miserably.

"In fact, I am beginning to agree with your brother that your aunt is the last person to have charge of you. If you had been chaperoned as you should be there would have been no need for this discussion."

"But—it's not Aunt Chloe's fault!" she cried, aghast.

"You are mistaken! Whatever her virtues, she seems to have not the slightest idea how to protect a young lady in London. If she is not aware of your disastrous propensity to throw yourself headlong into danger whenever you think that precious brother of yours is threatened, she should be. In fact, during my last conversation with your brother, he made it clear he meant to remove you from her care almost immediately. If he had done so, you might have been spared a highly unpleasant ordeal."

"He meant to. But neither of you understands that it's my fault, not Aunt Chloe's!" she said wretchedly.

He put out a hand, and then abruptly withdrew it. "My child—my dear Miss Ainsley, I understand your gratitude toward your aunt, perhaps more than you know. But that can't alter the fact that I have twice now found you in circumstances not only improper but that could well have been extremely dangerous." He hesitated, conscious, if she was not, of the absurdity of the situation. "You make me feel an hundred years old! It is not my place, nor is it my wish, to scold you. As you have pointed out, in both cases you emerged more or less unharmed. But you should never have been confronted with such situations, or been left so unguarded that you invite the unwelcome attentions of such men as you have today encountered. Can you understand that?"

"Yes," she whispered, her eyes downcast.

He grimaced again. "I am beginning to entertain a certain grudging respect for your brother, Miss Ainsley. You leave me at a loss as to what to do with you."

That brought her eyes up. "Do with me? But what should you do with me? It cannot matter to you, after all, what becomes of me?"

He was once more silent. He had certainly believed so, but however little he liked being drawn into the Ainsleys' affairs, no man of conscience could stand by and see this child ruined, or worse. At least he discovered he could not. He said ruefully, "I don't know whether to be grateful to you, or not, Miss Ainsley. Certainly I have been complaining lately that nothing out of the ordinary ever happens to me—at least until you came into my life. It remains only for you to divulge the name of your recent assailant and we need never allude to this unpleasant subject again."

He was unprepared for the guilty flush that stained her cheeks, or the stricken eyes she raised to his face. "Oh—oh, what does it matter?" she begged. "Please, please, I would much rather not tell you."

"Very well, Miss Ainsley," he said at last. "I cannot compel you to do so. But you may rest assured I have every intention of discovering it for myself. Now I think we had better go. I sincerely trust your aunt will have long since begun to worry about you."

12

The journey home was a silent one. At first sight of the Nonpareil Phila had been astonished at the gladness she felt, for she had been half expecting Mr. Drumm to come back after her, and at the very least, faced a long walk home. But it was impossible to feel, in Mr. James's calm presence, that anything bad could happen to her.

That first instinctive joy had not long survived her realization that she was in an even worse scrape than before, and that she would have preferred almost anyone else to have rescued her. Mr. James might be wholly reliable, but she was deeply ashamed to have him discover her in such a predicament, after he had already been so kind to her. And she would have died rather than reveal Mr. Drumm's name to him.

She had considered making him take her to the Royal Academy, as she had Mr. Shelby, but since she suspected Priddy would have long since given up on her and gone home, and she doubted very much if her present escort would have been as amenable as his secretary to such a suggestion, she did not dare to make it. But she was curiously reluctant, on top of everything else, to have him see the shabby house in Hanford Square.

There was no help for it, of course. Mr. James was a very different driver from Mr. Drumm, and she had no fear he might overturn her or collide with another vehicle in London's crowded streets, and they arrived in Hanford Square far too soon for her comfort. Seeing it through his eyes, it looked worse to her than it ever had before, and even Priddy's face, seen hanging out an upstairs window before the curtain was abruptly twitched back in place, seemed vulgar and middle class to her. Her only relief was that she might soon escape from him. Even Aunt Chloe's inevitable questions seemed preferable.

He had scarcely pulled up before she was slipping down, mumbling the stilted words of thanks she had been rehearsing for the last mile.

He ignored them. "I cannot leave my horses, Miss Ainsley, or I would certainly escort you to the door. I have discovered in myself a very strong desire to have some words with your aunt!"

He hesitated, seeing the shame and alarm in her face, and added unwillingly, "Don't look so absurdly guilty, my dear. Whatever I may have said, I don't blame you. In fact, I find myself in considerable admiration of your courage. And I am the last person to wish you to curb that remarkable loyalty of yours, for I find it—oddly touching. I wish only to ensure you never have cause to regret your impulsiveness. Now go inside, for it is clear your cousin Priddy is waiting for you."

She fled without another word.

Luckily, Priddy was the only one to have noticed Phila's absence, and she had stationed herself in the front hall, full of curiosity at seeing Phila return with the Nonpareil.

"Oh, pray, don't ask," begged Phila, "at least not now! Is my aunt very angry with me? Did you wait very long for me?"

Priddy shrugged those matters aside. "That doesn't matter, silly. Anyway, I told Mama your brother had taken you for a ride. Not that she'd have noticed you were missing," she added sarcastically. "Miss Woodyard has invited Lydia to her ball at last, and that's all that can be talked of. But you'd better change before Mama sees you or she will be suspicious."

Phila impulsively hugged her. "Thank you! Oh, Priddy, I wish we had never come to London!"

When she at last emerged, after having guiltily hidden her ruined gown in the back of her wardrobe until she could dispose of it later, it was to discover that Priddy had spoken the truth. Lydia and Aunt Chloe were already deep into copies of the *Belle Assemblée*, trying to decide what gown Lydia should wear for this all-important event, and no one had noticed Phila's absence.

Aunt Chloe did look up when Phila came in and said kindly, "Are you back, love? Did you have a nice visit with your brother? Lydie-love, I'm sure you'll roast decked out in swansdown in June. Whatever would your papa say to such an idea? Now this would be nice, if you ask me." She pointed to a simple gown composed of a pale blue underskirt and an overdress of white trimmed in simple pearl buttons which Lydia had no hesitation in dismissing as countrified. It was plain that Phila had already been forgotten, a circumstance she could only be grateful for.

The discussion continued throughout dinner and afterward. Apparently Lydia intended to dazzle all the gentlemen at Miss Woodyard's ball, and not all Aunt Chloe's protestations could convince her that young ladies, particularly unmarried ones, were supposed to dress simply, even in London. Nor was anyone much surprised when Aunt Chloe, desperately holding the line against swansdown, was brought to consent to an elaborate gown of pink satin with a rather daring décolletage and rhinestone fastenings worn with an aigrette of diamonds and feathers.

"Oh, for God's sake!" interrupted Letty at last. "You'd think she was going to the Palace at least, instead of some stupid ball, and I for one am sick of the subject already!"

Aunt Chloe looked surprised. "Now, Letty, it's not like you to be jealous of your sister's good fortune."

Letty abruptly rose and took a hasty step across the room. "Jealous?" she cried. "Of Lydia? Don't make me laugh! Oh—oh, never mind! I'm going to bed!"

Aunt Chloe stared after her, troubled. "Whatever do you suppose is the matter with her? It's not like her to be moody."

Lydia gave an unkind laugh. "It's exactly like her. If you ask me, she's getting entirely out of hand lately, Mama. You'd better do something about it before she embarrasses all of us and ruins my chances. I'll have to have a new evening wrap as well. I saw something that would do, if we had it made up in pink and substituted rhinestones for the pearl fastenings. What do you think?"

After a moment Aunt Chloe reluctantly returned her attention to an illustration of a spangled evening cloak which, as Aunt Chloe afterward confided to Phila, she trusted Mr. Coates would never catch sight of, for it was as improper as it was expensive, and reminded her of nothing so much as a garment to be worn by the type respectable women didn't talk about.

"Not that she won't have it in the end," she added gloomily, "for stand up to her I never could, not even when she was little. If she makes a fool of herself, as I fear, she'll have no one to blame but herself. Ah, well. What do you suppose has gotten into Letty lately? I vow and declare I almost wish we'd never come to London at all."

Phila was unable to enlighten her, for Lettice had never confided in her. And since at the moment she had no desire for a tête-à-tête with her aunt, she soon made an excuse to go up to bed, especially when Aunt Chloe, peering at her for the first time that evening, said unexpectedly, "You're not sickening or something, are you? You look feverish. That brother of yours didn't keep you out in the sun too long, did he?"

Phila quickly disclaimed any illness and fled, fearing Aunt Chloe's sharp eyes.

But after that she began to watch Lettice, and had to admit that something was plainly the matter. She was moody, which was unlike her, though even Phila soon tired of hearing about plans for the ball, and the rival merits of gauze over satin, and whether Lydia should choose diamanté over paste. And she was gone a good deal, returning late to dinner and either vague or irritated if anyone asked her about her day.

Once, as Phila was coming in from running an errand for Lydia, she encountered Lettice just going out and said impulsively, "How pretty you look! Is that a new gown?"

Lettice blushed for some reason. "Yes—no! I bought it before we came. If you want Miss High-and-Mighty, she's in the drawing room, holding court as usual. If I were you, Phila, I'd tell her to run her own errands. You're not her servant."

Phila stared at her, surprised, for that was unlike Letty. After a moment Letty flushed again, and brushed past. "Oh, never mind! Tell Mama, if she asks, that I'm going shopping with Lizzie. Not that I think she will. I'll be glad when this stupid ball is over so we can all have some peace again around here."

Derry, in the meantime, as yet blissfully unaware of his sister's latest escapade, was strolling with his friend Corny the next afternoon when Corny tugged at his sleeve. "Beg pardon," he said uncomfortably, "but you did say you settled up with the Nonpareil? He's staring at you in a dashed unpleasant way. Thought you ought to know."

Derry colored and looked around. The Nonpareil had evidently just come from White's, and he was with several other gentlemen, but he was indeed staring across the street toward Derry. Even as Derry watched he excused himself and started toward them, his expression far from friendly.

Derry stiffened, a little nervous despite himself, but stood his ground, having no reason to avoid such a meeting.

The Nonpareil did not waste words. "I want a word with you. Now, if it's convenient—oh, damnation! I have an appointment I can't get out of. Very well, tomorrow morning. Let us say nine o'clock. I'll expect you."

Derry stared after him, at the same time irritated by such high-handedness and beginning to feel a tinge of alarm. He was tempted to claim an earlier engagement, but when he said as much, Corny, his own slightly protuberant blue eyes betraying his astonishment at the exchange he had just witnessed, said hurriedly, "Wouldn't do that, if I was you. Don't I keep telling you he's the Nonpareil? In fact, take my advice, you'll take care to be on time, too."

Derry bristled at the suggestion he should have any reason to be afraid of Mr. James, but on second thought decided to keep the appointment after all.

But if Mr. Naseby was startled that the Nonpareil would have singled out his friend in so public a manner, he was even more astonished when, some hours later while he was finishing up a snug dinner at one of the ordinaries enjoying his frequent custom, he looked up to see the Nonpareil walking toward him.

So surprised was he that he looked around instinctively, expecting to see one of Mr. James's cronies, though it was far from being a fashionable restaurant. There was only a rather stout merchant consuming a beefsteak behind him, and he looked back quickly, wondering if his eyes could have deceived him.

There was no mistake. The Nonpareil had by now reached his table, and was saying mockingly, "Yes, it is really you

I've come to see! In future I would appreciate it if you would inform your landlady of your plans for the evening. I have visited no fewer than three establishments already in search of you, and I am due at a dinner party in little less than an hour.''

Corny gaped at him, then gathered his scattered wits and hastily begged him to sit down. He found himself on the verge of begging Mr. James's pardon for having put him to so much inconvenience, and stopped himself just in time. "I—that is, you were looking for *me*, sir?"

"I was, if you are Mr. Naseby, as I presume. I am hoping you will be able to give me some information about young Ainsley. I am told he is a particular friend of yours."

Corny began to look even more uncomfortable. "Happy to oblige, sir, but—well—friend of mine, as you say," he explained unhappily.

"You may relieve your conscience, Mr. Naseby. My interest in your young friend is minimal at best. Or I will correct that: If he has, as I suspect, fallen into the sort of company I have every reason to fear he has, my interest grows more acute.''

Corny immediately thought of Montague Drumm and his expressive face must have given him away, for Mr. James said dryly, "As bad as that, eh? You alarm me! Allow me to assure you that anything you tell me will naturally go no further, and that more than you know may depend upon your help. Is young Ainsley in debt?"

Corny gave up the unequal struggle with his conscience. He was extremely curious why so great a man should take such an interest in Derry, but the temptation to unburden himself of his own worries was too great. "If he ain't, he soon will be," he answered gloomily. "I mean—you're a man of the world, sir! What would you think of his plan to set himself up on his winnings? Not that I don't grant you he seems to have the devil's own luck—if it is luck."

"I take it you suspect it is not?"

"Well, some of it must be," amended Mr. Naseby grudgingly. "Some of the places he goes are perfectly respectable. But some of the places he's taken to frequenting are far from it. And even if they were, what man ever made his fortune at the tables? Lord, I ain't one of you clever coves, but even I know nothing's more certain to queer a man's luck.''

"You're right. Who introduced him to such places? If you mean the establishments I think you do, they don't usually cater to impecunious youths fresh from the country.''

"Cubby Farnsworth, for one,'' answered Mr. Naseby with a certain bitterness.

Mr. James raised his brows slightly. "You surprise me. It would seem he's moving in select circles indeed. I hold no particular brief for young Farnsworth. He's a reckless young fool who's been spoiled from birth. But I was not aware he numbered luring penniless young fools in over their heads among his vices.''

"No. At least, he enjoys devilish deep play, and he has introduced young Ainsley to some of the worst of the hells. But it's innocent enough, I daresay. *He* has no reason to encourage him other than supreme indifference to anyone not born with a silver spoon in his mouth.''

"I take it you believe someone does have a reason to encourage him?'' prompted Mr. James.

Corny hesitated. "I don't know anything, mind. I only know he's taken great care to introduce him into a set of company *I* don't care to mix with, and I'd give a good deal to know why.''

"So would I. Who is this Pied Piper? Anyone I know?''

"I don't know if he's come to your notice,'' said Mr. Naseby, burning his boats. "But as I said, you may meet him anywhere. If you must know, it's Jack Kingsley, and you needn't tell Derry I told you!''

"I won't. A captain in the Light Bobs?'' he asked thoughtfully. "Yes, I've seen him around. A pleasant-enough-seeming chap. Do you have any real reason, other than your obvious dislike, to suspect him of an ulterior motive for his friendship with Ainsley?''

"No, except that he's always hanging about an oily fellow by the name of Drumm. Even Derry don't much care for *him*, but if you ask me, it's Carlton House to a Charley's shelter they're as thick as thieves, and in it together, whatever it may be.''

"You begin to interest me very much indeed.'' said Mr. James grimly. "Has this Drumm ever made the acquaintance of Miss Ainsley? Yes, I can see that he has! In fact, you have now told me all that I need to know. I'm indebted to you! One more thing. Have you met the uncle and aunt who are giving a home to Miss Ainsley?''

For some reason Mr. Naseby reddened self-consciously. ''Not the uncle, but I've met the aunt. As vulgar as she can stare, of course, but she seemed kind enough. I know Derry seems to think his sister is fond enough of her.''

''But then it seems to take remarkably little to spark Miss Ainsley's sympathy,'' remarked the Nonpareil dryly, pulling on his gloves. He rose, and took up his hat and stick. ''You may oblige me by answering one more question if you will. In your opinion, is Ainsley serious about a military career?''

Corny's face cleared. ''Lord yes! He seldom talks of anything else. Well, you may not know, but his father was a military man. Seems to have died a hero at some place or another, I forget the story. But at any rate, he's sincere enough about that.''

''Then it seems clear that for the sake of all our sanities, the sooner he takes up his military career, the better. I must go. Thank you again.''

Corny stared after his elegant figure, more mystified than ever.

13

Derry might tell himself he was not in the least afraid of the Nonpareil, but nevertheless he presented himself on time in South Audley Street the next morning.

He was admitted by the same fish-eyed butler, who regarded him in a way that made Derry wonder uneasily if he had forgotten to polish his boots, or if his shirt-points had wilted in the heat. But after a moment he merely bowed and conducted Derry up a pair of stairs to a door on the first floor.

It was opened almost immediately to his knock, but the small, rather nondescript gentleman put one finger to his lips before beckoning Derry in, as though he were interrupting some important meeting or church service.

This was disconcerting enough, but to his surprise Derry found himself in a bedchamber. The reason for silence was soon discovered, however, for the Nonpareil was seated before his dressing table engaged in putting the finishing touches to his cravat.

At any other time Derry would have been interested in watching this procedure, for however much he might dislike Mr. James, he could not doubt that his air of quiet elegance was worthy of envy. At the moment, however, he merely thought it ridiculous, and turned his attention to the room in which he found himself. If he had ever considered the matter, which of course he had not, he would have presumed so wealthy a man would possess an opulent bedchamber, but this room bore no resemblance to what he would have expected. It was certainly large enough, and possessed the same air of quiet elegance as its owner, but it was plain almost to the point of asceticism. There was a single small painting hung over the huge bed. Derry, whose interest in such things was almost nonexistent, supposed vaguely it must be valuable, but missed the jewel-like tones that to the knowledgeable would have identified it unmistakably as an Italian Master. On a prominent pedestal in front of an alcove at the windows was placed a bowl of some sort with cracked finish. Derry supposed it was a pretty enough color, but naturally failed to recognize a piece of rare T'ang porcelain. There was a curious screen in one corner, and another vase on a small table by the door.

"Are you interested in cloisonné, Mr. Ainsley?" inquired Mr. James's cool voice behind him.

He started, then flushed. "Not particularly. You wished to see me?"

The Nonpareil rose and permitted his valet, the nondescript little man, to hand him into his coat. For a moment Derry was moved to genuine admiration despite himself, for he had never had a coat that fit so well. He was tempted to ask the Nonpareil for the name of his tailor, then thought better of it.

"Thank you, Nims, that will be all. I am lunching with my brother-in-law. Be so good as to inform West of the fact. I shan't need you for anything else."

When the valet had bowed himself out, the Nonpareil calmly took up a gold knife and began paring his fingernails. "I did. When—"

They were interrupted by a knock on the door. At his answer the slight figure of Mr. James's secretary, whom Derry recognized from his previous visit, came in, and hesitated. "Oh, I beg your pardon, sir. I didn't realize you had anyone with you. I can easily come back later."

"No need, Charles. Did you attend to that matter we discussed?"

The secretary hesitated again, as if aware of Derry's growing resentment, but answered readily enough, "Yes, sir, that's what I wished to speak to you about. I am on my way to see Wilson now, and wished to know how high you are prepared to go. I thought I ought also to warn you that His Royal Highness is said to be interested in the pair himself."

"If he wishes to pay more than five hundred, he's welcome to them," said the Nonpareil indifferently. "A pretty pair, but I'm afraid the glaze is damaged."

The secretary gave his shy smile. "I had the distinct impression you had taken one of your fancies to them, sir."

"I have, but you may rest easy. I have no intention of trying to outbid Prinny for them."

The secretary laughed this time, which surprised Derry. He would not have thought Mr. James stood on such easy terms with his employees. He himself had only seen him at his most forbidding, and would not have expected him to unbend so much with a mere dependent. "I will confess it always shocks me a little to pay so much for so small an item, but then I am a hopeless Philistine," said Mr. Shelby easily. "I'll be off then, unless you have any further commissions for me?"

Having been given none, he smiled at Derry, a touch of sympathy in his eyes, and took his leave. Derry ignored the smile, fuming at having been kept waiting for business that might very well have been conducted at a later time. It was a deliberate slight, and he was well aware of it; but short of making a scene and storming out, there was little he could do about it.

Certainly, when the Nonpareil at last put down his knife and turned to him all trace of friendliness had disappeared from his face. "Now, Mr. Ainsley. Be so good as to tell me when was the last time you saw your sister?"

Derry bridled at the tone, and would have liked to have slammed the words down his throat, but he was conscious, as the day before, of a chill of premonition, and said quickly, "You mean Phila?"

"I was not aware you possessed any other sister. In fact, I sincerely trust not! Of course I mean Phila."

The premonition grew to a certainty. "Oh my God! She hasn't been back here, has she?"

"I should take my whip to you for that," said Mr. James pleasantly. "Your sister is in every way your superior, both in wit and courage."

Derry was scarcely listening, for a new and even more horrible thought had struck him. "What is it? Has something happened to Phila?"

"Your concern is touching, if somewhat tardy. In fact, the last time we met, Mr. Ainsley, you assured me you meant to remove your sister from the care of an aunt I can only classify as criminally lax in her duties as chaperone. Had you done so, your sister might have been spared an extremely unpleasant experience. I might add that if it had not been for her somewhat remarkable courage and ingenuity, she might have suffered serious harm."

Derry sat down without waiting for an invitation. "Oh, my God," he managed. "What happened?"

The Nonpareil told him, not mincing his words. By the time he was through Derry was decidedly pale.

"Oh, God! How—how did you come to be involved, sir?"

"I encountered her on the roadside. I need hardly add that it was the merest good fortune, I, and not someone more unscrupulous, did so."

"Oh God! It doesn't bear thinking of! I can never be grateful enough, sir! When I think of little Phila . . .!" He was indeed feeling a little ill, and some of the details were only now beginning to sink in. "Who—one of *my* friends, you said?"

"I have every reason to suspect so, for she was certainly engaged in her fatal predilection for protecting you. She would not tell me who it was, but I think I can guess."

So could Derry. The memory of Drumm leering at Phila

and promising to keep a lookout for her filled him with hot rage, and it was all he could do to prevent himself from rushing out right then and choking the life out of the fat man.

He managed to say with difficulty, "I—I have an idea who it may be, sir. She did meet him through me, though you may not believe that I tried my best to prevent the meeting. But to think that he—never mind! I am grateful to you for telling me."

"I take it your sister had not done so?" inquired the Nonpareil a trifle grimly.

For some reason Derry flushed up. "No, but that's my fault as well, sir. I have not kept as close a watch on her as I should have since coming to London."

The Nonpareil might be angry with young Ainsley for his neglect of his sister, but he was conscious of a slight twinge of sympathy. He was very young himself, after all, and at the moment was looking more than a little sick. He said in a kinder tone, "I have no intention of making light of the incident, but you can hardly be expected to guard your sister night and day." His face hardened again. "What I do expect is for you to place her in the care of someone capable of protecting her as she deserves, and where she will be happy."

Derry rose unsteadily to his feet. It did not occur to him to point out in his defense that at the time the arrangement with Aunt Chloe had been made he had still been at Cambridge, or that at any rate it was none of the Nonpareil's business. He only knew that he had himself already seen, since coming to London, that the arrangement would not do and yet had let it slide while he enjoyed himself. If anything had happened to Phila . . .!

He looked up, his youthful countenance hardening. "I mean to do so, sir! As for the other, I think I know who it was, and you may believe it will never happen again. I am grateful to you for the information and for—for rescuing my sister, but you may trust me to take care of her from now on!"

14

The Nonpareil, very aware it was none of his business, said rather bitterly sometime later, "What else was I to do? He as much as told me to mind my own business. Damned young fool!"

Mr. Shelby, who had been told at least part of the story by then, looked suitably grave. "I know, but the situation as you describe it, sir, is a dangerous one. Do you suppose he really knows who did it?"

"If he does not, I trust he may be able to drag it out of his sister, as I could not. And I suspect the situation may be even more dangerous than you suppose. If I had any sense I would wash my hands of the whole affair right now, for it is likely to pitchfork me into exactly the sort of scandal I most wish to avoid."

His secretary regarded him doubtfully. "I don't see how you could be involved, sir, even if there were a scandal."

"Then it is clear you don't know Miss Ainsley!" said the Nonpareil grimly. "Or her brother. Both seem to go out of their way to collect disasters. It is no wonder their parents had the good sense to die at an early age."

Mr. Shelby knew his employer was not serious, but he could not help saying, "Surely you are a little unkind, sir?"

"Not at all. Miss Ainsley is an enchanting young lady, but if she continues down her present path she will one day cross the line between what is innocently appealing and what can no longer be condoned. And her brother, unless I much mistake the matter, is even a greater fool than I had thought him! As I said, if I had any sense I would leave town immediately."

After a moment Mr. Shelby swallowed what he had been about to say, and said merely, "I assume you will be attending the Derby this year, sir, as always? Will you be inviting anyone up to stay with you?"

"Yes, Alvanley and perhaps one or two others. Pray make the necessary arrangements. I have a horse running, by the way."

Charles looked surprised. "Do you? I knew you were backing Phalanx, but I had no idea you meant to enter your own colors this year."

"I own Phalanx. It is not generally known yet and I have my reasons for preferring it not to be for a while longer. I have become the target of too many attempts to influence the outcome of a race by other than legal means, as you know."

"Yes, sir. No one will learn of it from me, sir."

"Thank you, Charles. You are as usual wholly to be relied upon. I will probably be out until late. By all means take the day off."

Charles watched him go, torn. It was like Mr. James to be carelessly kind, as he had been in giving his secretary the day off for no reason, and at the same time utter so cruelly dispassionate a condemnation of a child like Miss Ainsley, all the more chilling for being true. Given her present circumstances and a brother good-natured enough but intrinsically weak, and it was not hard to imagine what her future must be. The Nonpareil had been there to rescue her once, but he was unlikely to be on hand the next time; and it was perfectly true that even if he had been inclined to interfere, there was very little he could do. Possessing a chivalrous nature himself, Charles had rebelled at the thought of leaving her brother to deal with so obviously black a villain but he was forced to acknowledge now that his employer had neither legal nor moral grounds for interfering. Not only did she possess a brother who might be expected to protect her, but any hint that so prominent a gentleman as the Nonpareil was interested in Miss Ainsley could only do her reputation irreparable harm. Charles knew that it was absurd to think Mr. James could have developed a tendre for so innocent a lady, but the world cared very little for veracity where it saw a juicy scandal to enjoy.

On the other hand, Charles Shelby could never before remember his employer calling any young lady enchanting.

The thought disturbed him, for some reason. Charles had long believed Mr. James ought to marry, but it was out of the question that he would ever look to a young lady of modest background, no very remarkable beauty, and who, as he said, seemed indeed to spring from one disastrous scrape to another. Charles was not privy to his employer's plans, but like the rest of the world he was well aware that there was more than a casual understanding between him and the beauteous Lady Antonia Burke. They had grown up next door to each other, she was in every way suited to be his wife, nor could there be any other reason for her to have rejected one flattering proposal after another, as she was known to have done. Further, Charles had frequently seen them together, and if he was not prepared to swear either was deeply in love with the other, he had recognized an ease between them that spoke of long friendship and similar backgrounds. He was not certain his employer was capable of more.

Yes, it might be just as well if his employer were to wash his hands of the young Ainsleys, both brother and sister, as he had said.

Having reached that decision. Mr. Shelby might not have been reassured by his employer's subsequent actions. James was far from showing any signs of washing his hands of the young Ainsleys, as they were the chief topic of conversation during his luncheon engagement.

Sir Adrian Barbeaux, married to the Nonpareil's only sister, was a sleepy looking individual whose habitually placid manner hid an intellect of considerable shrewdness. Few would have guessed, on meeting him for the first time, that he was a pillar of the Home Office, whose quiet working behind the scenes had more than once staved off national disasters threatened by the vagaries of politics or an autocratic and highly unstable King.

At the moment he looked merely like a well-fed gentleman settling down to enjoy a pipe after a meal. He filled his pipe, tamped it down in a meditative way, and took some time to light it and get it drawing to his satisfaction.

That done, he refilled his glass with a rare old port that had been a gift from his brother-in-law and passed him the decanter. "I remember Drumm, of course," he said at last. "Try some of this, by the way. I had it from your cellars, as I recall. Do you have any reason to suspect Drumm means to make an attempt on your entry for the Derby?"

"It wouldn't surprise me, since Drumm hates me like poison since our last encounter. I'm not worried about that. I think I have taken sufficient steps to prevent him or anyone from reaching Phalanx. But Drumm's name has cropped up in another context recently, and I'll admit I don't like the coincidence."

That said, he seemed in no particular hurry to go on. He refilled his glass and sat swirling the liquid for some moments, frowning a little, while his host smoked peacefully, watching him. At last the Nonpareil seemed to come to himself, for he drained his glass and said shortly, "In fact, I don't know whether I'm allowing my dislike of Drumm and his ilk to color my thinking, or for . . . other reasons, am putting unrelated events together and seeing a sum where none exists. But I thought I could do worse than to dump the whole in your lap, Adrian. Don't hesitate to tell me if you think I'm crazy. Have you run across a certain Captain Kingsley?"

"Should I have?"

"No, except that he may be met anywhere. A Peninsular officer, on the face of it charming, well liked by younger men—you know the sort I mean. He seems to be invalided out at the moment, but I gather there was some sort of scandal, all hushed up, of course. You know how close-mouthed you people in government are! I only know that he seems to have struck up an unexpected friendship with Drumm."

"Not so unexpected, after all," pointed out Sir Adrian mildly. "I don't doubt Drumm would be very useful to an expensive young officer."

"Precisely. But Kingsley seems also to have gone out of his way to cultivate a young man by the name of Ainsley who one would have said lacks any such immediate usefulness. He is fresh from the country, possesses neither wealth nor social position, and his only recommendation seems to be that he is army-mad. Nevertheless, Kingsley seems to have taken him up to a remarkable degree. He has certainly introduced him to Drumm—again not so remarkable, you will say! But perhaps you will be more interested when I tell you he has also brought him to the attention of young Cubby Farnsworth, with predictable results."

Sir Adrian frowned a little, and sat forward, but did not lose his habitual calm. "Barnstoke's heir? I will grant you your point, but Barnstoke's not as great a fool as he's been painted. You may be sure, whatever else you may think of him, he is not in the habit of leaving military secrets lying around for casual visitors to his house to find."

"Can I?" inquired the Nonpareil bluntly. "I happen to know he did something very much the same not too long ago. Don't look so shocked, my dear Adrian. I regret not all politicians are as discreet as you are. But you may be sure if I came to hear of it, others did too, however it was hushed up. And I find the combination of a known villain such as Drumm, an expensive and questionable officer such as Kingsley, and a naive and vulnerable young fool like Ainsley to be highly explosive. Particularly when you throw in friendship with the son of a man known both to be privy to high-ranking military secrets and notoriously indiscreet."

Sir Adrian busied himself with relighting his pipe, which seemed to have gone out. "I will admit—between these four walls—that Barnstoke is a liability," he conceded at last. "But do you have any reason—presuming, for a moment, that we accept everything you have said, which I am far from doing—that this young man—this Ainsley, didn't you say?—is inclined to cooperate with such a plot? I thought you said he was army-mad, which doesn't fit, somehow."

"He is. Keep in mind, however, that he is also greatly in awe of Captain Kingsley, whom he must see as the embodiment of everything he wishes to be himself. He also possesses a younger sister who renders him unpleasantly vulnerable to threats of blackmail or coercion. Their parents are both dead, and she seems to be his sole responsibility, except for some distant relations who have her in charge, and who seem to be wholly unequal to the task. Perhaps you will understand my alarm when I tell you I have reason to believe Drumm has already made an attempt to abduct Miss Ainsley. It may be only an attempt to take advantage of her unprotected state, but I don't like it. Had not Miss Ainsley been remarkably quick-witted for her age, he might have succeeded."

He had all Sir Adrian's attention now. "Upon my word! You say Drumm actually abducted her?"

"I warned you she is almost wholly unprotected. Her only

chaperone is a twelve-year old child. I hope, after this episode, that will have a stop put to it, but she is also disastrously prone to protecting her brother. Someone has only to hint to her that he may be in trouble and she does not hesitate to leap into trouble. I myself made her acquaintance when she came to my house, unescorted, to ask me to forgive her brother's gambling debt. Certainly she should be wary of Drumm after this, but I have no expectation that were someone to tell her they had information regarding her brother, or that he had sent them to take her to him, she would not go with them instantly," he ended grimly.

"Good God! What do you mean to do?" asked Sir Adrian, regarding him curiously.

The other grimaced. "There is little I can do. I have informed her brother of the attempt, and to give him his due he was genuinely shocked. But it would be fatal to let Drumm know I have any interest in the young lady myself, as you know. I must rely on her brother to see that she is kept more closely. I can, and intend to let it be known, particularly by her aunt, that Miss Ainsley is not quite so friendless as she appears. I am relying upon you to scotch any danger at the other end. Or tell me I am imagining plots where none exist!"

There was a moment of silence. "No, I won't insult your intelligence by pretending that what you suggest is impossible," conceded Sir Adrian unwillingly. "Wellington maintains, with some justification, that we lose as many battles off the field as on. Barnstoke will obviously have to be warned, but he may be relied upon to cause as much of an uproar as possible. I'll do what I can to keep your young friends' names out of it, but the whole will be damned awkward. Particularly since—well, never mind, but there are reasons why it could not have happened at a worse time."

"I imagine there is seldom a good time for military espionage. I won't apologize for dropping it in your lap, Adrian, for I know no one more capable of handling it. Thank you! I must go. You might, while you're at it, use your influence to look into Kingsley's military record for me. In the meantime I'll do what I can to keep Miss Ainsley out of danger, which is much the harder task, you may believe me!"

Sir Adrian was still regarding him with rather curiously,

but at that moment the door opened and a charming voice inquired from the doorway, "Believe what? My dear, why didn't you tell me Locke was coming, for there's something I particularly wanted to ask him! Or are you two talking secrets? Shall I go away?"

Lady Barbeaux may have been married for more than twenty years, and possess a grown son and daughter, but it was a fact that few, looking at her youthful figure and lively countenance, found easy to remember. She did not much resemble her brother, possessing his gray eyes but little of his dignity or reserve. She was as flighty as her husband was sedate, and though she spent her days in an endless round of visits, teas, and balls while her husband pursued his own interests, it was a combination that seemed to have succeeded, for they were known to be devoted to each other.

She had evidently just come in from an engagement of her own, for she had a charming chip straw bonnet set at a dashing angle on her head, and was wearing a becoming and extremely expensive walking dress of patterned silk.

"Very dashing," observed her brother, regarding her critically through his glass.

"Yes, and wickedly expensive!" She twinkled up at him. "Perhaps you were wise never to marry, for then you might have been required to spend money on something other than your own pleasure. Which reminds me, how much should I put on that horse of yours in the Derby? Is he going to win? I saw a hat today that was even more wickedly expensive, that I'm longing to buy. Unless, of course, you care to make me a present of it?"

"My dear," pointed out her husband mildly, "it is not generally known yet that Locke owns Phalanx."

"Oh, pooh! Well, what do you say? I happen to know you spent a fortune on that dazzling creature I saw you with at the opera last year," his sister said with familial frankness. "What I want to know is when you mean settle down at last and make me an aunt. I am running out of excuses."

"Now, dear—"

"Nonsense, Adrian! Locke and I understand each other very well! At any rate, I'm tired of being discreet. I loved Caroline, too, but if you are still wearing the willow for her after all these years . . .!"

"My dear Eliza," said her long-suffering brother. "When were you ever discreet? Adrian, I must go. I will rely upon you about that other matter we spoke of. Don't bother to see me out."

"Oh, drat!" said his sister feelingly, blinking back sudden tears. "Very well, I'm done! Pray don't go on my account."

"I'm not. I'm late already for an appointment. I will make you a present of the hat, my dear Eliza, but there is a condition attached. I wish you to seem to take an interest in a particular young lady. Oh, don't look so alarmed!" he added mockingly. "Your interest need only be of the most nominal. In fact, owing to the press of Lizzie's come-out this year, I think it would be natural enough if you asked me to deliver your card to her aunt. Now I wonder where can you have met her? Ah, I have no doubt you attended school with her mother. You have only recently learned of her presence in London, and of course are eager to meet the daughter of such an old friend."

She was staring at him in some surprise, but retorted indignantly. "If I am that eager to meet her, I would hardly send you in my stead!"

"Ah, but that is an honor you promise yourself soon. Thank you, Eliza, I knew I might rely upon you!"

Lady Barbeaux was left regarding the panels of the gently shut door in some astonishment, "But—but who is she?" she wailed. "I don't even know her name. What on earth is he up to?"

"I haven't the faintest notion, my dear," responded her husband frankly. "You had better ask him."

"Much good it will do me if he doesn't wish to tell me! Oh, I could just murder him. Nothing is more certain than that I shall meet her and cut her dead—if I haven't already! And what am I to do? It's all very well to say I needn't put myself out, but if he means to let it be known I was at school with this girl's mother, whoever she may be, I must at least have her to tea. I was never more annoyed with him! Ought I to invite her to Lizzie's ball?" A new thought struck her. "Good God," she said rather blankly. "You don't suppose. . .?"

"No, I do not." Sir Adrian had gone to pour himself another glass of port. "If you must know, it is her brother

Locke is primarily interested in," he added, by no means sure it was the truth. "And don't ask me anything more, for that's all I know, my dear."

"Her brother!" She sounded almost disappointed. "Oh, well, I should have known it was too good to be true. I almost wish my elegant brother might fall in love with some wholly ineligible female. At least it would prove he was human."

15

Derry, in the meantime, had left Mr. James filled with an almost equal mixture of guilt and rage. No more than the Nonpareil did he doubt for a moment that it had been Drumm responsible for Phila's abduction, and while he wanted to smash the teeth down that oily throat, he could not forget that it had been through him Drumm had met Phila in the first place. He had wished to avoid the meeting, it was true, but that was mere quibbling.

At the moment his duty was clear, and he did not hesitate. Since he had no idea where Drumm might live, he went straight to Captain Kingsley's lodgings in King Street. It was still early, and he had to knock a number of times before he was at last admitted by the captain's batman, hastily dressed and looking much the worse for wear.

Hooks, in normal times, was something of a favorite with the captain's many friends, since he was cheerfully and incurably Cockney, and possessed an impertinent manner he treated everyone to, including his master. He was lazy, only nominally subservient, and held just closely enough in line by the captain to still be amusing; but at the moment Derry was in no mood for his humor. "Where's the captain?" he demanded shortly.

Hooks grinned and scratched his head. "'E's in, in a manner o' speakin', that is. But you don' want to see 'im.

Powerful angry 'e is when 'e's woke unnatural-like. We 'ad a
party last night, as you might say.''

The evidence was everywhere. The captain's lodgings were
always cluttered, but now overturned chairs and bottles littered the floor, and the smell of cigar smoke and stale gin
was unmistakable. Someone had left a major's dress tunic
hung on a wall sconce. Derry looked around impatiently. "I
don't care for that! Wake him! I've got to speak to him."

"You wake 'im, if you're so anxious," invited the servant.
"I've 'ad the candlestick chucked at me head." He began
desultorily to pick up the place.

"Oh—go soak your head, you fool! You're still drunk."
Derry impatiently pushed past him. The captain's bedchamber was in a little better order, but he had apparently dropped
his clothes where he discarded them, and Hooks had made no
attempt to put them away. A messy pile of papers and bills
littered the dressing table, a cup of cold tea had been forgotten on the bedside table, and a military sword had somehow
become entangled in the bedclothes at the foot of the bed.
Derry ignored the mess and shook the slumbering figure of
his friend.

At the first hand on his arm Jack started up violently,
cursing. "Hooks, you bastard, I told you I was . . ."

Derry rescued the candlestick he had instinctively grabbed
up, a little amused despite himself. "Good God, Jack, it's
me! Were you really going to chuck the candlestick at me?"

"Aye, werry violent 'e is, when 'e's woken out of a sound
sleep," observed Hooks piously from the doorway. "Don't
say I didn't warn you."

Jack had by that time managed to focus his bleary gaze on
Derry's face. "What the devil? What do you mean by waking
me up at . . ." He peered at the clock, but it had not been
wound. "Never mind. Go away again and let me get some
sleep. You should have been here last night, by the way. I
can remember very little of it, but it seems to have been a
great party."

Derry forcibly prevented him from turning over and going
back to sleep. "So it would appear. Don't go to sleep again.
I've got to talk to you."

Jack yawned, but after a moment pulled himself up to lean
against his pillows. "Oh, very well, if you must! What's

o'clock by the way? Mine seems to have stopped, and I can't find my watch anywhere.''

"Lieutenant Fitzroy threw it out the window," observed Hooks from his vantage point at the doorway.

"Are you still here? In that case, bring me some coffee, since it appears I'm up, and then see what you can do about this place. It looks like a pigsty." He yawned again and rubbed his unshaven jaw, but looked more alert, for he added as Hooks at last shuffled away, "Now, you fool, what's all this about? You look ready to do murder."

"I am!" exclaimed Derry, his eyes fulminating again at the memory. "Where can I find Drumm?"

The captain looked very little better than his servant, but he sat up more fully at that, and reached for his cigar case. "Monty?" he asked casually. "He has lodgings in the City somewhere. I suppose I could find out if it were important. Is this what you woke me out of a sound sleep to ask me?"

"Yes. I haven't time to explain now, but—I told you he was a complete villain!" he burst out. "Good God, when I think—I'd like to get my fingers around that fat neck of his!"

"Good God, you're bloodthirsty for this early in the morning. What's he done? On second thought, you'd better wait till I've had my coffee to tell me. My stomach's none too steady at the moment."

Hooks sidled in then with a tray, which he made room for on the bedside table by the simple expedient of sweeping everything on it onto the floor. He then grinned and winked at Derry before removing himself again, ignoring the disorder in the room.

Jack leaned over and poured himself a cup of coffee. "I ought to dismiss the bastard," he said, yawning. "He was as drunk as I was last night. Now, cut rope and tell me what's up, you young hothead. Now that you've spoiled my sleep it's the least you can do."

Derry hesitated, but the urge to confide in his friend was too great. He told him, stuttering a little in his rage, unable to remain still but pacing up and down in agitation. "I told you not to let him hang around," he finished grimly. "Nor I won't soon be able to forget that I was the one to introduce him to my sister."

"In point of fact, I was," observed Jack mildly. "But

steady on, old fellow. I'll admit on the face of it it looks pretty bad, but I'd advise you to consider it a little more closely before you rush off to issue your challenge."

"Bad?" repeated Derry furiously. "I tell you the bastard abducted my sister! You were the last one I would have expected to defend him."

"I'm not defending him. I am merely trying to prevent you from making a fool of yourself, at least until you hear the whole story. You say he abducted her, but I have to say, at the risk of angering you even further, that it sounds unlike Drumm. Oh, I don't say he may not have gotten a little out of line, but you must admit your sister is extremely naive, however charming she may be. Can you be sure she didn't merely misunderstand, or took panic when his attentions became too marked? And—well—to be perfectly frank, dear boy, she shouldn't have gotten up with him in the first place, you know. No one's going to believe she didn't encourage him, I fear."

Derry stared at him. "My God, I can't believe this! I thought you, at least, would understand!" But in the face of his friend's calm reason, he was himself confronted by a sudden doubt. Drumm was an out-and-out villain, he firmly believed, but it was true that Phila was extremely inexperienced. He knew what James had said, but it was not beyond possibility that she had overreacted. Certainly she should never have gotten up with him in the first place, and that, coupled with the almost complete freedom she enjoyed to come and go as she wished, might very well have misled Drumm as to her quality and experience. Damn the Coateses! He had been right to believe them criminally negligent in their duties as chaperones.

As if sensing his growing indecision, Jack said persuasively, "Come, now. At least admit it might be so. I hold no particular brief for Drumm, but he must have known he could never get away with it! At any rate, true or false, you can't call him out you know."

"Why can't I?" demanded Derry belligerently.

"Because I assume you have no desire to have your sister's name bandied about, as you may be sure it will be if you challenge him. Challenge him! Good God, the man is no gentleman. You'd only emerge looking ridiculous from such an affair.''

Derry sat down abruptly. He was by no means ready to relinquish his just fury, but the force of the captain's arguments were having their inevitable effect and his uncomfortable doubts were growing. "I don't care," he said, looking mutinous. "What do I care for points of etiquette when the man's a menace to society? Anyone would call him out on his taste in coats alone! I don't need an excuse."

"An interesting point," grinned Jack. "I'll even admit that the world would be a decidedly better place without Drumm in it. But leaving aside every other trifling objection, I'm afraid you can't go about killing off men you owe money to.''

Derry stared at him. "I don't owe Drumm any money!"

"I dislike being the bearer of bad tidings, but I'm afraid you do. Do you remember that sure thing I put you onto a couple of weeks ago? The horse that my tipsters said couldn't lose, and managed to go dead lame in the last furlong? Yes, I dislike being reminded of it as well, for I lost a bundle myself! But the fact is, Drumm handled the transaction for us. He hasn't been pressing me for payment, so I've been in no hurry to repay him under the circumstances. But it does present a slight obstacle now, I'm afraid. Though it's a solution for getting out of debt that is tempting, I'll admit.

"Then I'll pay him back! In fact, I wish you had told me at the time, for you know my feelings toward Drumm. I would never have gone in on it if you'd told me who was involved.''

"I wish now I had resisted as well, but it's easy to be wise after the event. At any rate, if you pay him the two hundred pounds you owe him, I'll admit that removes that particular objection, at least. You can pay it, I suppose? I couldn't, God knows, but then I've suffered a number of rather serious reversals lately, I fear. We can't all have your phenomenal luck.''

"Y-yes. I mean, yes of course!" He could, but it would place a serious dent in his nest egg, nor could he remember ever having placed a wager that large. Since it was Jack, of course, he did not question it, and he had a vague recollection of a horse that had been unplaced. In the last few weeks he had perhaps gone a little overboard, recklessly convinced, despite Corny's warning, that he could not lose, and thus less careful than he should have been. But he certainly would never have agreed to join in any wager with Drumm, for he had mistrusted him from the first.

"Well, that's settled, then," said Jack lightly. "It may prove somewhat embarrassing for me, I'll admit, but by all means don't let that stop you."

"Embarrassing for you?" repeated Derry, flushing slightly. "How can it be embarrassing for you?"

"Because, my fledgling, I will find it rather harder to lay my hands on such a sum readily. But I suppose it must be done, if you are to call him out."

It occurred to Derry that his friend Jack was not taking the matter as seriously as he would have wished. He had come there full of the murderous intention of righting his sister's wrongs, but somehow matters had changed until he almost felt himself on the defensive. That was ridiculous, of course, but he found himself saying stiffly, "If it's a matter of money, I could advance you some, you know that."

"It is *always* a matter of money, my dear boy, as I fear you will learn to your cost. It remains only for you to make certain the crime did, in fact, take place, and then you may remove him with my blessing. I've told you I'm not in disagreement that a world without Drumm in it won't be an infinitely superior place. I only wonder if—" Abruptly his eyes narrowed and he sat up. "Wait a minute! What a fool I am! I know how you can pay Drumm back, and in his own coin, too, and in such a way that your sister's name will never come into it! It was already in the back of my mind, but I was prepared to see you kill the goose that was to lay the golden egg in the interests of justice. But this will kill both birds with one stone. It will also hurt Drumm where he's the most vulnerable—his pocketbook! I tell you it's foolproof."

Derry stared at him, torn. He was reluctant to give up his desire to see Drumm come to a deservedly violent end, but he was aware that his resolve had suffered an uneasy check. If he could have choked the fat life out of Drumm when he had first heard, it would have been easy. The delay had merely given him time to remember all the objections to so blood-thirsty and satisfactory a plan and lose his first, white-hot certainty. The thought that Jack had intended that from the first he dismissed as unworthy, but he could not quite dismiss the suspicion that from talking about calling a man out to merely causing him to suffer financial reverses was an ignoble leap. Still, he said somewhat sullenly, "I don't know. It doesn't sound right, somehow."

"If you mean it's not bloodthirsty enough for you, that's all to the good. I tell you, it's perfect. You'll teach Drumm a lesson he won't soon forget and do both of us a good turn at the same time. Enough of one, I hope, to see your sister settled for life. I'm sorry, old boy, I wouldn't say anything before, but I'm afraid your sister's just asking for it in her present situation. Do you want to be revenged on Drumm, or see that it doesn't happen again? With my plan you can have both, believe me."

"All right," said Derry, abruptly taking the plunge. "What do you have in mind?"

16

Phila, in the meantime, was suffering all the natural reactions to her unpleasant adventure. She had been more shaken than bruised by her untimely exit from Mr. Drumm's carriage, and suffered no real harm—not even Aunt Chloe's questions. But it was long before she could bring her spirits to the point of acknowledging that fact.

She had endured a trying interview with her brother the next morning, which might have something to do with it. It did not take Derry long to drag the whole story out of her, and even she could see that it only added fuel to his argument that Aunt Chloe was an inadequate chaperone.

"My God, Phila, have you no sense?" he demanded explosively when she had stammered to a finish. "Even if you did meet Drumm through me, you must have known better than to get up with him!"

She could not answer him, and after a moment he confirmed her worst fears by adding, "Well, it merely shows how impossible it is for you to stay here any longer! You've no business being out unescorted, but why didn't you at least tell me the damn fellow had approached you again?''

"I'm sorry," she said miserably. "I didn't think—and anyway, I haven't seen very much of you lately.''

He took that to be criticism of his neglect of her and colored up hotly. "Good God, can't I turn my back on you at all without your getting into trouble? And as for thinking I was in debt to him, all I can say is that if I were it would be none of your business! What did you think you could do about it, anyway? I tell you what it is, Phila, it's more than time I removed you from your cousins' influence, for if you ask me you're becoming as hoydenish as they are! This is the second time I've had to learn from someone else that you've tumbled into a harebrained scrape. It makes me look a complete fool! It's getting to the point I can't have a moment's peace for wondering what you might get up to next!''

"Was Mr. James very angry with me?" she asked miserably.

"Angry? Why should he be angry with you? I don't doubt he thinks you completely out of control by now," said Derry, unintentionally contributing to her depression, "but you may be sure it's me he blames! Good God, it would have to be him who came to your rescue a second time! I could wish it had been anyone else.''

Then abruptly he flushed. "No, no, of course I don't mean that! In fact, I must be damned grateful to him. Even if I did have to endure a damned officious lecture from him and have been made to feel a complete villain. Well, it does no good to talk of it! The thing is, you needn't worry about Drumm anymore. I intend to take care of him. In the meantime, don't go out alone, and tell me if he should dare to approach you again. And for God's sake, don't get into any more strange gentlemen's carriages!''

She ignored the last remark to ask fearfully, "Oh, Derry, what do you mean to do?''

But he was irritated once more. "Nothing to make you look like that! I'll admit I wanted to call him out when I first heard, but Jack convinced me otherwise. It's a good thing he did, since he was right: You as much as invited him to insult you by getting up with him. A fine fool I should have looked.''

This was palpably unfair, but Phila was so relieved to learn he had abandoned the notion of calling Mr. Drumm out that she made no protest. In fact, she had never expected to be so grateful to Captain Kingsley. "Oh, no, you mustn't!" she cried. "He isn't worth it anyway. In fact, since I made him overturn, I expect he will be happy never to see me again. But what do you mean to do? Please tell me!"

But that Derry would not do, adding unkindly that obviously the less she knew the better, since any time he confided in her it only led to trouble. Unfortunately, it was a charge she could not defend herself against, and so she did not press him, having to be content with his promise that he did not intend any violence.

But the interview had not been calculated to cheer her already drooping spirits, until in the end even Aunt Chloe commented on it. "If you're not sickening for something, I don't know what it is!" she said in her usual forthright way. "Drat the place; between you and Letty, and the heat, London don't seem to agree with any of us. Well, it's a cinch we'll none of us be able to go home until this famous ball is over. Not that I begrudge Lydia her chance as I hope you know! But it's true I'm beginning to think longingly of Somerset and your uncle. I hope you are not to be sick on top of everything else!"

Phila reassured her, and after that made an effort to appear more normal. But it was true that Letty was also in far from her usual spirits.

Phila, at least, had reason to be grateful to Lydia, and the preparations for her ball. It gave her something to do, since she was kept busy fetching and carrying and running errands for Lydia, and since Lydia now demanded her escort whenever she was to go walking in the Park, or to meet Miss Woodyard, she had little leisure in which to mope.

This last task Phila would have preferred to be excused from, since she had met Miss Woodyard by now and did not like her. She was a pale, supercilious young woman with a sharp profile and a haughty manner, and she had questioned Phila closely about her family and her relationship to the Coateses. She had obviously then dismissed her as being beneath her notice, for after that she seldom could be bothered to address any but the most trifling of remarks to her.

Toward Lydia she was considerably warmer, but Phila was at a loss to know why. Miss Woodyard was full of flattery about Lydia's beauty and gowns and jewels, but her manner was naturally cold, and it was almost as if she were forcing herself to affect a friendship she did not feel. Certainly she was a complete snob, and Phila could not help but suspect that ordinarily Miss Woodyard would never have condescended to befriend anyone so far beneath her own social stratum.

Nor did it take her long to discover the real reason behind Miss Woodyard's uncharacteristic lapse. She possessed a cousin of whom she was particularly fond, and who just happened, with increasing frequency, to escort her whenever she was to meet Lydia. Phila liked Mr. Bevis even less than Miss Woodyard, but at least the scales had dropped from her eyes. Mr. Bevis was bored and condescending, but he made no secret of the fact he was hanging out for a rich wife. He would no doubt have preferred one of his own social standing, but beggars can't be choosers, and some of his debts were growing pressing. He had clearly come to look Lydia over, and having approved, meant to waste no time in coming to terms with the most likely candidate his cousin had yet found for him.

Phila was appalled, for she thought that once his ring was on Lydia's finger and they were sure of Uncle Jos's money, neither would trouble to hide their contempt any longer. But when she at last steeled herself to broach the subject to Lydia, it was clear she might have spared herself the pains.

"Did you really think I didn't know?" demanded Lydia unkindly. "You are a fool, Phila! I am by no means decided to take Mr. Bevis yet, for this ball should give me the chance I need, and I may do even better for myself. But if not, you may depend upon it I shall be very careful never to let him forget who holds the purse strings. So long as that's understood, what do I care what his motives may be, so long as we both get what we want?"

Thoroughly chilled, Phila said no more.

But she was unable to remain quiet when Lydia said carelessly that same evening, "Phila had best have a new ballgown as well, Mama, if she is to come with me. Miss Woodyard will be expecting me to have a chaperone, and she doesn't object to Phila.''

Phila had been paying very little attention to the conversation, her fingers desultorily occupied in mending a tear in one of Priddy's muslins, but her mind far away, when she was recalled with a jerk by that. ''But—but—I naturally assumed Aunt Chloe . . .''

''Oh, Mama doesn't want to come, do you, Mama?'' said Lydia in her unkind way. ''And I can't go with no more than a maid to escort me.''

''Then Letty . . .?''

But both sisters repudiated that suggestion with loathing. ''Don't worry, Phila,'' said Letty. ''I don't aspire to such circles, believe me. You may have my place and welcome.''

''Oh, yes, you'd prefer to marry some red-faced merchant and produce a passel of dirty brats, I have no doubt! If, that is, marriage even enters your plans these days, which I'm beginning to doubt.''

''Now, girls!'' protested Aunt Chloe unhappily. ''But Lydia's right, for once. I've given it a good deal of thought, and I agree that Phila is the one to go with her.''

''No—oh, no!'' cried Phila before she could prevent herself. ''Oh, Aunt Chloe, please don't make me!''

Even Aunt Chloe stared at her, and Lydia said furiously, ''Make you! You should be grateful to me, for it's the closest you'll ever get to the polite world otherwise, despite your much-vaunted breeding! And if not, you can at least remember what you owe to us and make yourself useful for once in your life!''

Phila bit her tongue and said no more, but later, alone with Aunt Chloe, she tried to explain, though without much success.

Aunt Chloe merely patted her cheek fondly. ''Now, my dear, Lydia didn't mean to be unkind. Or rather, I daresay she did, but I hope you've too much sense to regard it. You don't need me to tell you that she's got this bee in her bonnet about being a fine lady someday, and nothing is to stand in her way. Between you and me, I suspect if she does succeed in her ambitions she'll have precious little to do with her family after that, but that's neither here nor there, after all. It's not her pa's and my way to deny her if it's what she wants. Lor', child, I don't say that to get your sympathy, but to let you know I'm not blind to any of my children's faults. And if her ambition can help you at the same time, however little it may be her intention, then it's even better.''

"But I don't want to go!'' cried Phila desperately. "It should be you or Letty instead, you know it should.''

"Now, that's like your kind heart, my dear, but I've given this a great deal of thought, you may believe. And for all I treat you as one of my own, I haven't forgotten you aren't, as I hope you know. It should be you, not Lydia, mixing with the Miss Woodyards of this world, as we all know.''

"Oh, Aunt Chloe, you mean to be kind,'' said Phila helplessly, "but what good does it do me to have been born a lady if I must live on your and Uncle Jos's kind charity? I don't belong in that world even as much as Lydia, for at least she has beauty and money! I have nothing! I've learned that, at least, since coming to London. Oh, don't you see? If you make me go with Lydia, I shall feel miserable and out of place, and Miss Woodyard despises me and—anyway, the sooner I accept the truth that I shall never escape from being a burden on you and my brother, the better!''

This was so unlike Phila that Aunt Chloe's jaw dropped, but she made a rapid recovery. "Now, let me hear no more of such talk! Charity, indeed! And as for the rest nothing could be further from the truth. I hope I'm not one to shortchange my own daughters, and there's no denying Lydia's a mighty pretty girl. But no amount of beauty, or her papa's money, will ever succeed in making her a lady-born, and we both know it, more's the pity. Why else do you think she's resented you all of these years, if not because you have what she would give anything to possess? If she succeeds in marrying above her station, as the saying is, and I'm sure I hope she may, she'll never be able to forget that her ma and pa were nothing but good yeoman stock, and proud of it; nor you may be sure will anyone else let her forget it either. Well, that's her cross to bear. But as for you, all you need is some fine gentleman to fall head over heels in love with you and you'll soon forget this talk of not belonging.''

Phila surprised both of them very much by bursting into tears.

17

Phila soon recovered from this uncharacteristic lapse, however, and apologized.

Aunt Chloe patted her hand and said kindly, "We'll say no more! A new ball dress will soon set you to rights, I'll warrant. And let's hear none of your protests, my dear! It's been in my mind since we came to order you one, for Heaven knows you deserve it, if anyone does. And once you're decked out to rival Lydia, as I mean to see you are, you won't feel the poor relation any longer, I promise you! Let's only hope that you don't put her nose out of joint, for you're a very pretty girl, as I hope you know. Now, let's say no more, as I said. It's the heat that's affecting us all, I shouldn't wonder. I feel decidedly glumpish myself."

Phila knew it was not the heat, but she wisely said no more. Nor did she think she was in any danger of putting Lydia's nose out of joint, new ballgown or no. She only wished she could go back to Somerset now and forget everything that had happened in London.

Then something occurred to put the ball out of everyone's mind for good, and make Phila indeed wish that she could have gone away when she had wanted to.

Notwithstanding their brief quarrel Lydia still expected Phila's escort whenever she was to meet Miss Woodyard, for as she had said, she was doing Phila a favor, after all, and if Phila was unwilling, or unable to appreciate it, then she might just remember what she owed to the family. It obviously had not occurred to Lydia to regard Phila in the light of a rival, for Phila had never shown well in the company of her more outspoken cousins; and in the presence of Miss Woodyard and Mr. Bevis she was rendered almost invisible by shyness and dislike.

Lydia was perfectly content with this state of things, and they had long since ceased even making a pretense of including Phila in their conversations. Phila, in turn, seldom bothered to listen, so that the introduction of the Nonpareil's name one day while they were walking in the Park was all the more startling.

She had no idea what had gone before, but her wandering thoughts were jerked to attention in time to hear Miss Woodyard say, in her condescending way, "Mama is acquainted with him, of course, and I stood up with him for one dance at Lady Castlereigh's ridotto. I've sent him a card to my ball, but I daresay he won't come. He's one of the Leaders of Fashion, you know. Mama says he suffered a tragic love affair in his youth, which is why all the beauties have thrown their caps at him year after year to no avail. But of course everyone expects him to wed Lady Antonia Burke sooner or later, for they are imminently suited."

Phila was now frankly listening with a sort of sick compulsion. She had not known the Nonpareil was shortly to be wed, but she had occupied herself at least once in gloomily imagining the sort of female who would appeal to Mr. James. The opposite of herself in every respect, of course: beautiful and well-born, sure of herself and wholly unlikely to fall into painful and humiliating scrapes. Her conduct would doubtless be as proper as her lineage, and she would certainly have no embarrassing relations, or ever drag Mr. James into improper situations.

This depressing picture was abruptly dispelled by Miss Woodyard's saying with something almost approaching animation. "Oh, but he's coming over! I didn't think—but of course he knows Mama, as I said. It is a great honor to be introduced to him, my dear Miss Coates, for he is normally quite a high stickler."

Phila felt anything but honored, but it was quite true that Mr. James, mounted on a glossy black, was making his way deliberately toward them. She did not know how she had come not to see him before, but there was now no escape, for he had clearly seen her. She could only pray that he was indeed acquainted with Miss Woodyard, and would ignore herself altogether. Or that she could sink into the earth where she stood.

She was unaware of the mute appeal in her eyes as she looked up at him, but she was very aware of her heightened heartbeat. Even overshadowing her embarrassed memory of their last meeting was the sudden conviction that Lydia was going to be very angry indeed if she ever learned that Phila could have introduced her to the Nonpareil himself. Even Miss Woodyard seemed to be in awe of him. Worse, Aunt Chloe was going to be hurt, for neither of them would ever understand the truth, or be able to see that, far from having any desire to help Lydia in her social ambitions, Mr. James blamed the Coateses for Phila's shortcomings.

He had reached them by then, and was swinging easily down from the saddle. and it very quickly became apparent that Phila's prayers were not to be answered. Miss Woodyard's gracious smile was wasted as well, for if Mr. James recalled dancing with her at Lady Castlereigh's ridotto he did not reveal it, but said instead, his eyes taking in both of Phila's companions with an equal lack of recognition, "Miss Ainsley, we are well met, for I have been wondering how you were getting on. In fact, I have been meaning to call on your aunt, but unfortunately I was called out of town for a few days. Are these your cousins?"

Phila felt the calm of total despair overtake her and thus was able to make the necessary introductions. She was aware of Miss Woodyard's astonishment, on one side, and if it would almost have been worth it to see that imperious damsal thrown for a loss for once, Phila had only to steal a glance at Lydia's rigid features on the other to lose all inclination to enjoy her triumph.

It was Miss Woodyard who recovered first, all trace of her usual condescension absent from her manner. "I believe, you are acquainted with my mother, Lady Woodyard," she said brightly. "But I was not aware you knew Miss Ainsley."

"Weren't you?" he observed politely. "But then there was no particular reason you should be, after all. As it happens, her mother was at school with my sister. Since my sister is at present almost wholly tied up with her elder daughter's debut this Season, she asked me to keep an eye on Miss Ainsley for her."

"Dear Lady Barbeaux!" gushed Miss Woodyard. "I am sure Miss Barbeaux and I are the best of friends! I am so looking forward to her ball—next week, is it not? Speaking of which, I am sure my mother sent you a card for mine on the fourteenth. I do hope you will be able to come. Miss Ainsley will be attending, so you may be sure of renewing your acquaintance there.''

At any other time Phila would have been amazed at the change that had come over Miss Woodyard, for even to Lydia she had not bothered to put herself out very much. In fact, Phila found it a little disgusting that anyone could have so little pride as to make up to the Nonpareil so basely simply because of his wealth and position. It showed more than ever how little she belonged in their world.

Perhaps fortunately the Nonpareil was not required to answer Miss Woodyard's question, for at that moment a husky, attractive voice inquired behind him, ''Locke? Forgive me, but if you are going to be another few minutes, I think I shall have a gallop.''

Phila found herself looking up at the most beautiful creature she had ever encountered. She was riding a spirited-looking bay that looked far too strong for any lady to hold, and was dressed in a dashing habit that set off her splendid figure to admiration, and on any other woman would have looked decidedly fast. A daring military shako was set on her golden curls, a feather curling down to caress her cheek and set off her brilliantly blue eyes. At the moment she was smiling a little quizzically down at her escort, and Phila, still gripped by that odd fatalism that seemed to have come over her, did not need to be told that this was Lady Antonia Burke. The contrast to her own childish figure and tongue-tied manners could not have been greater, and at the moment not even Lydia's certain fury could make Phila any more miserable than she already was.

That did not last, unfortunately. Mr. James gracefully made the introductions, and if Lady Antonia was surprised to learn that the Nonpareil's sister, whom she knew very well, had been to school with Miss Ainsley's mother, she did not reveal it. She said instead, in her enchantingly husky voice, ''see! How delightful! I hope you are enjoying your stay in London, Miss Ainsley? You must come and drink tea with me one afternoon. Locke will bring you.''

It was too much. Lydia had remained silent till now, for in fact it had taken some moments for the extent of Phila's perfidy to sink into her. Not only had Phila remained silent about her grand acquaintances while she, Lydia, had worked and schemed only to meet someone as unimportant as Miss Woodyard; but even now her insignificant little cousin was receiving all the attention and had even been invited to take tea with the famous Lady Antonia Burke, while she, far more beautiful and rich, had been totally ignored. The fact that Miss Woodyard had been ignored as well clearly made no difference.

Lydia had never been made to consider the consequences of her actions, but she was no fool, and seldom forgot where her own best interests lay. Her temper might be violent, and she had been allowed to vent it on her family for so long that she was out of the habit of biting her tongue; but even a moment's consideration would have convinced her of the inadvisability of alienating so important a figure as the Nonpareil.

However, for once she was far too angry to consider her best interests. "Certainly, if my mother can spare her, of course!" she said, the venom in her voice unmistakable. "I fear you somewhat misunderstand my cousin's position. Since her parents' death she has served as my mother's companion. But I'm sure Mama will be delighted to give her the time off to visit you under the circumstances, even though we were both unaware she had any acquaintance in London!"

Even Miss Woodyard gasped slightly. There was surprise, and then pity in Lady Antonia's eyes, but Phila did not dare to see what Mr. James's expression might be. What made it worse was that what Lydia had said was true, however cruel it had been. She was little better than an unpaid companion in the Coateses' household.

She tried to say something, anything to relieve the awful moment. But there was nothing to say, for nothing could recall those words or make them any less true. Knowing she was perilously close to losing control completely, Phila completed her disgrace by ignominiously turning and running away, almost blinded by tears.

18

She might have been a little comforted, however, had she seen the Nonpareil's face before her disastrous flight. Not even Derry would have recognized it, since for all his unpleasantness the Nonpareil had never lost his temper with him, or come close to doing so.

He had lost his temper now, however. He looked Lydia up and down, making no attempt to hide the contempt in his expression and said shortly, "I would have thought your cousin was a wholly unworthy target, Miss Coates, since she is almost pathetically grateful to your family. Or did you believe her to be as friendless as she appears, and so open to your vindictiveness?"

Lydia was goggling at him, for once brought to a sense of her own folly. But the Nonpareil did not wait for her to answer, "She may not be able to defend herself, but you have gone too far this time. In fact, I would advise you to reconsider your present ambitions, for I can't help but think you'll find London an unfriendly place from now on. I hope I make myself clear?"

Once they had ridden away Lady Antonia said frankly, "What a shrew! That poor child. I hope she was not too wounded, but I fear otherwise."

"So do I," said the Nonpareil grimly. "Unfortunately Miss Ainsley is already morbidly sensitive about her unfortunate circumstances, and absurdly grateful to her relations, the quality of whose kindness I'm afraid we have just seen an example of."

"Poor child," said Lady Antonia again. "Will she be all right?"

"I doubt even Miss Coates would dare to abandon her in the Park," he said drily, his eyes still unusually hard. "Though I fear I have only made matters worse by my bungling attempt to help."

Lady Antonia stared at him in some surprise. It was indeed unlike him to behave so clumsily, for anyone with sense could have predicted the outcome of his well-meaning but unwise interference. It was even more unlike Locke to go out of his way to be kind to so unlikely a young lady, however much to be pitied.

Lady Antonia had known Locke since she had been a scruffy brat tagging after him whenever she got the opportunity, and she flattered herself she knew him better than perhaps anyone else.

"Well, yes, rather," she conceded. "Who is she? And don't repeat that nonsensical tale of her mother's having been at school with Eliza, for I don't believe a word of it."

"Perhaps someday I will tell you how I came to make her acquaintance," he said. "It was something that not even you, with all your vaunted courage, would do, my dear Tony.

"Suffice it to say she is an orphan, as you no doubt gathered. There is a brother, but he seems wholly incapable of providing for her, or even of controlling the more disastrous of her impulses. At the moment she resides with the Coateses, whom I believe are some sort of distant relations. Unfortunately, she has been made to feel very much the poor relation, as you just saw. I only regret her sex made it impossible for me to deal with her cousin as I would have liked."

Lady Antonia glanced at him again, aware of a faint, wholly unworthy sense of pique. She was not in love with her old friend. But she had long ago determined that when she was at last ready to settle down, she could do far worse than such a marriage of friendship, rather than passion. She suspected, in fact, that neither of them were particularly capable of passion. Certainly they were both far too clear-eyed and self-absorbed to ever give in to the willfully blind, self-deluding state the world called love.

Though nothing had ever been said, she had believed Locke to be of the same mind. Nor did she, after some consideration, believe that he was in love with the childish Miss Ainsley. But like Mr. Shelby, she had never known him to speak in quite such terms of anyone before, or go to such extraordinary lengths to help one who, one would have thought, was wholly beneath his notice.

Annoyed with her own line of thought she said, her mocking drawl more pronounced even than usual, "That was evident, my dear! But you may well have had your revenge. I presume you are unacquainted with your Miss Coates's companion?"

"The languid blond? Should I know her?"

She smiled. "No, except that her mama is greatly desirous that you should, and I know for a fact that you stood up with her at least once at Arabella Castlereigh's ball."

"Did I? Very likely!" he said indifferently. "I can't remember a worse crush. In fact, I can't think why I went."

"You went because I asked you," she supplied unresentfully. "But never mind that! The point is, besides having a languid daughter to dispose of, Elvira Woodyard—a most unpleasant woman!—has an exceedingly expensive and equally languid nephew on her hands, and everyone knows Woodyard is all to pieces! Believe me, there is no other reason I can think of why the Woodyards, an old family, however unpleasant, would stoop to cultivate your Miss Coates. They mean—or rather meant!—her to rescue Reginald Bevis from the worst of his embarrassments. I say meant, because judging from the look on Miss Woodyard's face when we left them, they are about to reconsider, in the face of your so-obvious disapproval. So you see, you are likely to have your revenge even sooner than you were expecting, if that was your intent."

"Good God! Where on earth do you learn all this?" he asked, amused in spite of himself. "Never mind, my sister is just the same! But I fear you overestimate both my influence and my vindictiveness. Miss Coates may marry your Mr. Bevis with my compliments—in fact, it sounds as if they deserve each other. And it might, at least, precipitate the removal of my Miss Ainsley, as you call her, from London, which is a circumstance devoutly to be wished, at the moment. But for God's sake, let us change the subject! I am finding a career of philanthropy extremely exhausting. I can't think what can have possessed me to embark on it in the first place."

That sounded more like the Locke she knew. She glanced at him, a little relieved in spite of herself, and readily changed the subject, embarking on a lively account of a hunt she had been on, and making him laugh, as she always could. But even as she did so she felt a twinge of self-contempt that she should feel it necessary to compete with so absurd a young lady. Nor could she be wholly satisfied that she had his whole attention, a thing that had never happened to her before.

In the meantime Phila, blinded by her tears, had only succeeded in losing herself among the maze of paths criss-crossing the Park. By the time she had recovered herself somewhat, and acknowledged the extent of her folly, since she had only succeeded in making an even greater fool of herself by running, and must eventually confront Lydia any-way, it took her some little time again to find a path that was familiar to her, and led to the right gate.

Unlike the Nonpareil, it did not even occur to her that Lydia and Miss Woodyard would have waited for her; and thus she was not doomed to be disappointed. But since as usual Phila had come out quite without any money, she had no choice but to walk the long distance home.

To add to her misery it presently began to rain. She trudged on, her muslin gown soon soaked, and tried not to think of the scene that undoubtedly awaited her at home.

That Lydia was furious there could be no doubt. But even more than Lydia's anger did Phila fear that Aunt Chloe, too, was likely to be very hurt, at the very least. She had no idea why the Nonpareil should have said such a thing, but if he had been bent on punishing her for her previous folly, he could not have hit upon a better plan. It was going to be impossible now to make Aunt Chloe believe that she had not refused to help Lydia by introducing her to so acknowledged a leader of the "ton!"

By the time she at last reached home, she was soaked to the skin and thoroughly miserable. To her relief Priddy let her in, her freckled face flushed with some strong emotion. "I was on the watch for you," she said hurriedly. "Hush! They're in there. You'd best come up and get out of your wet things."

"Oh, Priddy! What's happened? Is Aunt Chloe very angry with me?" she asked, dreading the answer.

"Don't be silly! We all know what Lydia is. Anyway, that's not what she's really angry about, though she won't admit it, of course. In fact, if you ask me, she ruined herself. Oh, but you don't know that part yet! After you left, it seems your Mr. James let her know he found her as poisonous as I do, and that from now on she was likely to find London a great deal more unfriendly than before. Not surprisingly, after that her precious Miss Woodyard found urgent reason to be someplace else, and left her in the lurch,'' she said with a certain satisfaction, ''which is why her highness is having hysterics in the parlor right now. But if you ask me, she deserved everything that's coming to her.''

"Oh, Priddy!" breathed Phila in horror. "I never meant—oh, what am I going to do?"

She was given no opportunity to discover, for at that moment the parlor doors were flung open, and Lydia cried shrilly, "I thought it was you! So you dared to show your face back here after all? But then I have discovered we none of us knew what a clever little schemer you really are, beneath that demure exterior!" She took in Phila's bedraggled appearance and shrinking stance and added unkindly, "I wish your great Nonpareil could see you now! It's clear she means to have him for herself, of course, which would be hilarious if it weren't so pathetic! What did you do, make him feel sorry for you with your pitiful little ways? We've all seen them, haven't we, Mama? The pitiful Miss Philadelphia Ainsley, always so eager to please, with her well-bred air and shy eyes. While all the time she was obviously planning to stab us in the back at the first opportunity. Well, your Mr. James may feel sorry for you, but did you really think he would stoop to marrying a penniless little guttersnipe obliged to live on other people's charity? Don't make me laugh! You heard Miss Woodyard: the whole world knows he's going to marry Lady Antonia Burke.''

"I told you how she came to meet him!" cried Priddy furiously. "And anyway, what all this is really about is that you ruined yourself by letting him see what an ill-natured beast you are.''

"No, Priddy, please . . .!" begged Phila.

Unexpectedly, Aunt Chloe took charge. "Now that's enough,'' she said in an unusually firm voice. "I don't know what difference it makes whether Phila should be acquainted with this Nonparole or not, which is a mighty funny name for a grown man anyway, if you ask me. What I do know is that I've heard more than enough on the subject at the moment.

For now, Phila had better go upstairs and get out of those wet things, for it will do none of us any good if she catches her death. And as for you, Lydia, if your chances are ruined as you say, I'll wager Priddy is right and you've only yourself to blame. I've warned you time and again about that temper of yours, but you'd never believe me that a beautiful face is not enough. I'm sure I'm sorry if Miss Woodyard was unkind to you, but perhaps it will teach you a much-needed lesson, and that's all I have to say on the subject for now."

Her eldest daughter relieved her feelings somewhat by taking up a vase and flinging it against the wall.

19

Phila gratefully fled to her room, and thought it prudent to remain there. She was sick that she could have caused so much trouble, and had to dismally face the fact that even without Derry's determination it was doubtful if she could remain much longer with the Coateses. Even if Aunt Chloe really did not blame her, they must naturally think of Lydia first, and it was unlikely Lydia would be content with the status quo after this.

She went to bed on that dreary thought, and somewhat to her surprise slept almost immediately. It was well after midnight when she woke with a start, uncertain what had aroused her but with the echo of some sound in her ears.

For a moment she lay straining her ears, half-believing she had imagined it. Then she became aware of the sound of pebbles spattering against her window.

She was up in a flash and had tumbled to the window to throw it open. It was still raining, but even as she craned her head out the window she had to duck to avoid another shower of stones. Then Derry's voice, somewhere below her, said warningly, "Shh-h-h! I thought you were never going to wake up. Come down and let me in."

She gaped at him for a minute, then hurried to put on her

wrapper and feel her way downstairs, afraid to light a candle in case anyone should see it.

It took her some moments to pull back the heavy bolt on the door, but at last it was free and she pulled the door open to admit a Derry as thoroughly soaked as she had been earlier.

"Derry! Oh, how soaked you are!" she cried. "Come into the breakfast room. There should be a fire laid there."

Without a word he followed her to the back of the house, and stood wearily as she ran to light the fire and then several candles. Her heart was beating a little fast with dread, and when she saw his face in the soft candlelight he looked so white and defeated that she cried out instinctively, "Oh, Derry, what is it?"

"I'm sorry, Phila," he said tiredly. "I shouldn't have come, but I didn't know what else to do. I've been walking for hours, trying to think, but I don't seem able to. I've made such a mess of everything. It seems ironic, doesn't it, that I accused you of being the one always in a scrape."

Wordlessly she went into his arms, despite how wet he was. He returned the hug rather convulsively, but after a moment pulled away. "Don't! I'm soaked. I only came to tell you—to tell you that I have to go away for a while. I don't know yet for how long, but I'll write and give you an address, and then as soon as I can I'll send for you."

This was worse than anything she had expected. "What— oh what is it?" she whispered. "You haven't—you haven't killed Mr. Drumm, have you?"

He gave a strangled laugh. "I only wish I had! My *friend* Jack talked me out of it. We were to pay him back in his own coin and ruin him, but it turns out I was the one to be ruined instead. I thought myself such a knowing one, when all the time I was no better than a Bartholomew Baby, a pigeon for their plucking. And the worst of it is, I *trusted* him!"

Phila was unexpectedly calm now, especially since her own fevered imaginings had made her fear far worse. "It doesn't matter" she said urgently. "You couldn't expect to be on guard against two such dreadful men!"

"But you were, weren't you?" Derry demanded with a weary smile. "Jack said you didn't like him, but I didn't believe him. Even Corny saw through them from the first, and he hasn't a brain in his head. I can scarcely take it in, even after I heard them discussing it with my own ears. We were—well, it doesn't matter now, but Jack told me that Drumm meant to interfere with one of the favorites in the Derby next week. The catch was that Jack knew who actually owned him, and knew Drumm and his villainous cronies would never get near him, so we were going to back the horse heavily and ruin Drumm. Only as I told you, it was all a trick, and I was the one to be ruined instead. They were in on it together from the beginning.''

"Yes, but why, Derry?'' she asked in bewilderment. "They must know you're not rich. Why go to so much trouble for so little?''

"Oh, I haven't told you the worst, yet!'' he said bitterly. "In fact, it makes me sick even to think about it. Phila, they wanted me to spy for them! Evidently, they suspected I wouldn't go along with it otherwise—I should be grateful at least for that compliment!—so they intended to put me so thoroughly in debt to them that I daren't refuse or they'd publicly expose me. Yes, I know it sounds incredible! And Jack is an *officer*, too! I can't—but I tell you, I heard them with my own ears. Cubby—well, you don't know him, but he's a friend of mine. It turns out his father is something big in the Foreign Office, and I was to steal military secrets and pass them on to them.''

"Oh, Derry, no! Oh you must stop them!''

"Do you think I haven't thought of that?'' he said heavily. "But no one is likely to believe me. It's so preposterous I can scarcely believe it myself. And Jack—well, Jack is both well-known and liked. Who's going to believe me, an unknown, against him? I've even thought of going to Mr. James, since it's his horse they mean to tamper with, but he thinks I'm a complete fool alrea—.''

But she had gone completely white and clutched at his sleeve. "Mr. James?'' she managed. "It's his horse they mean to tamper with?''

"Yes. Evidently it's not generally known that he owns the horse, since he's something of a target for attempts like this. Jack said Drumm didn't know, and that James had seen to it that no one could get near the animal before the race. but that was before—when they still meant to drag me into their nefarious plans. I don't know what the truth is now.''

She was still clutching at his sleeve. "Oh, Derry, we must warn him!" she cried desperately.

"Good God, Phila, how? Tell him that in the course of overhearing two traitors discuss stealing military secrets, I learned they meant to tamper with his entry in the Derby? Even if I wanted to, he'd never believe me! I tell you he already thinks I'm a complete fool.''

"Oh, what does that matter? We can't just let them get by with it after all the kind things he's done for us. Oh, don't you see? He thinks we're both complete fools, but we can't just stand by and do nothing.''

For the first time it occurred to Derry that Phila was hardly looking her usual cheerful self, and her obsession with warning Mr. James seemed unnatural in light of his other news. But he knew he himself was not looking his best either at the moment, and after a struggle with himself said merely, "Yes, all right. If you think it's so important.''

"Yes, and now that I come to think of it," she added with unexpected good sense, "I think you should tell him everything. No, I know—I don't want him to know either, but he's very influential. Very likely he can do something to stop them; but whether he can or not, we have to try. At least it's better than running away, knowing that if they fail with you, they'll only try it with someone else.''

After a moment Derry gave up the unequal struggle with his conscience, miserably aware it should have been him, not Phila, to insist. "Yes. I think I always knew I couldn't go away without at least trying to—but I warn you, it won't change anything, Phila. Whether or not they manage to catch Drumm and Kingsley—and it's only my word against theirs, remember—I shall still have to go away. If no one believes me I'll be ruined, since I told Jack to go ahead with the wager. And even if they do, well, I don't think I can bear to have everyone know what a fool I was. I thought I might enlist after all. You know that's always been in the back of my mind, and if the war doesn't end too quickly there's every chance I'll see advancement. You'll have to remain with Aunt Chloe and Uncle Jos for a little longer, but as soon as I can I'll make other arrangements.''

She did not tell him that she might not be able to remain with the Coateses after her own folly, but said with a little catch in her voice, "Yes, I know! Don't think about that. Oh, Derry! What a mess we've both made of everything!"

Once again it vaguely occurred to him that she was looking unlike herself, but he was too wrapped up in his own misery for the fact to impinge much on his consciousness. "Yes. Funny, isn't it? Corny was right, I've been the king of all fools. I should have stayed in old Ligget's office where I belonged. Never mind! It does no good to talk of it. I'm only sorry I've failed you."

"Oh, no, Derry, you mustn't think that!"

They were both perilously near to tears. Derry cleared his throat and tried to say more normally, "I must go. I'll—let you know where I am as soon as I can. Only if—if for some reason I should fail to reach Mr. James, you must tell him what you know. Once I'm gone, there should be no reason for Drumm or Jack to bother you anymore, but perhaps it would be safest if you were to go back to Somerset. You should be able to think of some excuse for Aunt Chloe."

"Yes, of course, but why should you fail?" she inquired a little sharply. "Oh, Derry, what is it? They don't know you overheard them, do they?"

He denied it, but after much probing at last confessed that he was not certain, but he thought someone had been following him all evening. "They didn't hear me, so—well, he may have been there before today, just general insurance. But of course I had no reason to be suspicious before. Phila, don't look like that. I only told you in case—well in case they should not let me get to the Nonpareil."

But she had flown to the window to peep out. "Oh, Derry," she cried in alarm. "There *is* someone there!"

"Don't be so scared. Very likely I can manage to lose him." He did not sound very sure himself, though.

But Phila had turned back, her face unexpectedly determined. It had occurred to her, in fact, that if they had had Derry followed, they must know he had overhead them, and since it had been her insistence that they should tell Mr. James, it only seemed fair that she should be the one to go. "No, no! You stay here. I'll go. They have no reason to be suspicious of me."

Derry thought they would have every reason to be suspicious if a young girl slipped out at night unescorted, but he knew that look. He said, compromising, "I oughtn't to let you, but—well, they might very well try to interfere if I were to go to the Nonpareil. But I must distract my watchdog first. I'll go first, and send a cab back for you. But whatever you do, don't get in until he gives you the password, and tells you that *Priddy* sent him! Have you got that? Oh, and Phila—you're a brick! I don't think I ever realized how much until now."

20

By the time Derry had left to draw off his shadow, and Phila had tiptoed upstairs to dress and then come down again, nearly half an hour had elapsed. The rain had slackened, but nevertheless she had put on a heavy cloak with a hood, as much for concealment as for protection against the weather. She slipped out, feeling guilty at having to leave the door unbolted and the sleeping household vulnerable to the thieves and murderers that Aunt Chloe was determined lurked around every corner in London. But she reassured herself that her and Derry's need was greater at the moment, and with any luck she would not be gone all that long.

To her relief she saw that a hansom cab was drawn up to the curb, its side lanterns reassuring in the wet darkness. Its driver also looked reassuringly solid, and as she approached he leaned down to say with evident disgust, "I was told to take you straight to South Audley Street, and to wait until you came out again, but not to let you get up until I had told you that *Priddy* sent me! All I can say is, it's a mighty strange name for the young *gentleman* as hired me, and if this is in the way o' bein' an elopement, then Jonathan Crawley's not your man. I've three daughters o' my own about your age, and I couldn't square it with my conscience if I'd been paid twice as much as that young gentleman give me."

Phila had to bite back a nervous giggle at the incongruity of his suspicions. "Oh, *please*!" she begged. "It's not what you think at all! That—that was my brother who sent you, and I—I've been called out to visit a sick relative. My aunt! Oh, please, hurry! There's no time!"

Whether satisifed with her story, which was the best she could think of at the moment, or merely uncertain enough to withhold judgment for the moment, Mr. Crawley at last climbed down and opened the door for her. The interior of his cab smelled unpleasantly stale and close, but since it had begun to rain harder again she was glad of its protection and huddled gratefully into one corner as they set off.

She was both impatient and dreading the ordeal facing her, but at that hour and in that weather the streets were mostly empty, and she was surprised at how little time it took to travel from Hanford Square to South Audley Street, since a world of style and substance lay between them. All too soon, it seemed, they had pulled up, and she could recognize the house she had once before visited, though it seemed far longer ago than a few weeks.

She did not wait for the jarvey to open the door, but clambered down herself, grateful to see that several lights still showed at the windows. Despite the urgency of her mission, she was not certain she would have had the courage to bang on the knocker until she had managed to rouse the household and demand to see Mr. James.

The jarvey, apparently having had time to consider the matter, said bluntly now, "It's all very well to talk o' sick aunts, but you can't tell me you're not quality, and I know enough to know that quality don't allow young ladies of your age to jaunter around by themselves till all hours o' the night! It's in my mind that if this *ain't* an elopement, you're up to some sort of mischief, young Miss, begging your pardon, I'm sure. And if you was my daughter I'd hold any sensible man to blame that helped you to do it."

Phila was no longer inclined to be amused. "Oh—this is absurd! I am *not* eloping, and I must go in here! It— it's a matter of life and death! Please, I'm grateful for your concern, but you must believe that I know what I'm doing."

He was still scratching his head, looking both uncertain

and mulish, when they both became aware of footsteps coming toward them, echoing on the wet pavement.

Phila started nervously, terrified it would be the watch, and dreading his inevitable involvement in the present altercation. Instead it was the Nonpareil, in evening clothes and looking remarkably normal, despite the hour.

He had seen them as well by then, and if he was startled to find Phila on his doorstep in the rain, engaged in lengthy conversation with a cabdriver, he did not reveal it, but merely came swiftly toward them.

"Oh—oh, *Uncle!*" cried Phila nervously, wishing to forestall whatever he might be about to say. "Thank goodness you've come!"

He accepted the role thrust upon him, though he cast a swift, hard look at her face. "I am rather glad of it myself, as it happens." he said dryly. "What's the matter? Have you forgotten your purse and can't pay your driver?"

"No, oh no! He—it's just that he doesn't believe that you are really my uncle, and that I have come to visit my *sick aunt!*" she said desperately, grateful for his quick wit.

He transferred his gaze to the unfortunate driver, now beginning to look somewhat ill at ease. "Indeed? I can't say I blame him, since he must wonder what sort of uncle I can be to allow you to come out alone at such an hour. I wonder myself! But I can assure you I am really the child's uncle. I am grateful for your concern, but you may safely leave her in my care."

The Nonpareil's obvious wealth and breeding were having their inevitable effect, but Mr. Crawley was not quite yet prepared to abandon his self-appointed role of watchdog, and said gruffly, "That's as may be, sir, but I'll wait here for her all the same, as I was hired to do. Begging your pardon I'm sure if I've offended you."

Mr. James allowed himself a slight, genuine smile. "I am only relieved my niece found so ready a protector. I need not tell you, I know, that in her—devotion to her aunt, she quite misunderstood the need for haste, and took a foolish risk in coming out at such an hour. I suspect you must have daughters of your own, so you know what young girls are like. But you need not remain, for you may rest assured that I will see her home myself."

Mr. Crawley allowed himself to relax, and accept the very handsome sum bestowed upon him by the swell mort. "Aye, I suspicioned it was something like that," he said, not wholly truthfully. "I've three daughters myself, as you've guessed, and everyone o' 'em up to mischief when they get the chance. I hope no offense was taken, as I said, for none was intended. It's just that you can't be too careful these days."

They parted on the best of terms, Mr. Crawley climbing back up onto his seat and lifting his whip before giving his horse the office, while the Nonpareil and Phila remained on the curbside until he had driven off.

"A most remarkable man," observed the Nonpareil. "But then I should be familiar by now with your extraordinary capacity for making friends wherever you go. But let us get out of this rain. No, it can wait until we get inside. I'm afraid you're soaked."

"Not for the first time today," said Phila, feeling completely foolish. But she obediently followed him inside, a little surprised to see no sign of the butler or footmen that had been so very much in evidence the first time she had visited him.

As if divining her curiosity he remarked conversationally, as he lit a branch of candles from the lantern left burning for him on a low table in the hall and then led the way to the room she had once before seen, "I dislike keeping my staff up to all hours merely because I should choose to stay out late. An idiosyncracy of mine, I'm afraid, and not always appreciated. I once had to dismiss a valet who refused to go to bed before he had attended me nightly. Of course, he never let me forget that I was to blame for keeping him from his just slumbers while he did it. In the end it was either dismiss him or retire faithfully every night at ten, which I refused to do. Thankfully, the rest of my staff does not feel the need to make martyrs of themselves in my behalf."

A fire still burned in the grate, and she was grateful for the room's warmth. She could not quite make herself meet the Nonpareil's eyes yet, though she was aware that for all his seeming calmness, he was regarding her with an uncomfortably penetrating stare.

After a moment he went quietly to pour a glass of brandy,

and put it into her hand. "Not usually recommended for young ladies, I know," he said ruefully. "but it should help warm you up."

She sipped experimentally at it, grateful to be given a moment to recover her courage. She did not much like it, but it indeed helped to warm her, spreading in a glow from her stomach outwards.

He had gone to stand by the fire, and said now, in a graver voice than any she had yet heard from him, "Now, Miss Ainsley, what is it? I well know only some emergency could bring you here on such a night."

The brandy had given her the courage to lift her eyes to his face, but she was to regret it, since he was regarding her with none of his usual amusement. She even thought he looked a little pale, but that was nonsense, of course. As once before, she could only blurt out the truth, dreading to see that look of concern change to something very different. "They mean to make your horse lose the Derby, and D-derry steal government secrets for them!"

Oddly enough, she thought he relaxed. He certainly came to sit beside her, taking the glass from her hand and putting it on the table beside him. "Ah, you relieve me, Miss Ainsley. I feared your aunt had cast you out as a result of this afternoon."

She gaped at him. "You thought—did you *hear* what I said?"

"Certainly. I have suspected something of the kind for some time, now."

"You suspected—you *know* about Mr. Drumm?"

He had taken her cold hands and was warming them between his own. "My poor child, you are frozen! But I warned you, did I not, that I had every intention of discovering the name of your abductor. Once I knew that, it was not a remarkable step to guess at the whole. I have had dealings with Drumm before, in fact. I am less acquainted with Captain Kingsley, but there had to be some reason they both were at such pains to cultivate your brother."

She was staring up at him with such wonder that he was once more a little amused. "Don't look so astonished. It was, as I have said, not so very difficult to figure out. I am more interested in your aunt's reaction. I hope you will believe that

I had no intention of making things even more unpleasant for you.''

"No—oh, no!'' she managed. "It—was a little unpleasant, but I don't think Aunt Chloe blames me, which is what I feared the most. But even if she did, she is far too kind to ever throw me out as you imagined.''

"I am glad to hear it. Will you believe also that if she should ever do so, or if you should ever find yourself in need of help, I hope you will come to me?''

He sounded almost stiff, for some reason, Since she could not know what alarm he had experienced at first seeing her, or that he had never before made such an offer in his life, she merely said faintly, blushing a little, "Yes. I don't know why, or why you have been so kind to both Derry and me, but it seems natural for some reason to come to you with my troubles.'' After a moment she plucked up her courage to add, "And Derry? He doesn't have to go away after all?''

There was unaccustomed self-mockery in his expression as he said, "Yes, I thought it would not be long 'til we get back to your brother! He has all your loyalty, I know.''

Despite her protests he insisted upon seeing her home himself. His carriage was a great deal more luxurious than the cab she had come in, and since the day had been an exhausting one, she found it difficult to keep her eyes open.

When they reached Hanford Square again she almost stumbled to the door, no longer particularly caring whether anyone should hear her.

He started to say something, but then took one look at her weary face, and said instead, "Go to bed, you absurd child! And don't worry. I shall see your brother comes to no harm.''

Then, to her utter amazement, he raised her hand and kissed it, holding it a moment longer in his warm one, before patting it and turning away.

21

When informed, at what he considered an unseasonable hour the next morning, of the turn of events, Sir Adrian Barbeaux was at first astonished and then as disturbed as was possible for one of his even temperament. "My dear Locke! I must confess I never really believed—but this is terrible! You say the boy overheard them planning it? We must be grateful, of course, especially that he had enough sense to come to you, but I will admit frankly that a scandal at this juncture is the last thing we need."

"I am hoping one won't be necessary. Keep in mind that so far as we know no attempt has yet been made. And we are indebted to Miss Ainsley, not her brother, for the news."

"You don't say so? Well, as I recall, you said she was a rather remarkable young lady. But the very fact that such a thing was planned shows clearly that Barnstoke can no longer be tolerated."

"I will leave that to you, Adrian. But I must confess I am less concerned with avoiding a political scandal than I am with seeing these two brought to justice."

"Naturally. But, well, you see the difficulties!" Sir Adrian had resorted to his pipe, as he did at most moments of stress, and now regarded his brother-in-law over the bowl with one of his shrewd looks. "What's on your mind? I know you too well to be deceived."

"To lay a trap for them," answered the Nonpareil calmly. "As you so rightly point out, no crime has yet been committed, so far as we know. You know as well as I do that the government's primary goal will be to avoid a political scandal it can ill afford, given the war's growing unpopularity at home. Oh, I don't doubt things will be tightened up for the moment, but it's unlikely to last. In the meantime, our two would-be traitors will likely never even be questioned."

"It's risky," observed Sir Adrian thoughtfully. "Extremely

risky. But I'll admit it does somewhat stick in my craw that your friends remain at large to try it again. But I hope you are not actually proposing we should hand over military secrets in an attempt to catch them red-handed?''

"At the moment I am proposing no more than that they should be permitted to continue to think young Ainsley a pigeon as ripe for the plucking as they obviously believe him. In fact, I intend to let them believe they have succeeded in tampering with Phalanx, if that is their plan. If an attempt is made, and he is subsequently scratched from the Derby, they will be free to blackmail young Ainsley into going along with their plans. Whether or not it is allowed to go any further than that is, of course, up to you and your contacts in the government, but at least we shall have gained more concrete evidence of guilt.''

"Good God! You'd actually go so far?'' exclaimed Sir Adrian, forgetting the larger issues for the moment. "It's the Derby, man!''

Mr. James shrugged. "There will be other Derbies.''

"Yes, but not—oh, well, never mind! If your mind is made up, I must not attempt to dissuade you. As for the other, as you say, it will need to be cleared with the highest levels, and I needn't remind you they are unlikely to be very enthusiastic. You're sure the boy can be trusted, I suppose?''

"Reasonably sure. His father was a military man, killed at Talavera, and he himself has military ambitions, I understand. It must surely count in his favor as well that he—or rather his sister—came to me with the information as soon as he learned what was planned. I think he will be more than eager to help clear his name.''

"Yes, well, I must take your word for it at the moment. I'm not making any promises, but I'll see what I can—''

"Talking secrets again?'' inquired Lady Barbeaux' amused voice from the doorway. "My dear Locke, I haven't seen so much of you in years. Which reminds me, I should be angry with you, you know. I really had no idea you meant to make quite so public a protestation of my supposed interest in your Miss Ainsley. I shall have to call on her, and at the very least invite her to Lizzie's ball. But let it never be said I am an undutiful sister—particularly since I have already been repaid so handsomely. The hat was ravishing. Thank you. I can see I shall have to put you in my debt more often.''

"You're remarkably cheerful this morning, Eliza," responded her unfilial brother. "I can see you've been gossiping with Tony. Pray spare me whatever highly unlikely conclusion you've arrived at. At any rate, Miss Ainsley will very probably have returned to Somerset by the time of Lizzie's ball, so you need not put yourself to such sacrifice.''

When he had gone her husband remarked perceptively, "Locke is right, my dear. You look remarkably like a cat that's got at the cream this morning. What are you up to?"

"Don't be so ridiculous, my love! I hope I am always cheerful in the morning," protested his wife of some twenty years not very convincingly. An impish smile betrayed her. "But you needn't think you can keep anything from me! I know it all, and I couldn't be more delighted!''

Sir Adrian looked somewhat astonished. "What do you mean, you know it all?"

"Tony has told me everything. I tell you I was never more diverted!''

Sir Adrian regarded her a little searchingly, but said nothing.

She gave her silvery laugh. "My dear, you are transparent! Of course Locke is not in love with her! Did you really think I knew my brother so little as to think that? My dear, Tony tells me she's a pretty enough child, but shy to the point of gaucheness, impulsive, absurdly tongue-tied, and worst of all, possesses impossibly vulgar relations. Can you really see Locke so far forgetting what is owed to our illustrious ancestors? No, no! I am just delighted that he seems to have gotten over Caroline at long last.''

"You elude me, my dear," said Sir Adrian dryly. "I thought you did not believe him to have developed a tendre for Miss Ainsley?''

"No, of course not! But how long has it been since you have seen him put himself to so much trouble for anyone? Surely you must have noticed that after Caro died Locke just—went away. Oh, I don't mean literally, of course! He smiles and carries on conversations with you and all the time is perfectly charming as only he can be, but he hasn't let anyone near him for years." Abruptly she blinked. "Oh, it's absurd to cry, at this late date! But if this child has at last succeeded in embroiling him in her absurd adventures, I shall be eternally grateful to her. I only hope she may lead him a merry dance!''

This wish, at least, showed every sign of being fulfilled. From Sir Adrian's the Nonpareil drove himself immediately to Derry's lodgings in Duke Street, only to be rewarded with the information that he had gone out early that morning and wasn't back yet.

Mr. James swore, and could only hope he had not done anything so foolish as to leave town already. He left his card with a note on it that he would return later, but in fact it was not until late in the afternoon that he at last succeeded in running his quarry to earth.

Derry had not left town yet, but his rented chambers showed every sign of hurried packing when Mr. James was escorted upstairs by the landlady. Derry had swung around in quick alarm when the door opened, but when he recognized Mr. James he relaxed, though his expression remained guarded.

''Did Phila . . .? Yes, of course she did, or you wouldn't be here,'' he answered himself when the landlady had gone. ''And you needn't say it, for I know I should never have let her do it!''

''You shouldn't, but that's not what I came to discuss,'' said the Nonpareil, removing a pile of shirts from a chair so he could sit down, and calmly doing so without an invitation. ''My short acquaintance with your sister has taught me that she is immovable when her mind is made up. I am relieved, by the way, to find you have not already taken flight, but I would be interested to hear where you have been all day.''

''If you must know, I got on a boat to Richmond!'' said Derry defensively. ''I couldn't leave until I knew Phila was safe, and I wanted to avoid any chance of running into—well, you know. But I'm leaving tonight on the midnight mail.''

''I hope to persuade you to not to do anything so foolish.'' said the Nonpareil calmly.

Derry glanced up quickly, hope and pride warring within him. ''Does that mean you actually believe me, sir?''

''I not only believe you, I have come to ask your help. I have no intention of engaging in recriminations, but I think you will admit you owe it both to your country and to your sister to stay and fight instead of running away.''

Derry stared at him wordlessly for a moment, as if he did not quite dare to believe what he was hearing. He was pale, and slightly unkempt, and he looked as if he had not slept at all the night before. In fact, he seemed to have aged several years in the last week, for he no longer much resembled the carefree youth he had been. The Nonpareil had not been able to summon up in himself either a great deal of interest or pity for so irresponsible a youth until that moment, but he made the rather interesting discovery then that Miss Philadelphia Ainsley was not the only member of her family capable of appealing to one's more human instincts, however reluctant.

"Oh, God! Do you mean it, sir? I'll do anything—anything! Did you think I wanted to run away? It was the only way I could think of to foil their plan. It never occurred to me that you or anyone else would actually believe me. It's only my word against theirs, after all, and Jack, at least—well, you know! But if you believe me, and I can help to bring them to justice, then I don't care what happens to me after that," he ended passionately. "Even if I never—well, it doesn't matter, but you may believe I don't care how dangerous it may be, so long as I can help see them exposed for the traitors they are."

"An admirable sentiment," said the Nonpareil dryly. "It might have been as well if you had remembered it sooner, instead of proposing to leave your sister to face the music all alone, but that is neither here nor there at the moment. I have every intention of ensuring that you are placed in no particular danger, but your role should be difficult enough to suit your present expiatory mood. In short, I expect you to continue to play the dupe for as long as possible, without letting either of them suspect you are on to their game. I warned you it would not be easy! It would be useful if you could also manage to let it appear as if you will not be as difficult to persuade as they may perhaps believe. You will see that everything depends on your acting ability. Are you up to it, do you suppose?"

"I don't know," said Derry frankly. Then his open face hardened. "Never mind! I *will* do it! At the moment I find it difficult to contemplate even meeting Jack again without betraying my—but you needn't worry! In fact, I'll be glad to deceive them if it means getting a little of my own back again, not to mention repaying them for what they tried to do to my sister!''

Mr. James rose and picked up his hat and gloves. ''Good. I am relying upon you more than you perhaps realize. I will be in touch shortly, and in the meantime you are to let me know if anything in the least suspicious occurs.''

Derry paled as he remembered something. ''Oh, God, sir. I was forgetting—I'm afraid they may already be on to me. At any rate, I was certainly being followed last night. I—I didn't say anything before, but that's the reason I allowed Phila to come to see you last night instead of coming myself. I'm ready to swear they can't have known I was outside listening when I overheard them discussing their plans, but do you think they're suspicious of me already?''

''I doubt it. I set that watchdog onto you. Don't look so insulted. I have been acquainted with Drumm, at least, a great deal longer than you have, and have suspected their involvement with you for some time. If you are wise, you will take advantage of your watchdog, for he will provide not only a measure of protection but an additional witness as well. I must be off. I am going out of town for a few days. If anything should happen, inform my secretary. If necessary, he will know where to find me.''

He paused at the door. ''Oh, yes. It would be best if your sister were removed from temptation, at least for the moment. She is rather inclined to leap into danger if she suspects you may be threatened. For what it's worth, I believe Drumm's earlier attempt to abduct her was no part of their plans. But I'd rather be safe than sorry.''

''Good God, yes!'' agreed Derry with something like a shudder. ''But—well, I'm not sure she'll be willing to leave,'' he confessed unwillingly. ''You know what she is. But I'll do my best, sir!''

''You have my sympathy,'' said the Nonpareil, and took his leave.

22

As it happened, however, there was little likelihood of Phila's being sent anywhere, at least for some days. She came downstairs the next morning with an aching head, her eyes hot and heavy and her cheeks unnaturally flushed.

A harrassed Aunt Chloe took one look at her and ordered her upstairs again immediately. "In fact, I've suspected you've been sickening for something for days now," she said frankly. "It's plain you've got that influenza that's been going about, though I shall no doubt have to send for a doctor to tell me what I already know. As if that wasn't all that was needed on top of everything else! Well, it's not your fault, my dear, and there's no help for it. You get back in bed and I'll send your breakfast up to you. You shouldn't have come down in the first place, feeling as you do."

Since Phila had reasons of her own, aside from any inconvenience to the household, for not wishing to be thought ill, she protested that it was just a head cold, and she would be better shortly. She was profoundly grateful that no one had heard her midnight foray the night before, but since it was imperative she call on Derry as soon as possible to prevent his doing anything desperate, she could not afford to go to bed, much as her aching head and limbs might long for it.

But when Aunt Chloe heard that Phila proposed to go out, she put her foot down, for once moved to firmness. "And what am I to tell your brother when you very likely contract pneumonia because of it, I'd like to know?" she demanded. "Lordy, Lordy, who'd have guessed, when we came, that it'd come to this? Here's Lydia carrying on as if her life was ruined all because some man I'd never heard of until yesterday snubbed her, and now you taken ill. I'm sure I wish I'd never heard of London!"

Letty, who had been a curious spectator to this scene, said

unexpectedly, "I'll take a message to your brother for you, if it's so important. I have to go out anyway."

Since Phila was, by that time, feeling decidedly ill, in the end she allowed herself to be persuaded. Nor, when Letty returned sometime later in the day to tell her that Derry had not been at his lodgings and his landlady didn't know when he was expected back, did the news, though dismaying, have the capability to stir her as it would ordinarily have done. She was far too conscious at the moment of her bodily ills to have much room to spare for anyone else.

The doctor arrived around four, and duly confirmed Aunt Chloe's diagnosis. Phila, by then in the throes of a high fever, and alternately chilled and then burning hot, allowed herself to be helped up to drink the saline draught he prescribed, wishing only to be left alone to die in peace. Her head felt as if someone were pounding on it from the inside, her body as if it had been stretched on a rack, and even the slight exertion required for the doctor's examination left her feeling so exhausted she desired nothing more than to be allowed to sleep for a week.

The doctor's draught helped somewhat, though, and when Derry came up to see her sometime later she was weakly relieved and clung a little tearfully to his hand.

For his part, Derry was shocked to see his sister looking so ill, and suffered all the guilt of one convinced that if he had not let her go out alone in the rain the night before, she would never have contracted influenza. Aunt Chloe had reassured him a little on that point, by telling him that she had seen it coming on for days, now; but still, Phila looked so very ill and feverish it was difficult for him not to blame himself. Particularly since, now that he remembered it, he himself had noticed she was not looking herself last night, though he had been far too wrapped up in his own misery to pay much attention to the fact at the time.

He patted her hand a little awkwardly and assured her that everything was all right. Mr. James had been to see him, and it seemed there was no reason for him to go away after all. In the meantime she was not to worry, and should concentrate on getting well, for the Nonpareil had everything under control.

She seemed to accept that, saying merely a little feverishly, "And you promise not to go away, at least until I'm better? I

shall be better directly. I never meant to be sick on top of
everything else! If only my head didn't ache so! I can't seem
to concentrate properly. I know there are things I meant to
ask you—oh, the Derby! You did say everything was all
right? I don't think I could bear it if Mr. James should lose
the Derby because of us. And they'll prevent them from
stealing military secrets?''

Derry once more reassured her, a little alarmed at the way
her words wandered, and beginning to be afraid that matters
were more grave than Aunt Chloe had led him to believe.

But Letty, whom he met coming to give Phila another of
Dr. Claycross's draughts, was able to allay the worst of his
fears. To tell the truth, Derry had always disliked both his
older cousins, but on this occasion Letty did not seem nearly
as objectionable as he had always thought her. She told him
calmly that Phila was very feverish, and not acting quite like
herself, but that he needn't worry, the doctor was convinced
it was no more than a particularly virulent case of influenza.

"I shall stay with her tonight, and Priddy, of course, can
scarcely be prised from her side. I'm glad you've come,
though, for something seemed to be preying on her mind
earlier. In fact, I went to your lodgings to speak to you, but
you were out. At any rate, it's probably just as well Phila's
fallen ill, for my dear sister would have made her life miserable otherwise. I must go. The doctor said she was to have this
every four hours.''

The same thought had occurred guiltily to Derry. He was
genuinely sorry to see Phila so ill, but he had been dreading
this meeting with Phila, since he was by no means convinced
of his ability to keep the Nonpareil's plans, and his role in
them, from her. As it was, he need not have worried, since
she had asked him very little and accepted his vague reassur-
ances with a readiness he could never have hoped for had she
been feeling herself. Even more important, it had been unnecessary for him to try to send her home, since she could be in
no danger as long as she remained in bed.

Unaware that her illness was viewed as a blessing on more
than one side, Phila continued for more than a week to have
very little interest in anything outside her bedchamber. She
remembered Derry's visit, and was aware the doctor returned
several more times, to poke and prod her and look grave

before going away again; and that whenever she woke up, Priddy, or sometimes Aunt Chloe, or even Lettice, was at her side. But mostly she slept, or lay in misery, unable to separate the aches of her body from the tumbled images in her head.

These were vivid and troubled, but she seldom could recall them on the few occasions when her mind was clear and she knew where she was. Several times she dreamed vividly that Papa was home, coming in late to kiss her good night as he had sometimes done when he and Mama had been out for the evening, or catching her up in one of his great hugs. When she woke it took her several long moments to remember that Papa was dead, and so was Mama, and that she would never again go to sleep in her safe little bed at home. Once Papa lifted her up to carry her, but when she put her arms around his neck, he did not have Papa's laughing eyes, but a pair of much graver gray ones, and his face had somehow become inexplicably confused with the Nonpareil's.

Once, to Letty's astonishment, she sat up and cried urgently, "I had forgotten . . .! The Derby! Oh, I must know when it is! What day is it?"

"The Derby?" repeated Letty. "What on earth does that matter? I never knew you were interested in horses."

Phila woke properly then. "What . . .? Oh, I must have been dreaming!" she mumbled. "I thought—never mind. It doesn't matter. Only I thought for a moment it was over, and I'd been too late after all. I'm so hot and thirsty."

Letty obligingly helped her sit up to drink some lemonade left ready on the table beside the bed. It seemed to Phila she had never tasted anything so delicious.

She was grateful to lie back down, however. "Thank you," she said humbly. "I never meant to be so much trouble."

"I'd just as soon be here as downstairs, if you want the truth. Why did you want to know about the Derby?"

"Never mind," repeated Phila weakly. "There's nothing I can do anyway. I alway thought you resented me as much as Lydia did," she added inconsequently. "Why are you being so kind to me?"

For some reason Letty blushed. "I never resented you. We

just never had that much in common. It's late. You'd better
go back to sleep now.''

Phila soon did so, too apathetic to pursue the subject. And
inevitably, of course, she soon stopped feeling as if she had
been beaten over every inch of her body and her head belonged to someone else. Her mind stopped wandering, and
though she still slept a great deal, she recalled everything that
had led up to her illness.

Unfortunately, that included that disastrous meeting with
Mr. James, and Lydia's justified fury, as well as Derry's
horrifying news. While she had been ill neither of these
things had much mattered, but once her mind was clear she
was filled with questions and renewed fears.

It was true that Derry had told her she was not to worry,
and that Mr. James was taking care of everything. But that
did not solve the problem of her own immediate future,
which loomed exceedingly harshly before her of a sudden. It
was very unlikely she would be able to continue to live with
the Coateses after all that had happened. Aunt Chloe had
been to see her frequently, of course, and her manner had
been as kind as ever, but it was clear that her thoughts were
elsewhere. Nor did Priddy, usually so outspoken, have anything to say about Lydia, which led Phila to guess that
conditions had not eased during her enforced absence.

If it did not take the entire two weeks the doctor had
predicted, it was nearly ten days before she was at last
allowed downstairs again, watched over by a hovering Priddy.
She was amazed how weak she was, and was glad to settle
herself on a sofa in the front parlor while Priddy sketched
beside her and Aunt Chloe knitted desultorily. There was no
sign of Letty or Lydia, and Phila could only be glad. She had
not seen Lydia since before she became ill, and she dreaded
meeting her again.

When the front doorbell rang, no one suspected disaster. In
a moment the housemaid, Betty, came in with a note and
handed it to Aunt Chloe with the information that a gent'man
had just brought this, and hadn't waited for a reply. Would
Madame be requiring her any further that morning, for if not
Cook was wishful for her to go around to the fishmonger's,
since no delivery had yet been made that day.

Aunt Chloe dismissed her with exasperation, predicting

quite rightly, as it turned out, that she would take that as an excuse to take an unscheduled holiday, and they'd be lucky if they saw her again before dinnertime.

Priddy was paying no attention at all to her mother's words, and though Phila made the proper responses, she was, in truth, having trouble keeping her eyes open. Aunt Chloe's sudden strangled scream was thus all the more startling. Phila's eyes shot open in alarm, while Priddy looked up, her own round with astonishment.

The sight that greeted both of them was hardly reassuring. Aunt Chloe stood in the center of the room, one hand at her throat and her face as pale as was possible for one of her robust constitution. The other hand held a crumpled note.

Both Phila and Priddy rushed to her, but it was Priddy who had the presence of mind to take the note from her Mama's hand and read it, while Phila chafed her hands and made her sit down. When Priddy at last looked up, her freckles were standing out unnaturally, and she said flatly to Phila's unspoken question, "Lydia's eloped with Mr. Bevis."

23

There was very little anyone could say or do, of course, and it was long before Aunt Chloe would be comforted.

"Lordy, Lordy!" she moaned from the depths of the chair Phila had helped her into. "What am I to tell her papa? To think she could do a thing like this without a thought to us and nothing but a cold note to say she'll let me know where they'll be living. I never thought a daughter of mine could so forget her upbringing. Good middle class stock we've always been, and proud of it, with never a hint of scandal till now. I tell you, it will about break her poor old pa's heart!"

Fortunately, since Phila felt stricken with guilt over her own responsibility for Lydia's elopement, and even Priddy seemed a little overcome by the sight of her mama alternately wiping at her eyes and giving vent to her despair, Letty soon came in and took unexpectedly capable charge.

Since the fear that Mr. Bevis was merely deceiving her poor Lydia and had no intention of doing the right thing by her had taken unfortunate possession of Aunt Chloe's mind, Letty said with her usual bluntness, "Don't be ridiculous, Mama! He'll have to marry her if he hopes to get his hands on Papa's money, which I presume is the point of an elopement. At any rate, it's what Lydia wanted, so we must hope she'll be happy."

This forthright speech, far from offending Aunt Chloe, seemed to have a beneficial effect. She could not prevent herself from moaning again and crying unhappily, "I can scarcely bear to hear the word at the moment. Nor it's not as if we would have forbidden the banns, though her papa would have made sure he was a decent man and meant to treat her right before he would ever have consented to such a match. But she must know we'd never refuse her anything she had her heart set on. To run off like this, without a word, is what makes it hardest to bear."

But after a moment she blew her nose and sat up with a little of her old energy. "Well, there's no use crying over spilt milk, as the saying is, and we must learn to live with it. Even if a special messenger were sent off to Papa immediately, he could not hope to set out before nightfall, and by then the damage will be done. We must just hope he does mean to marry her. But Letty's right, if he *is* marrying her for her money, and I'm sure I never thought to be grateful for such a thing, then he must know he can't hope to touch any of it until the ring is on her finger. Not that that's much comfort," she added, momentarily relapsing into gloom once more, "for that's no guarantee he'll treat her as he ought. What do we know of this Mr. Bevis anyway?"

Since Phila was the only one of them actually to have met Mr. Bevis, it fell to her lot to try to reassure Aunt Chloe. This was difficult, since Phila had only met him a few times and had not liked him, but by dint of exaggerating his good looks and birth, and minimizing his expensive habits and snobbery, she had the satisfaction of seeing Aunt Chloe looking slightly more cheerful.

"Well, I don't say he's the son-in-law I'd have chosen—in

fact, from the sound of it, for all his fine birth and Town polish he might be the very last I'd have chosen, for you can't fool me you didn't like him, my dear. I daresay I won't like him either, but that's neither here nor there and I daresay I won't be given the opportunity, for I doubt he'll want to have much to do with his new relations! But I'm not the one who's marrying him, and her papa and me made up our minds long ago not to stand in her way.'' She mopped at her eyes again. "If only we could be sure he meant to be good to her, I'd say no more. That's what's worrying me now. That and how her poor papa will take the news.''

Since not even Letty could reassure her on that head, they all remained guiltily silent. Priddy had said very little till now, but she burst out abruptly, her face suspiciously red, "I don't care! I hope they will have nothing to do with us, for if you ask me we're better off without her!'' She then grew even redder and surprised them all very much by running out of the room.

Aunt Chloe tsk-tsked over this, but was soon sufficiently recovered to go off to write immediately to her husband, and get the unpleasant task over. Letty went with her, and Phila, feeling unnecessary and still miserably guilty, went upstairs to see Priddy.

She found her, predictably, thrown down on her bed with her feet kicking together. She was not crying, and said resentfully as Phila came in to sit on her bed, "I don't care what you say, I am glad she's gone! We'll be happier without her. I'm *glad* I'm not beautiful!''

Phila went away without a word, recognizing the grief that hid behind Priddy's scowl. She lay down on her own bed meaning only to rest for a few minutes. But in fact she fell asleep and did not hear the doorbell some hours later.

Aunt Chloe, however, still engaged in her dismal task of writing to her husband, lifted her head suddenly, hope leaping into her breast. "Oh, I knew it!'' she cried thankfully. "She's not done it after all, thank God!''

Letty was more doubtful, but since the housemaid had not returned yet, went to answer the door at the second imperious ring. Rather to her surprise she found herself confronting a distinguished-looking stranger, but before she could inquire his business her mother cried from just behind her, "Where is she? Where is my baby? Oh, what have you done with her, you brute? *Answer* me or I'll have the law on you, gentleman or no gentleman!"

The gentleman stiffened, and seemed to turn pale, before barking out, "Good God! When was she last seen? Don't stand there staring or I'll do more than have the law on you, for you must know every minute is vital! How long has she been gone?"

Aunt Chloe was indeed gaping at him. Then she seemed to lose all control. "*You* can dare to say *that* to me?" she gasped. "Oh my poor baby! Have you abandoned her already, you overbred icy-faced excuse for a man? I don't care, for I wouldn't have her wed you if you was the last man on earth now, you—you—"

She was rapidly descending into an exchange of personalities in a manner that revealed her humble origins, her voice shrill and her stout body almost quivering with rage, when Letty interrupted. "Mama, I think there's been some mistake. I don't think this is Mr. Bevis."

The Nonpareil, at the moment in no mood to enjoy a spectacle that at any other time might have been expected to appeal to his sense of the ridiculous, snapped shortly, "I neither know nor care who Mr. Bevis may be. I am still waiting to be told how long Miss Ainsley has been gone, and what, if anything, has been done to find her."

It was Lettice's turn to gape now. "Phila? You thought we were talking about *Phila?* Good Lord no! She's upstairs in her room."

The Nonpareil was conscious of a relief so intense it was as out of proportion as his earlier fright had been. In fact, all the time the stout harridan had been screeching at him, he had stood as if turned to stone, unprepared for the strength of the cold dread that seemed to grip his heart, and repeating blankly to himself, "My God, what have I done? What have I *done?*"

Letty, observing the rapid play of emotions across his face with curiosity, took pity on him after a moment and said, "You must be Phila's Mr. James. I think you'd better come in."

"Yes, I'm James," he confirmed, recovering himself a

little. "I beg your pardon! It would seem we've been engaged in a comedy of errors. If it's not Miss Ainsley, may I ask who has disappeared?"

Letty studied him. Aunt Chloe was still gaping in astonishment as if unable to take in this turn of events, and Letty glanced at her before reaching a sudden decision. "You may as well know, since the whole world will know soon enough, I'm afraid," she said dryly. "My sister has eloped with a man by the name of Bevis. That's who Mama mistook you for."

His brows rose slightly, but he betrayed no other emotion. "I'm very sorry to hear that, and can only apologize again for intruding at such a moment. If you would be so kind as to tell Miss Ainsley that I called—"

"No," said Aunt Chloe surprisingly, having concluded her own scrutiny of the newcomer and reached a decision. "You may as well come in. The whole world will soon know of the scandal as my daughter says, so there's no point in pretending otherwise. So you're this Mr. James I've heard so much about? I can't say I expected it, but you've the look of a sensible man, despite whatever it is they call you. And I'm sorry if I said anything I shouldn't have," she ended handsomely.

His own fears allayed, the Nonpareil was rapidly recovering his sense of the ridiculous. His lips twitched slightly, but he said gravely, "On the contrary, it is I who should apologize, ma'am. As I said, we seemed both to have been laboring under a considerable misapprehension. You are, of course, Miss Ainsley's aunt and this must be Miss Lettice Coates. I am happy to make both of your acquaintances, and can only wish it had been under less unfortunate circumstances."

He hesitated, aware the sensible man he had certainly always prided himself on being would undoubtedly withdraw at this point with renewed apologies, before he could be drawn into the sort of family crisis he most deplored. But it seemed the last half hour had held more than one revelation for him, for he was no longer convinced he was in the least sensible. "Forgive me," he said abruptly, "but why do you fear a scandal? If your daughter has indeed eloped it's unfortunate, but the world need not know the true facts of the case unless you choose to advertise them, surely?"

Aunt Chloe's massive bosom swelled visibly. "And you think it's not a scandal when my daughter elopes with a fortunehunter I've never even laid eyes on? If you think that can be hushed up, you've less sense than I gave you credit for, even *I* know that."

He did smile then. "If that is all that's troubling you, then you may take my word for it that such stories are quickly forgotten in London. There may well be some talk, I'll admit, but there will always be some new on-dit, and in six months no one will remember it any longer."

"Hmph! But even if what you say is true, it don't change the fact that we know nothing about this Mr. Bevis. He could be a bluebeard for all that we know!"

"Yes, but it's occurred to me that Mr. James may be able to help us there, Mama," said Letty. "Do you know Mr. Bevis, sir?"

"We certainly are not intimates, Miss Coates," he said frankly. "From all I know of him he was certainly on the lookout to marry a fortune, but in my world that is not so very rare, I fear. I know nothing else to his discredit, I assure you. His manners are not particularly to my taste, I'll admit, but I believe he is generally considered an asset by hostesses, and his birth and breeding are impeccable."

"As if being a fortunehunter were not to his discredit!" grumbled Aunt Chloe. But she was a little impressed in spite of herself, for she added grudgingly, "But at least that's something. Mr. Coates don't mind paying highly for what he wants, but it's something else entirely to pay through the nose for mutton dressed up to look like beef."

"Very true," agreed the Nonpareil, once more amused. "I can guarantee he is at least beef, though whether he is a bargain is something else again."

"What Mama's really afraid of is that he'll mistreat her," said Letty bluntly.

"Then do something about it," answered Mr. James calmly.

24

Aunt Chloe stared hard at the Nonpareil, her face suddenly intent. "Do you think I haven't thought of that? But a woman's fortune becomes the property of her husband, even I know that! And I won't see my daughter starve, not even to thwart him. Are you saying there is a way?"

"Certainly. I'm no lawyer, of course, but I believe such arrangements are by no means uncommon. You need only place your daughter's fortune in a trust to be controlled by you and your husband. That way you can be certain it will not all be squandered in the first year, and even see that Bevis gets not one penny if the marriage should not be a happy one."

After a moment Aunt Chloe gave a crack of laughter. "If what you say is true, then I'm obliged to you! It will kill two birds with one stone, for leaving aside all other considerations, Lydia has yet to learn money don't grow on trees in the spring. They'll neither of 'em like it, o' course, but they'll put up with it if they expect Mr. Coates to support 'em, as I've no doubt they do. Well, I'm obliged to you as I said, and so will be my husband, I can promise you. They may not wish to acknowledge her ungenteel relations, but they'll soon learn we're not such fools as they obviously think us."

"Mama, Mr. James doesn't wish to hear all this. He's come to see Phila. She's been ill, in fact today's the first day she's been allowed downstairs, but I know she'll want to see you. I'll go get her."

When Phila came down, some ten minutes later, she was looking shy and more than a little curious, but both emotions were overcome by her astonishment in discovering her aunt and Mr. James hobnobbing as if they were old friends.

When Aunt Chloe had at last pulled her bulk to her feet, and thanked Mr. James profusely once more before going off, as she said, to write her husband a far happier letter than she had feared she would be obliged to send, Phila stared after her disbelievingly for a moment. It was hard enough to believe Mr. James was actually seated in Aunt Chloe's parlor, even harder given Mr. James's opinion of her aunt, to believe they had reached such intimate terms so quickly. "What—what did you say to Aunt Chloe?" she managed. "What was she thanking you for?"

For his part, Mr. James was a little shocked at his reaction to her appearance. He had been told she had been ill, but he had been unprepared to find Phila looking quite so pale and drawn still, even more unprepared for his desire to catch her up in his arms and carry her to the sofa, which it looked like she should not yet have left.

He resisted the temptation, but could not prevent himself from going quickly to her and taking both her cold hands in his, and leading her to the sofa. "My poor child, what have they been doing to you? Your cousin told me you had been ill, but I had no notion it was as bad as this. Are you certain you should be up?"

She blushed, but after a moment shyly withdrew her hands. "Yes, oh yes! I am much better now. It was nothing but the stupid influenza, anyway."

"Contracted, no doubt, the night of your late and very wet journey to my house. I should not have asked what your *relations* had been doing to you," he said ruefully.

She blushed still more. "No—at least, I did come down with it the next day, but my aunt tells me I had obviously been sickening for days. But what were you and Aunt Chloe talking about?"

"I have been advising her on a way to tie up your cousin Lydia's fortune so that your aunt and uncle will have final say over its disposition."

"You *have*?" asked Phila in astonishment. "Aunt Chloe told you about that?"

"She had very little choice, I fear. She mistook me for Mr. Bevis when I arrived, a curious misapprehension which, I might add, I find far from flattering."

"Mistook you for Mr. Bevis?" repeated Phila in even more astonishment.

"Yes, but I can't really blame her. You see, *I* first thought it was you who was missing. Fortunately, your cousin Lettice perceived the confusion and straightened it up before your aunt and I forgot ourselves entirely. I liked your cousin Lettice, by the way. Much more than your cousin Lydia, I must admit. I thought her a sensible girl. I liked your aunt as well, as a matter of fact. She is obviously a practical woman who wastes little time on polite insincerities.''

"You *did*?" repeated Phila, feeling a little as if she must still be asleep and dreaming.

He smiled and came to sit down beside her. "Because I don't happen to believe her the best guardian for you doesn't mean I am incapable of perceiving her good qualities.''

His smile faded, and he searched her face a little intently, recognizing the shadows that lay behind the more obvious signs of ill health. "What's the matter?" he inquired gently after a moment. "You're not still worried about your brother, I hope?"

She started and looked quickly away, blushing. "No. At least—I am a little worried about him, but he came to see me again yesterday, and assured me that he has nothing to fear from those awful men now." She turned her head back shyly. "I know I have you to thank for that.''

He felt a twinge of guilt, since he was in effect using her brother to trap Drumm and Kingsley. But since if things went as planned she need never know anything about it, he successfully stifled it. "You have already done so more than once, I recall. But if it's not your brother, what is it? You can't deceive me you're not unhappy over something. Surely your aunt doesn't blame you for your cousin's elopement?"

"No," she said truthfully. "At least—it was my fault, for if it hadn't been for me, she would never have done it."

"In that case it is *my* fault," he said calmly. "I made it clear that she was unlikely to succeed in her ambitions in London. Nor do I regret it, since she has made your life miserable for years."

She stole a look up at him, her expression a little troubled. But all she said was, "But I can't help wondering what is to become of me."

He hesitated, once more at a loss, as he seemed so often to be with her. "Would it make you so very unhappy to be obliged to leave the Coates?" he asked at last. "I know you are fond of your cousin Priddy, and your aunt, too, but—

forgive me—I had not gathered your life had been completely comfortable with them.''

She tried to smile, though it was a very poor effort. ''No. At least I *would* be sad to leave them, but not if I were going to a place I really belonged.'' She added almost inconsequently, ''While I was sick, aside from feeling so wretched, all I could think of was that I had no right to be ill, especially at such a time, when poor Aunt Chloe had so much to worry her already. And then it occurred to me that it will never be any different. Wherever I go, I shall always be there on sufferance. Even if I found a job, which is what I have been thinking lately I should do, I still could be turned out at a moment's notice.''

He was both troubled and a little alarmed, for this was indeed unlike her, and said bracingly, ''My dear, you are merely blue-devilled! Apart from every other consideration, has it never occurred to you, in this pathetic future you've envisioned for yourself, that you will one day marry, and have a home of your own?''

''No, for I won't ever marry. I have known that for a long time. How can I? I don't fit in with my cousins' friends, and—and being in London has taught me that I don't fit in here either. Aunt Chloe thinks I have only to meet some young man who will fall desperately in love with me, but I am neither pretty enough nor well-born enough to have him overlook all my other disadvantages. And even if he would, *I* cannot. Can you understand that? I would still feel the poor relation.''

''My dear—!'' But he found he could not utter the trite words of comfort on his lips, that someday there would come along a man who would love her for herself, and care not a button for her disadvantages. He did not believe it himself. A man would have to be deeply and irrevocably in love with her to be able to overlook her lack of fortune, her vulgar relations, and her own impetuous tendencies to leap headlong into trouble.

The Nonpareil had been aware for some time, since the night she had come to his house in the rain to tell him of the plot against her brother, in fact, that Miss Philadelphia Ainsley had managed to touch him in a way no one ever had before. He told himself it was pity, for then he had been concerned that his own actions, however kindly intended, might have caused her to lose her home with her aunt. And there was no denying that her warmth and impulsiveness, her ability to throw herself headlong into the affairs of those she cared about, had made an indelible impression on him, for he had no longer believed such selflessness existed. But if he had recognized the danger, he had been fully aware how foolish it would be to allow pity and admiration to be mistaken for any warmer emotion.

But from the moment he had arrived this evening his actions and emotions seemed no longer to be those of the rational man he knew himself to be. When he had believed her missing, and himself to blame, it had seemed to him as if he had received a mortal blow from which he was not likely to recover. And when he had seen her, looking so pale and ill, he had wanted to sweep her up in his arms and protect her, conscious of an irrational resentment toward her relatives for taking no better care of her than that.

Now she was in far more need of comfort, for everything she said was true, but he could not give it to her. If he was conscious of a strong desire to forget everything that was owed to his birth and breeding, and throw his heart and fortune at her feet, so that she need never be made unhappy again, he retained just enough sanity to know that his emotions, evidently, were no longer to be trusted.

He was not some callow youth, in love for the first time, after all. He was not even certain he was in love at all. It was true that for all her youth and folly he found her oddly—the word that sprang to his mind was gallant, but it was not a term usually applied to women. It was oddly fitting, though. Her own circumstances could hardly be more unhappy, and yet, or perhaps because of that, she threw herself passionately to the defense of those she loved. And in doing so she had shown him exactly how barren his own life had become. He had friends, relatives, every comfort that wealth could possess, but he had somehow, since Caroline died, perhaps, increasingly divorced himself from any real contact with either love or hate, joy or sorrow, or any of the emotions that made one human and vulnerable to others.

But the very fact that he had existed happily for so many years, uninclined to accept any of the lures thrown out to him by far more practiced beauties showed how wise he was to be cautious now, before he found himself tied to a charming girl who was not of his world, and would make him the worst possible wife.

Nor did he have any need to imagine what his world would say of such a match. He, who had once been engaged to the reigning Toast, and who might have had his pick of any of the beauties over a dozen Seasons, to be brought to his knees at last by an impetuous child who would turn his life upside down, fill his house with her impossible relations, and reveal him to the world as exactly the besotted fool he himself had been so contemptuous of in the past.

None of that should matter, of course, if he were truly in love. But he was not yet certain he was in love, or would not recover from this fit of temporary insanity. And until he was, it would be folly to proceed, at the risk of making them both miserable, and himself a complete fool.

Uncomfortably aware he had allowed the silence to extend too long, and for perhaps the first time in a great many years thrown out of his usual cool command, he said more stiffly than he had intended, "Phila—Miss Ainsley, this is indeed your illness talking, you know. In a few days, when you are feeling better, you will be amazed at how gloomy you have allowed yourself to become, all for no reason."

She blushed, always absurdly sensitive to snubs as he well knew, and said painfully, "Yes, of course! I don't know how I came to—I'm sorry! I don't even know why you came. N-not to give Aunt Chloe advice, or to listen to my self-pity, I know."

He felt like a murderer, but told himself it was better for her to be hurt a little now, than a great deal later. "I have never known you to indulge in self-pity," he said, trying to bring the conversation back to a more normal footing. "But I'm afraid you won't like what I have to tell you. I had no wish for you to hear it from someone else first, however. My horse did not compete in the Derby."

Her eyes widened, and she stared at him in horror for a moment. "Not—you were too late after all?"

"No," he said unwillingly. "I scratched him myself. And don't look like that! I have said your brother will come to no harm."

If it was doubtful that she wholly believed him, for once the Nonpareil was grateful to make his escape, bitterly aware that he was not the man he had believed himself to be.

25

If the Coates household was curious about Mr. James's visit, it got very little satisfaction from Phila. She emerged from the interview looking unlike herself, but since she almost immediately went up to bed, begging the excuse of her recent illness, and was not seen again until the next morning, by which time she looked pale, but composed, there was not much anyone could make of it.

Aunt Chloe did say, at breakfast the next morning, "Well, I won't deny I'm grateful to your Mr. James, or whatever it is he calls himself, Phila. He may have been indirectly responsible for Lydia's running away, but at least I slept better than I expected to, thanks to him, and was able to write to Mr. Coates with better news than I feared. I'll never be happy about it, especially that it was done in such a hole-and-corner fashion, but at least I needn't fear he'll mistreat her, or I'll know the reason why, you may be sure!"

"He's not my Mr. James," denied Phila calmly, though she had done little more than crumble the bread and butter on her plate.

Aunt Chloe, her mind on other matters, failed to notice what at any other time would have given her cause for alarm. "At any rate, I daresay there's no reason to remain in London now, except that I don't know if I can bear to go until we've at least heard from her. Drat the girl! It's the uncertainty that's unsettled me the most. Well, one thing's for sure, I won't think of doing anything until I've heard from Mr. Coates. Lord, Lord, to think our visit should have ended like this!"

They heard nothing more from Lydia for several days. Despite her words, or perhaps merely to give herself something to do since she hated waiting, as she said, Aunt Chloe began half-heartedly packing. Phila, also grateful to have something to occupy her thoughts, helped her, promising not to overdo and to lie down for several hours in the afternoon.

They were sorting through Lydia's things one afternoon since, as Aunt Chloe said sensibly, whatever happened she'd no doubt be wanting them sent on to her, when Letty came in unexpectedly, her cheeks unnaturally red and sounding a little out of breath. "Phila," she said oddly. "Can I see you for a moment?"

Aunt Chloe looked up from the depths of a trunk. "Is that you, Letty? Have you and Lizzie finished your shopping already? Goodness! I certainly never remember bringing so much when we came! I wonder if she'll be wanting it all right away, or if she mightn't wish us to send it home for her, at least for now? In fact, I'm right sorry I started this at all, for it only serves to bring it all home to me."

"You may as well pack up all her things and take them home, Mama," said Letty indifferently. "If I know Lydia, she'll be wanting a whole new trousseau as soon as she's back. Phila! It's urgent that I talk to you."

Phila followed her wonderingly, for Letty had never shown any particular desire for her company before, and since they had been in London had seemed more and more remote from the rest of the family.

Once they were in Letty's own room, and she had closed the door, for all her urgency, Letty seemed uncertain how to begin. "Oh Lord," she said at last in her blunt way. "I'm never any good at wrapping things up in clean linen. The truth is, I have—reason to believe your brother may be in danger. I don't even know why I'm telling you, except that somebody's obviously got to do something!"

For the moment Phila did not even wonder how Letty came to be involved, for she realized that Letty's news was no more than she had been expecting since last night. "Is it Mr. Drumm?" she managed. "Has—has he called in his debt already?"

Whatever she had been expecting, it was apparently not that, for Letty positively gaped at her. "Do you mean you *knew*?"

"Yes. Derry told me everything. Only—never mind. Tell me what you've learned."

Letty was still staring at her. "Good Lord, aren't you the sly one. You knew Drumm and Kinsgley meant to make your brother steal military secrets for them? I seem to have been wrong on a great many counts lately. But did you also know your brother was working with your Mr. James to try and trap them?"

As Phila turned suddenly pale and sank onto the bed, Letty said ruefully, "I'm sorry. I know I'm only making things worse. I—I guess I'd better tell you what I know, and how—how I came to overhear what I did."

"It doesn't matter," said Phila. "I knew—or at least I should have known. Oh, what a *fool* I've been!"

Letty stared again at the unusual bitterness in her tone, but said with a great deal less than her usual assurance, "If it's any comfort to you, you're not the only one." She actually even blushed. "I—well, I suppose I may as well tell you and get it over with! It's not Lizzie I've been meeting when I go out. As a matter of fact, it's your brother's friend Mr. Naseby, and you needn't tell me there's no future in it, for I know it!"

Phila showed no inclination to do so. "Mr. Naseby?" she repeated in astonishment.

Letty blushed again, and turned away impatiently. "I told you you weren't the only one who'd been a fool. I can't explain it, even to myself. I know he's not much to look at, and he's no brains to speak of. Even if we were of the same class, it would be ridiculous. But—well, we have fun together, and that's all that seems to matter."

Phila's eyes unexpectedly filled with tears. "Oh, Letty. I'm so sorry," she whispered.

Letty grimaced. "Good God, don't, or you'll have me bawling too! I don't know why you care anyway, for we've hardly been kind to you in this house. At any rate, it's not what you think. In fact, he'd marry me in a minute, or so he says. But well—he's not willing to forget he was born a gentleman and go into business with his uncle, who's been supporting him all these years anyway. And I'm not willing to starve on the allowance he gets from his uncle, or forever be looked down upon in his world. I told you it was hopeless. At any rate, if he's ashamed of his uncle's money, then he'd end by being ashamed of me, too, and so I've told him. But, well, I still visit him now and again—and I know it's improper, but I don't care. We may as well enjoy ourselves while we can! At any rate, I only told you to explain how I came to overhear what I did. I'd gone this afternoon to—well to tell him about Lydia. Corny knows Mr. Bevis and doesn't like him either, by the way. Anyway, there's a back entrance in his lodgings and I usually go that way to—well never mind. The point is, your brother was with Corny when I arrived today. I was annoyed, and waited, hoping he'd leave soon. But then when I realized what they were talking about, I listened deliberately. That's how I learned about Drumm and Kingsley and the Nonpareil's plan to trap them. Only I'm afraid your brother doesn't believe that Captain Kingsley can really be as black as he's painted. In fact, he suspects that he's as much a victim as your brother was meant to be, and so he means to give the great captain a chance to clear himself. Worse, he means to make poor Corny help him."

"Oh, *no!*" cried Phila, her hands at her cheeks.

Letty shrugged. "Yes, well, since I didn't like the captain any more than you apparently did, and can easily believe him a spy, if not worse, it occurred to me your brother could be getting in over his head. If Kingsley is guilty, as we suspect, at the very least it will tip them off that your brother's on to their plans. They may merely be frightened away, but on the other hand they might turn dangerous. I don't know about your brother, but even if I can't have Corny, I don't have any wish to see him murdered by the likes of them."

"Oh, no! Oh, what can Derry be thinking of? I can believe anything of *either* of them! Mr. Drumm even tried to abduct me once! Oh, we must try to stop him before it's too late!"

"Mr. Drumm tried to abdu— Good God!" said Letty faintly. "Corny said you was a dark horse, but I never—well, we can talk about that later. The point is, if we're agreed that something must be done to stop them, it's occurred to me we could do worse than go to your friend Mr. James. Certainly this seems to be no part of his plans, and whether or not you approve of his using your brother to try to trap them, it seems to me he's the only one likely to be able to talk some sense into them."

"No!" said Phila with unexpected violence.

As Letty stared at her once more, she had the grace to blush. "I'm sorry. I know—but you don't understand."

But how could she explain what she herself barely understood? Mr. James had made it more than clear, the other night that he was beginning to find the Ainsleys and their troubles a dead bore. If she had never imagined that a warmer relationship might exist between them, which was plainly absurd, she had come, insensibly, to think of him as someone to be trusted, and who understood, as no one ever had before, a little of her own feelings. That was the only excuse she could find for her maudlin display, imagining that Mr. James might care what was to become of her, or consider her with anything other than a certain pity.

But it was painful even to remember last night, and the fool she had made of herself. And the very fact that Mr. James could place Derry in danger as he had showed how very little real regard he had for her feelings.

Once she knew the truth, she was not even very surprised that they should have set a trap for Drumm and Kingsley, or that Derry should willingly take part in it. She had allowed her illness and her fear to blind her to what at any other time she would have suspected at once. But if she did not particularly blame Mr. James, she could not go to him now with the news that Derry meant to put all at risk in his foolish desire to clear his friend.

Letty was still looking at her a little oddly. "Are you sure? I thought—I mean, after the other night, Mama and I both suspected—well, that Mr. James was more than a little interested in you."

Phila's laugh was unexpectedly bitter. "You are mistaken! He thinks me a stupid child, and I can't blame him. I met him when I went unescorted to his home to beg him to forgive my brother's gambling debts. After that, it was he who was obliged to rescue me when Mr. Drumm tried to abduct me, and now, not only have we involved him in a plot to steal military secrets, but he has had to scratch his horse from the Derby when he was the favorite. At any rate, everyone knows he is soon to marry the daughter of a duke."

After a moment Letty kindly said no more. "But if we aren't to go to him, what else can we do?" she asked frankly. "They're hardly likely to listen to us, and it's planned for tonight. We've got to do something, but I confess I don't know what.''

Phila managed to surprise her most of all by saying unexpectedly, ''I do. I think I know exactly what to do.''

26

It had not taken long, in fact, for Derry, his soul still smarting from the discovery of what a fool he'd been, to begin to chafe at his limited role in Mr. James's plans. Worse, he was no longer convinced he *could* have been so completely mistaken in one he had considered a friend, and the notion, once taken root in his mind, that Jack was just as much a victim of Drumm as he had been intended to be, grew rapidly in such fertile soil.

If he had been able to go away as he had planned, he might have been able to control such doubts. Required, as he naturally was, to continue to meet Jack as if nothing had changed, it became increasingly impossible to make himself remember that Jack meant to betray his country and had intended to use him as a tool to do it.

And since he had received only one brief note from the Nonpareil, telling him that an attempt had indeed been made to drug Phalanx but had fortunately been discovered in time, it was easy enough to begin to resent being kept in the dark, while all the excitement happened to others.

Given all these circumstances, it was but a small step to the determination to take a more active role. They all thought him a fool, obviously, even Mr. James. But he was not a fool, and while an officer must, naturally, learn to obey orders, it was equally as important to use one's own judgment when those orders conflicted with what one increasingly suspected to be the truth. Military protocol aside, common decency demanded that if one's friend were about to be accused of something one believed him innocent of, one was bound, as a gentleman, to give him a chance to clear himself.

Unfortunately, this logic did not seem to impress Mr. Naseby. Derry had cautiously confided in him, and found his friend Corny a poor ally, since Corny found no difficulty whatsoever in believing Captain Kingsley a traitor to his country. Now he said simply, "If you take my advice, Der, you'll stay out of it. In fact, if you was to ask me, your Captain Kingsley is as likely to be the ringleader as Drumm— no, no! I've no intention of debating the matter with you because— well, for one thing, I ain't any good with words, and for another thing, it doesn't matter what I think! Point is, we oughtn't to meddle in the Nonpareil's plans. Told you he's got quite a nous-box on him. More important, brother-in-law's big in government, as I told you. Bound to know what they're doing."

Derry was irritated, but since he needed Corny's help, he controlled it. "I tell you he doesn't know Jack like I do! I'm not making any excuses for him, but—well, I happen to know he owes Drumm quite a bit. If there's the slightest chance that he's being blackmailed just as I was meant to be, then I've got to give him the chance to come forward and clear himself. If it was me—which it nearly was—or you, for example, wouldn't you wish for the same chance?"

Mr. Naseby found no answer for that, and after a moment Derry added, "At any rate, I have no intention of ruining anyone's plans. If anything, I'm merely accelerating things slightly. I'm supposed to make them think I'm as big a fool as they believe me, and I'd naturally be getting desperate, now that I think I owe Drumm all that money. If Jack uses the opportunity to—well, to turn the screws, then I'll know— Oh, it doesn't bear talking about! I only know I have to find out the truth for myself. If I'm wrong then—then nothing's changed and the plot will finish a little sooner, which I'll be damned glad of, I can tell you! Even if they are both guilty, I've discovered I have no particular liking for stabbing them in the back. If they are traitors, I hope they both hang for it, but I'm not cut out for the role of Judas. Oh, the devil! Enough talking, as I said. Are you going to help me or not, because if not, I must find some other way to do it."

Put in those terms, Mr. Naseby naturally had no choice. He might suspect that a true friend of Derry's would either talk him out of such a dangerous scheme, or failing that go immediately to warn the Nonpareil. But the first he had already failed at, as he had known he would before he opened his mouth; and the latter he had regretfully to dismiss as well, since Derry had sworn him to secrecy. And since his own role, as Derry pointed out, was really quite a minor one, merely to lure the Nonpareil's watchdog away so that Derry could meet undisturbed with Captain Kingsley, he gloomily allowed himself to be persuaded. And since neither had any reason to suspect they had been overheard, they set about their preparations with very different expectations: Mr. Naseby resigned and Derry, now that he was at last doing something positive, both nervously excited and apprehensive, and by no means as sure of himself as he had made Mr. Naseby believe.

It was nearly seven that night when they met again. To lull the suspicions of Mr. James's watchdog, they dined together at a snug hotel, Derry full of determined spirits and Mr. Naseby, now that he had had several hours in which to think it over, more uneasy than ever. At a quarter to nine they emerged and hailed a cab to drive them to Covent Garden, presumably to stroll in the stalls and ogle the opera dancers with the other young bucks during the performance, and then repair to the Green Room afterward in search of more promising entertainment. In reality, Derry meant to slip out as soon as the performance began and return to his lodgings where he was to meet Captain Kingsley at 9:30.

In the beginning, all went exactly as planned. They even took the added precaution of changing coats and hats in the cab, in case Derry's watchdog saw Derry slip out. They were much of a size, and in the dark he would have no reason to suspect any trickery, especially since it was clear that Derry knew of his presence.

When they arrived, Derry made sure his shadow was present before they emerged, looking very much as any other young blades in search of a spree. Derry even staggered realistically and put his arm around his friend, as if he had imbibed too well at dinner and needed momentary support. Mr. Naseby, by now sweating, saw that Derry was actually enjoying himself, for there was a glitter of excitement in his light blue eyes, and he laughed as he leaned on him, pretending momentary dizziness. The knowledge did nothing to improve Mr. Naseby's temper or his own performance, which even he recognized as wooden.

Once they were inside the theater he breathed a sigh of relief. He had nothing to do now but remain for the performance and wait for Derry to rejoin him, after which he might retire to his much deserved rest. But not before he had given his friend a piece of his mind for having involved him in such a harebrained scheme.

It was at that point things began to fall apart. Derry laughed again, his eyes fairly blazing with excitement by now, and saluted him briefly before slipping away to find the rear exit, as they had planned. The performance had already begun, but Mr. Naseby dutifully went to purchase his ticket, planning since he was by no means fond of singing, to sleep through the performance.

He reached for the pocket where he kept his notecase, only to find it empty. Only then remembering he was wearing Derry's coat, not his own, he began feeling in other pockets for where he might have put it when the exchange was made. They were all empty. He had evidently forgotten to remove his own pocketbook when the exchange was made, unlike Derry, who was even now making his way home with both purses in his pocket.

The ticketseller was becoming impatient, as he foolishly felt all his pockets again in growing panic. When the gentleman behind him complained he gave up his place, wondering desperately what he was to do now. He had no hope of finding Derry, for he had been gone some minutes already, and had a cab waiting for him in the back alley. In desperation Mr. Naseby looked around for some acquaintance to lend him the price of a ticket, but though several gentlemen had arrived this late, including the man who had become impatient and gave him an irate glare now as he passed, all were strangers to him.

He wiped the sweat from his brow with Derry's handkerchief and tried to think. The thought of skulking in the lobby until the performance was over was not one that appealed to him, but without the price of a ticket he would plainly get no further inside. Nor was it likely he would be allowed to remain, for already the ticketseller was eyeing him with suspicion, and one of the ushers was watching him as well.

Feeling absurdly guilty, Mr. Naseby slunk around to the exit Derry had taken, meaning to follow his example and walk home, abandoning Derry without further compunction. He had done his part after all, and Derry had been able to make his slip. It had never, in his estimation, been necessary to maintain the charade to the bitter end, once their object had been reached. That had been Derry's idea of course. Now that he came to think about it, the army was obviously the very place for Derry after all, since it would presumably offer him all the excitement he could wish, and his friends might thus be left in peace.

But he was not in peace at the moment, nor likely to be any time soon, he discovered. The exit Derry had taken led into a blind alley, which led back to the front of the theater. Derry, with a cab waiting, had evidently been able to slip by his watchdog, but Mr. Naseby, on foot, and dressed in Derry's coat, had little hope of doing so unless the watchdog was a great deal more inattentive than he had any reason to hope.

But since he shrank from returning to the lobby under the mistrustful eyes of those hired to guard the sacred portals of Covent Garden, he determined to brave it out. If the watchdog saw him, he would attempt to draw him off, still pretending to be Derry. But either way it was clear he had a long walk before him. He cursed Derry and set out.

The alley was both longer and darker than he had first thought. He reached the end, grateful for the dark night since he was by now feeling decidedly like a fugitive—and walked straight into the man he was trying to avoid.

It was so unexpected he was unable to gather his scattered wits enough to try to pass it off. He fell back, looking the picture of guilt, while the burly watchdog stared at him first in perplexity, then in growing wrath.

"Well, I'll be . . . !" he said. "Diddled! And that by a pair of cod's heads I wouldn't have said knew the time of day."

His face grew more severe, and he added reproachfully, "You hadn't ought to've done that, sir! Mr. James won't be pleased, he won't, and your young friend hasn't the least notion what he's stirring up with his foolish games. I only hope we all don't live to regret this night's piece of work!"

He then turned without another word and left the hapless
Mr. Naseby standing where he stood, without a single word
to say in his defense and unpleasantly aware the damned
fellow was right. By the time he recovered enough to notice,
the burly figure was lost in the gloom. "Here! Hi, I say!" he
cried, starting up from his embarrassment. "Wait for me, you
fool! You don't know where he's gone, and I haven't got my
purse on me! Oh—oh, devil take it! *Now* what am I to do? I
suppose I have no choice but to walk all the way to South
Audley Street and make a complete fool of myself. And let
that be a lesson to me!"

27

Mr. Japes, the Nonpareil's watchdog, reached South Audley
Street considerably ahead of Mr. Naseby, and operating under a strong sense of personal mortification. He had allowed
himself to be taken in by one of the oldest tricks in the book,
lulled by circumstances and the extreme youth of his quarry
into relaxing his usual vigilance, with the result that he now
had to confess his lapse and seek immediate advice from his
employer. He was a man who prided himself on his work,
and Mr. James could not be more contemptuous than he was
of himself. In fact, he berated himself all the way to his
employer's residence, dreading his inevitable reaction.

As it happened, Mr. James was dining out that evening,
according to the toffee-faced butler, who did not quite
manage to conceal his contempt of such a visitor to a gentleman's residence, however much he might be in his master's
employ. Mr. Japes considered the matter for a moment and
asked to see Mr. Shelby instead.

The butler looked even more disapproving, but consented
to take a message to the secretary at last. He moved off with
glacial slowness, however, obviously in no hurry to do so, and
Mr. Japes had to possess his soul in what patience that
remained to him.

He was rewarded, for however slow the messenger, Mr. Shelby seemed to waste no time, but came down the stairs quickly, his expression grave.

"Do I take it you've lost your quarry?" he asked. "Mr. James won't be pleased. What happened?"

"I didn't exactly *lose* him," said Mr. Japes bitterly, "though that's hardly any recommendation! Lulled, is what I was, and it ain't often Bartholomew Japes has to admit to such a thing."

"Are you saying young Ainsley gave you the slip? Good God!"

"Aye, I told you I was lulled. Ordinarily not even a child should have fallen for such a trick, but I'll admit that young varmint managed to pull the wool over my eyes. Knowing I was there, and all, and the reason it never occurred to me— but that's no excuse! I don't know when I've been so ashamed, and that's a fact!"

"Well, it doesn't do any good to dwell on it now. Mr. James is dining with Lord Carrington this evening, but I know he'll wish to be told right away. You'd best come with me, in case he has any questions for you. Where—oh, there you are, West! Have a carriage brought around immediately. I must—"

He was interrupted by the front doorbell sounding with unexpected force, startling him and stiffening the already offended butler into icy fury. He went with glacial steps to open the door and dispose summarily of this latest insult to his domain.

A greatly ruffled Mr. Naseby almost fell into the hall, obviously in the very act of making another violent assault upon the bell pull. "It's about time," he grumbled. "I must see Mr. James immediat—"

He seemed to spy the others then, for his expression changed, and he demanded in high dudgeon, "Oh, it's you, is it? I ought to plant you a facer for abandoning me like that!"

Mr. Japes, a figure of some bulk, and still smarting himself, stepped forward invitingly. "You're welcome to try, o'course. Better men than you has done it and failed."

Mr. Shelby intervened somewhat hastily. "Gentlemen, please! Do I understand you're Mr. Naseby? I am Mr. Shelby, Mr. James's secretary. I'm afraid Mr. James is out for the evening, but please come in. I've a notion you're just the man we want.''

Mr. Naseby allowed himself to be mollified slightly, but said with some bitterness, "Aye, I'll be bound I am! And if this fool had had the sense to realize it, I might have been spared having to spout Derry's watch to a damned thieving jarvey just to get here.''

"You—pawned Mr. Ainsley's watch?" asked Mr. Shelby, understandably all at sea.

"Since I had just discovered I left my purse in the pocket of my coat which he is now wearing, I had little choice in the matter! If I hadn't, your man here would never have discovered the trick, for I didn't have enough money on me to buy a ticket. I ain't saying I'm sorry it *was* discovered, for I never did approve of it, but I can tell you I've never spent such a dashed unpleasant afternoon, what with worrying if I was doing the right thing, and then being made to feel like a pickpocket by some ugly customer who called himself an usher, and then reduced to pledging my—Derry's—watch to as brazen a thief as it's been my misfortune to meet unhung. I should have known what would come of allowing myself to be persuaded to get involved against my better judgment.''

Mr. Japes was grinning openly by now, and even Mr. Shelby was having to struggle to keep a straight face. "I'm sorry for all your trials, but I'm glad you've come. We are on our way now to speak with Mr. James. If, as I suspect, you know where Mr. Ainsley was going, I hope you'll agree to come with us. I was just about to—but wait. If there's any chance your cab may still be here, it would save having to send around to the stables.''

"Oh, he's waiting all right," said Mr. Naseby even more bitterly. "Or at least he'd better be! It would serve Ainsley right if he did lose it, but I promised the bloodsucker out there that I'd redeem the watch as soon as I arrived.''

"Yes, of course!" Mr. Shelby immediately pulled out his pocketbook. "I'm sorry, I should have thought of that at once. I fear I lack the wit for such intrigue. Will this be enough?''

"A couple of coachwheels, and no more!" protested Mr. Naseby. "I told you the fellow's the biggest thief unhung! In fact, if you take my advice, if you insist upon giving him any further business, you'll settle on the price before hand!''

Derry's watch duly retrieved, and the grinning jarvey given directions, the three climbed into the rather malodorous interior, much to Mr. Naseby's evident disgust. The latter, still struggling with his conscience, flatly refused to divulge his friend's plans to anyone but Mr. James, so that it was a silent journey to Berkeley Square where Lord Carrington, an old friend of Mr. James's, resided.

It also began to look to have been a futile one. My lord Carrington's butler, opening the door at such an hour to three strangers, had no hesitation whatsoever in denying his lordship.

Mr. Shelby said patiently, ''I have no wish to disturb his lordship. I do, however, have need to speak with Mr. James, who I have reason to know is dining here this evening, since I am his secretary. Please inform him that Mr. Shelby is here, and that the matter is somewhat urgent.''

The butler remained unimpressed. ''That's as may be, but Mr. James—if indeed he were dining here this evening—left no instruction that he was to be distrubed. I can't take it upon myself to interrupt him, I'm afraid. You may leave a message, if you wish, of course.''

''No, of course he didn't, for he naturally had no notion such an emergency would arise! I can only tell you that he will be very angry indeed if you refuse to tell him I wish to speak with him.''

The butler looked on the verge of being persuaded by this argument, despite his better judgment, when Mr. Naseby, nearly at the end of his patience, made the mistake of exclaiming, ''Dash me, if I haven't descended into some madhouse or another! Of course he could hardly leave word that he was expecting an emergency to arise, you fool! I tell you, I don't know what the world is coming to when even a peer of the realm can keep such impertinent fools as servants!''

The butler stiffened visibly, looking the irate Mr. Naseby up and down with clear dismissal. ''Indeed, sir?'' he inquired. ''And who might you be, if I may inquire?''

''Who might I—dash it, this is the outside of enough!'' he cried, beginning furiously to search through his pockets for his cardcase. ''I'll tell you who I might be, and then we'll have no more of your . . .'' Only belatedly he recalled that his cardcase, like his purse, was undoubtedly still in his coat even now on Derry's back, and gave vent to his frustration by dashing his—or rather Derry's—hat on the ground.

Mr. Japes, who seemed to have taken no greater liking to his lordship's butler than Mr. Naseby had, said helpfully, "For once I agree with 'im! Just you say the word, sir, and I'll floor the mort—er—gentleman in a trice and fetch Mr. James myself."

"Good God, no! Oh, this is ridiculous," said a much-tried Mr. Shelby. "Be quiet, both of you! It doesn't matter who either of them are. What does matter is that you will be sorry indeed, my good man, if you don't take my message, and at once. I am myself a little acquainted with Lord Carrington, and I can assure you I will not hesitate to inform him of the matter if necessary."

Whether convinced by this threat, or, more likely, by the size of Mr. Japes, whose eagerness to intervene could not be mistaken, the butler at last bowed woodenly and announced that he would inform his lordship. He then took the precaution of closing the door in their faces, despite Mr. Japes's quick attempt to prevent him, obviously not trusting such questionable visitors not to rob its inhabitants.

"That's the last we'll see of him," pronounced Mr. Naseby gloomily. "Should have let this fellow floor him, if you ask me. Devil take me if I ever allow myself to be drawn into such a crack-pot scheme again. And I thought Mr. James a man of sense, too."

"He is a man of sense. If you must know, I don't blame that poor devil for not trusting us. But for God's sake, if he does come back, let me do the talking. If we're not careful, he'll have us arrested for suspicious behavior or something."

It began to seem as if Mr. Naseby had been correct in his prediction, for they were left to cool their heels on the steps for some minutes. Mr. Japes passed the time by whistling tunelessly between his teeth and eyeing the house with a professional eye, at last pronouncing judiciously that if it turned out the fellow had tipped them the double, he'd engage himself to gain entrance through the downstairs window before the cat could lick her ear. Always assuming, o'course, that he had Mr. Shelby's permission.

"You have *not* got my permission, you fool! We can't go breaking into houses!"

But Mr. Naseby's interest was caught. "Come to that, I'd back him to be inside in five minutes. All I can say is, your Mr. James keeps some mighty odd company. Never laid eyes on anyone who looked more like a second-story man."

"Now that's where you're wrong," corrected Mr. Japes, unoffended. "I don't say I couldn't get inside o' that window, *and* in two minutes, but milling kens was never in my line."

"You surprise me," said Mr. Naseby rather nastily. "What is your line, in that case?"

Mr. Japes scratched his head. "A little o' this and that. Mr. James keeps me busy, often enough. And seein' as how I'm grateful to 'im for rescuin' me from the ring, so to speak, I'm happy to oblige 'im."

"Bruiser, eh?" Mr. Naseby seemed momentarily to forget his animosity. "Thought you looked familiar. I may have seen you fight once. You were right to abandon the ring. And if that fool don't return soon, dashed if I won't *help* you break in that window."

Fortunately he was not put to the test, for almost at that moment the door reopened, and the butler said even more woodenly, "I beg your pardon, sir, for not having recognized you. Mr. James will see you—er—all of you in the study. If you'll step this way."

"Never mind, Farnes," interrupted the Nonpareil's calm voice. "I'll come out. Pray convey my apologies to Lord Carrington and explain that I was called away unexpectedly. Thank you."

When the butler had bowed frigidly once more and closed the door upon them, Mr. James looked from one to the other with slightly raised brows. "Charles, I'm surprised at you. Did you really threaten to do Farnes an injury? Ah, Japes, and Mr. Naseby! What a—pleasant surprise. perhaps someone will kindly explain to me what's going on."

They all tried to do so—at the same time. After a moment the Nonpareil held up one elegant hand. "Never mind, I think I can guess. Young Ainsley has slipped his leash, no doubt. I suspected he might attempt to do so."

Even Mr. Japes stared a little at that, and it was evidently too much for the much-tried Mr. Naseby, for he said with awful sarcasm, "You suspected he might do so? I wish the devil I might have known it, instead of running myself ragged all evening and making a complete fool of myself into the bargain!"

"I am much obliged to you if your—er—efforts were on my behalf," said the Nonpareil calmly. "But you must recall that I as yet know nothing except that one whom I trusted seems to have unaccountedly failed in what would have seemed a simple enough task."

It was Mr. Japes's turn to redden. Mr. James spoke quite pleasantly, but the ex-pugilist seemed to find it difficult to meet his eyes, and said bitterly, "Aye, and how I came to be taken in by so old a trick is more than I can tell you. But if you want to know how this gentleman's involved, sir, I can tell you that, at least, for he it was who helped that other one to pull the wool over my eyes. And if it hadn't been that I had no reason to suspect the young gentleman to wish to be rid of me, knowing as he did that I was there to protect him, I daresay I might have been more alert."

The Nonpareil ignored the slight accusation in Mr. Japes's tone, his eyes once more on Mr. Naseby, who grew uneasy under the scrutiny. "Did he indeed? In that case, I have even more reason to be grateful to you, Mr. Naseby, for I suspect you will save us a good deal of time."

"What do you mean to do?" inquired Mr. Shelby quickly.

"Spring the trap, of course. And to think that only a few weeks ago I was complaining that nothing out of the ordinary ever happened to me," said the Nonpareil.

Mr. Naseby, staring at him, was astonished to discover that one whom he had always believed to be the epitome of fashion and sense, was as crazy as his friend Derry. The Nonpareil was plainly enjoying himself.

28

In the meantime, Letty's new-found respect for her meek little cousin was increasing rapidly. It was Phila who made all the plans, and who slipped out only to return with the astonishing news that she had arranged for a cab to pick them up after dark, with a driver who could be trusted. And it was Phila who without a blush informed Aunt Chloe that Letty's friend Lizzie had invited them to meet some friends after dinner, if Aunt Chloe could spare them. They would not be late and Lizzie's brother had promised to see them home.

Aunt Chloe protested mildly that Phila was not yet well enough to be going out, but since she had received a long missive from her husband that afternoon, expressing disappointment but not surprise at her news, and instructing her to remain in London at least until Lydia returned, and in the meantime to confer with a firm of solicitors whose names he'd been given, and who might be able to help them on the matter she had mentioned, Aunt Chloe's thoughts were otherwhere, and she made no real objections. In fact, she seemed relieved to see Letty and Phila on such good terms, and urged them to enjoy themselves before hurrying off to write to the solicitors' office.

It was Priddy who said in her blunt way, as soon as her mama was out of the room, "I know you both are up to something. I'm not asking any questions, but you'd better be back when you say. Ever since Lydia left, Mama's been checking our rooms in the middle of the night to make sure we're there. I've seen her do it."

Phila blushed and hugged Priddy rather convulsively, and Letty said, "We're not eloping, if that's what you fear. In fact, I'll tell you all about it tomorrow. I'm just along for the ride, as a matter of fact. Phila's the one who's pulling the strings."

Phila blushed again and begged them to hush before Aunt Chloe came back and heard them.

It was also Phila who seemed the calmest at the appointed hour. Aunt Chloe accepted without protest the news that Lizzie was sending a cab for them, which was to meet them at the end of the street. Once out of the house, Phila walked them at a rapid rate, and seemed wholly unsurprised, as Letty had to confess she was, to find a cab waiting for them as promised, the driver a huge man who greeted Phila with the news that he had ought to have his head examined. In fact, only her threat to find another driver if he wouldn't help her had persuaded him, for he'd be bound she was up to mischief.

Phila blushed and reassured him that they meant only to call on her brother, and that he might drive them home again himself exactly as she'd promised. He seemed to be resigned, if not content with that answer, for he helped them in and climbed back up on the box himself. In a moment they had started off.

"Where on earth did you meet him?" inquired Letty curiously.

Phila blushed in the dark. "Mr. Crawley helped me once before. He didn't want to this time, but at least we can be sure he won't abandon us, and I suspect he might be useful if—well, it doesn't matter. But I'm sure we can trust him."

"Well that's something, anyway. What are you planning? You meant to say he might be useful if it came to a fight just then, didn't you? And to think I used to think you such a meek little thing! What excuse are we going to make to your brother, by the way, for dropping in at such an hour?"

"It doesn't matter," insisted Phila. "We'll tell him we were on the way home from friends'—that Aunt Chloe has been taken suddenly ill. Anything! They may think it odd, but there's nothing they can do as long as we're there. And either we'll stay until Captain Kingsley leaves, or insist upon taking Derry away with us. Derry may be furious as well, but I don't care, so long as we can prevent something dreadful from happening."

After a moment Letty laughed. "Well, as I remember, Corny said you were an unusual girl. I only hope Captain Kingsley isn't going to be as angry as I expect he will be. At any rate, what's to keep your brother from trying again, sometime when we're not around?"

"I'll worry about that later," said Phila stubbornly. "If I

have to I'll threaten to go to Mr. James. For the moment all I care about is keeping Derry out of danger tonight.''

Letty shivered a little despite herself. It had already occurred to her that such desperate traitors were unlikely to balk at violence, or even murder if necessary. But since she could think of no better plan she remained silent.

Everything looked perfectly normal when they arrived before Derry's building. They knew from what Letty had overheard that afternoon that Derry was to meet Captain Kingsley at 10:00, and it was a few minutes before that now, but there was yet no sign of his arrival. As soon as the cab they were in drew to a stop Phila opened the door and tumbled out, and Letty had no choice but to follow. Behind them, the jarvey scratched his head for a moment in indecision, and then followed as well, his face determined.

There was no sign of Derry's landlady in the hall. A lantern had been left burning on a low table, and without compunction Phila grabbed that up and hurried up the stairs, her shadow floating eerily behind her on the wall.

All was silent except for the noise they made on the stairs, which was considerable because of the jarvey's heavy boots. Phila looked back, as if annoyed he was there, but said nothing and hurried on. Letty, her heart beating with increasing and so-far unjustified panic in her breast, could detect no sign of hesitation in Phila's white face. She seemed wholly unaware that she might be putting herself or them in danger. Letty shook her head and went on.

Mr. Crawley was laboring heavily behind them, no longer able to keep up. For the moment he was out of sight, though they could hear his heavy steps on the uncarpeted stairs and the sound of his breathing.

Then Phila, at the top of the stairs, gave a little strangled cry. By the time Letty looked up, she was gone, or at least Letty could no longer see her. Letty's heart was wholly in her throat by now, but she hurried after her, trying to convince herself that Phila had just rounded the corner, and that nothing bad could have happened with herself just a few steps below her.

But when she reached the top of the stairs, there was no sign of Phila in the ill-lit hall, which was completely empty. All the doors were closed, and Letty, having no idea which one was Derry's, stood helplessly, even yet not believing that Phila could have disappeared almost before her very eyes.

She was sweating out of fear by then, and conscious of a desire to turn and run back down the stairs as fast as she could. Instead, she opened her mouth to shout for the figure on the stairs behind her.

Just then a heavy, smothering cloth was flung over her head, blinding her and making it impossible to get out any other than a strangled cry. Helplessly she felt herself lifted and carried, unable to struggle or even to warn their driver of danger.

She was carried for only a few moments. In the enveloping cloth she could hear very little, and see nothing, so she could not tell what had happened to Mr. Crawley behind her, but she had decided not to waste her strength until she could see what they were up against.

After another moment or two she was set down on her feet again, and the smothering cloth jerked off. Whatever she had expected to find, it was certainly not a room full of people, at least one of whom was very well known to her.

Letty gaped at Corny, who was looking a good deal astonished himself. Phila was standing in the middle of the room, looking as disoriented as Letty herself was feeling, while a perfectly normal young man was saying in some embarrassment, "I beg your pardon—both of your pardons! I had no idea— We had orders to prevent anyone else from going in, but we never dreamed—that is, I am sorry for any alarm you may have suffered."

"Good God!" said Letty. "You knew what her brother intended to do?"

"No," said the harrassed Mr. Shelby. "At least, Mr. James thought it possible, but Mr. Naseby warned us before he could—that is—er, in time."

"Yes, but what I want to know," put in Mr. Naseby suddenly, "is what the devil you're doing here, either of you? Good God, we might as well have invited the whole town!"

"I overheard you talking this afternoon, you see," supplied Letty dryly, and shrugged. "I'm sorry if we've gotten in the way, but I thought someone ought to keep you two fools from murdering yourselves."

"Will someone please tell me what's happened?" demanded Phila in a voice that shook a little. "Where's Derry? What is going on? I demand that someone tell me!"

Mr. Shelby and Mr. Naseby exchanged quick glances, but before they could answer a door had opened behind them and a familiar, elegant figure came in, looking absurdly out of place in that crowded room.

"Never mind, Charles! I will take care of Miss Ainsley. I can see, in fact, that I should have expected this. It did not occur to you, of course, Miss Ainsley, to come to me? Or even to trust me to take care of your brother, as I promised?"

Letty had thought he was perfectly calm, until she saw his eyes. She did not, of course, know him very well, but even she was rendered unexpectedly tongue-tied by the expression in them, especially when he turned on her and added, "I certainly did not expect Miss Coates, whom I thought a sensible woman, to aid and abet you in such folly."

Phila stood alone in the middle of the room, very pale. "My brother—?" she managed.

"Is perfectly safe," said the Nonpareil. "Charles—no, I may need you later. Mr. Naseby, oblige me by escorting Miss Ainsley and her cousin home, and making sure they remain there!"

Letty's eyes were wide, but to her surprise without another word Phila turned and left the room.

29

It was a silent journey home. Phila said nothing at all, and even Mr. Naseby was unnaturally subdued, but whether out of embarrassment that Phila should know about his relationship with her cousin, or for some other reason no one could tell.

Priddy was waiting up for them, full of questions; but out of consideration Letty waylaid her and told her in a few brief words what had happened while Phila went up to bed.

No one mentioned the matter at breakfast the next morning. The night's adventure might not have taken place, except that Aunt Chloe asked the two older girls kindly if they had enjoyed their evening out.

Letty glanced quickly at Phila before answering somewhat dryly for both of them, "Oh, yes, we had a wonderful time. I can't remember when I've enjoyed myself more, in fact."

Aunt Chloe seemed satisfied with that answer and the subject was allowed to drop.

Fortunately there was a diversion soon after breakfast that effectively put last night's adventure into the background for the moment. Shortly after ten there was the sound of a heavy carriage at the door, then the bell sounded, and there was unusual activity in the hallway. Phila and Letty were once more engaged in half-heartedly helping Aunt Chloe sort through Lydia's things and pack them, but after a moment a curious Letty went to the head of the stairs to see what all the commotion was about.

She was gone so long that Aunt Chloe, engaged in searching for a slipper that either in her haste Lydia had packed without its mate to take with her, or had not been put up with its mate, grew impatient and grumbled, "Drat the girl! I may as well have gone myself. Here it is! At least it relieves my mind to know Lydie's not hopping about on one sandal, though what it was doing in a drawer is more than I can answer. Good God, what is it? Don't give me such a scare, girl. My nerves ain't up to it."

For Letty was back in the doorway. "Mama," she said oddly. Then, "Oh, you may as well know! Lydia's back, though she might as well have stayed away as far as I'm concerned."

Aunt Chloe stared at her for a moment, then gave a shriek and dropped the shoe to plunge out the door. Left staring at a troubled Phila, Letty shrugged. "Well, at least it appears that he married her. She's wearing a new and extremely expensive traveling dress that she didn't own before she left. Though how she managed to have it made up so quickly, or whose money paid for it is yet to be discovered! We may as well go down. I've a feeling Mama's going to need support to stand the shock."

There was indeed already a visible change in Lydia when

the two girls followed Aunt Chloe's bulky figure down the
stairs. Aside from the new—and becoming—traveling dress
and a bonnet that afterward even Aunt Chloe speculated must
have cost fifty guineas at least, if a shilling, with an extravagant poke and enormous ostrich feathers that must have made
it difficult to climb into a carriage, she certainly looked as if
marriage agreed with her. She looked both extremely smug
(if she were a cat she'd be licking her whiskers, whispered
Letty into Phila's ear) and more animated than anyone could
remember ever seeing her, and had obviously decided to
conduct herself as if the elopement and her mother's distress
had never taken place, and she had returned from a conventional bride trip.

She was surrounded by boxes and bandboxes in the hall—
all of it new, no doubt, muttered Letty—and was impatiently
directing a postboy about their disposal, but she turned at her
mother's cry and allowed herself to be embraced and noisily
kissed. She disengaged herself quickly enough, however,
saying, "Take care, Mama. I am to meet my husband in an
hour. We're staying at the Clarendon until we can find somewhere suitable to live. Bevis says they have the best dinners
in London. I just stopped by to see you and drop off some
trinkets I purchased for you and the girls."

"So at least he married you," said Aunt Chloe, dabbing at
her eyes and accepting the rebuff with good grace.

"Mama!" Lydia briefly lost a little of her enforced good
humor and glanced at the postboy irritably, but after a moment she had recovered and dismissed the boy. "Yes, he
married me, if you had any doubts. You might have known
you could trust me for that. And I warned you, didn't I, that I
had no intention of going back to Somerset to rot away, or
marry some farmer. Since it had become more than apparent
that Phila's and not my wishes were all that counted around
here, I did what I had to and I'm not sorry for it."

Priddy had come out of the morning room at the back of
the house that had been given over to her for her lessons and
sketching to see what all the commotion was about, and she
now said hotly, "What you mean is you'd made London too
hot to hold you!

Aunt Chloe looked distressed, and Phila mortified, but
after a moment Lydia merely smiled rather unpleasantly.

"My dear little sister! Which reminds me, Mama, I shall have to have a talk with Papa right away and settle the matter of what money is to be mine now that I'm married. There's the matter of my portion as well, but Papa will have to settle an allowance on me over and above that, for you know yourself how expensive it is to live in London. But we can discuss that later. Come into the front room and see what I've brought you."

Priddy hung back, her face mutinous, and after a moment Phila quietly closed the door on them and remained behind with Priddy.

"I wish she hadn't come back!" said Priddy horribly. "I wish she'd stay with her new upper-class relations and not even bother to pretend she still has any interest in us, except for Papa's money."

"Yes, but your Mama doesn't wish she'd stay away," Phila reminded her gently.

When Priddy merely scowled and flatly refused to go in and as she put it make over Lydia and pretend that nothing had happened after Lydia had nearly broken their mama's heart, Phila thought it politic to invite Priddy to go for a walk with her until Lydia had gone again.

They had walked for nearly an hour, and Phila, at least, was extremely weary after her sleepness night, by the time she judged it safe to return. Priddy had said very little, except to kick at pebbles and say that as far as she was concerned Lydia needn't think to buy her off. But as they reached their street again, she looked up, and said with more interest than she had displayed that morning, "Isn't that your Mr. James coming toward us?"

Phila blanched and looked up quickly, her heart beginning to hammer against her ribs for some reason. It was indeed Mr. James, driving himself in a high-perch phaeton and looking magnificent in a huge, many-caped greatcoat. He was alone, not even a groom up beside him, and at sight of them he checked his high-spirited pair immediately.

"Miss Coates," he said calmly. "Miss Ainsley. I was coming in search of you, but this is even better. There are—certain matters I believe we must discuss, if you can spare me some ten minutes of your time."

He spoke evenly, and there was no trace of either emotion

or irritation in his face. Even so Phila had no wish to get up with him after last night, and said hastily and rather incoherently, "No, no! I mean, I mustn't leave Priddy. Perhaps another time."

Priddy was looking openly curious by this time and said promptly, "Don't be silly! It's only half a block." She grimaced. "If worse comes to worse, I can always lock myself in my room until she leaves!"

In the face of Priddy's disclaimer, and the hand the Nonpareil was already stretching down to her to so peremptorily, Phila was left with little choice but to take it. Once she was beside him in the awkward vehicle, he wasted no time, but nodded briefly to Priddy and gave his horses the office.

She had driven with him once before, and though she realized he must be a very good whip, on that occasion too she had been far too preoccupied to really enjoy the experience. She stole a furtive glance at his face, and still could read nothing in it. After a moment she said unwillingly, "You wished to speak to me?"

"In a moment, Miss Ainsley! Why should your cousin lock herself in her room?"

"Oh. My cousin Lydia returned this morning. Priddy doesn't want to see her yet, because she hasn't forgiven her for hurting Aunt Chloe so badly."

"I can't say that I blame her. I assume your Cousin Lydia is married, then? Has your aunt said anything more about my suggestion?"

His words and manner were perfectly pleasant, but Phila, perhaps morbidly sensitive, could detect no real friendliness in either. "Yes. She's very grateful to you, in fact, and has already written my uncle all about it. He's given her the name of a solicitor to see in London."

He made no comment, and an awkward silence fell. Phila was about to steel herself to ask again what he wanted to talk to her about when her distracted eye at last noticed, to her amazement, that they had gone in quite a different direction than she had expected. Even as she started, the river came into view, and it became obvious they were going to cross it.

"What are you doing?" she cried instinctively. "Why have you come this way?"

"I am taking you to Kent to my mother," he said calmly,

heading onto the bridge and successfully overcoming his leader's objection to a heavily laden cart coming toward them on the opposite side. "I intend to make sure this time that you remain safely out of trouble!"

She flushed up to the roots of her hair. "Kent? You can't be serious? I have nothing with me—my aunt—You can't—oh, take me back at once!"

He laughed in a way she thought unkind. "I not only can, I already have, Miss Ainsley. You needn't worry. I spoke with your aunt and she packed all that you will need immediately. She has promised to send your luggage on tomorrow. I have hopes that my mother will be able to control you, since no one else seems able to, but at any rate you will be out of London, where you can do the most harm."

She sat staring at her twisted hands, trying desperately not to cry and betray herself. It was clear now that he despised her, and she wanted only to crawl into a hole and die, or at least never be obliged to meet him again for as long as she lived. Certainly the last thing she wanted, under the circumstances, was to be thrust upon his mother like some child in disgrace. "Please . . ." she managed, "I beg of you, don't . . ."

He ignored her. "You may as well know it all at once! Your brother was wounded last night. No, he is in no danger, and he has, in fact, only himself to blame. If he had not seen fit to interfere in my plans, risking everything—but enough of that! He is under a doctor's care, and my sister is herself nursing him. He certainly does not require your assistance, though I know you will find that impossible to believe."

His unkind words, the news about Derry, her sleepness night all combined to make her lose whatever control she had on her emotions. She wanted only to escape from him and go to Derry, and before she could prevent herself she had grabbed at the reins, crying wildly, "Stop! Oh, why are you doing this? I must go to my brother! Let me out! Let me out now and I'll walk back."

The result was not quite what it had been with Mr. Drumm. There was very little traffic now, and they were moving at a fast clip, but Mr. James was an excellent whip, unlike Mr. Drumm. His grays stumbled slightly, startled by the unexpected pressure, but he held them up, sweeping around a particularly difficult turn at barely diminished speed.

Phila gave a desperate sob and would have jumped, despite their speed, all reason seeming to leave her, had he not pulled her back with a cruel grip on her arm and more or less anchored her in her seat.

"Oh, no, Miss Ainsley!" he panted, baring his teeth a little. The fury in his face was unexpected, and startled her out of her recent folly, so that she could only stare at him, white-faced and trembling. "You won't succeed in serving me the same trick as you did Drumm! I am, in fact, for the first time able to feel a little sympathy for your previous persecuter. From the first moment we met you have not hesitated to make *my* life a misery, or spare anyone else in your disastrous conduct."

She could not imagine why he was saying such things to her, or what she could have done to make him this angry with her. She was beyond any defense or dissimulation, her hot tears no longer to be contained, and her trembling so great that she might have had a fever.

As if this merely served to goad him further, he said, still in that unfamiliar harsh voice, "Yes, I am the villain now, am I not? Everything is always someone else's fault, never your own! From the moment we met you have not hesitated to thrust yourself into one disastrous and ill-bred scrape after another, or scrupled to drag others in behind you. Again and again I told myself it was due to your youth, and the disadvantages of your upbringing, but I can no longer so deceive myself. Since I first met you your behavior has been outrageous. You have never hesitated to go your length to demonstrate your total contempt of the normal canons of civilized behavior. In fact, the truest thing you ever said to me, though I doubt you meant it exactly that way, was that your aunt was in no way to blame for your excesses. Poor woman, she has my deepest sympathy. If you were in my charge, which I thank God you are not, I would not hesitate to lock you up somewhere in the country and throw away the key, for I am convinced it is the only way anyone around you will ever know any peace!"

29

Phila gave another sob, feeling as if she had stumbled into a nightmare, and that none of this could really be happening to her. Derry could not be lying wounded somewhere, perhaps even dying, while she was being foisted upon some elegant stranger who would despise her as her son clearly did. And the Nonpareil could not have said all those deliberately cruel things to her. It must be a nightmare, for whatever she had done she had not deserved that. He had been angry last night, yes, but this cold cutting stranger beside her was not the Mr. James she knew.

If she had been more herself or possessed more experience of the world, it might have occurred to her to wonder why the Nonpareil, with all his address, should have so far forgotten himself as to be deliberately unkind to one whose sex, age, and present unhappiness should have protected from his tongue, if his own dignity did not.

Phila, still struggling with the illusion that she must wake soon and discover that none of this had happened, only knew that if she had ever considered herself unhappy before, she had been mistaken. The thought of remaining beside him for several more hours, perhaps, filled her with a kind of sick panic. But her brain seemed numb, and incapable of anything but remembering again and again with shrinking horror the things he had said.

Beside her the Nonpareil, nearly as aghast as she was, stared straight ahead, his own emotions in nearly as much turmoil. He had meant to say none of those things, of course. He had thought himself well in control again, and beyond whatever madness had temporarily afflicted him. He had told himself that her behavior last night merely proved how wise he had been not to embark on a marriage that would be disastrous for them both. Once more she had flung herself into danger, wholly unnecessarily, and dragged her cousin in

after her this time. Worse, she had drawn him down to her
level, undermining his intention of remaining aloof but polite,
driving him by her white face and wounded eyes to say things
he had never intended. She was impulsive, ridiculously warm-
hearted, loyal to a fault, absurdly oversensitive, far too young
and unsophisticated, with neither conduct or polish— all the
things he least wanted in a wife. She should be glad he had
regained his sanity before it was too late.

"Oh, God, what's the use?" said the great Havelocke
James in a ragged voice. "Phila, my—"

But Phila interrupted him, suddenly furious. "While my
brother lies wounded, perhaps dying, I am to be packed off like
an unwanted parcel because it suits *your* convenience! But then
that's all we've ever been to you, isn't it, an inconvenience?"

She surprised an odd laugh from him. "A damnable inconvenience! Phila—"

"And that is all that matters, isn't it?" she demanded
pantingly. "My brother is in disgrace because he dared to
interfere with the great Havelocke James's plans. I did too,
and that is why I have been treated to this tirade today. And
why I'm to be packed off in disgrace, without regard to my
wishes, or my brother's, or even my aunt's. But then no
one's wishes matter but your own, do they? You have seldom
hesitated to make known to me your opinion of my relations,
so I should not be surprised at the contempt you feel for me
as well. If my brother had been killed, I've no doubt you
would merely have shrugged your shoulders in that well-bred
way of yours and gone on to your club. Wouldn't you?
Wouldn't you?"

There was an unaccustomed patch of color in his cheeks,
and he answered, a little stung in spite of himself, "You are
mistaken! If your brother had been killed it would have been
no more than he deserved for meddling in things he little
understood, but I would have been genuinely sorry. As for
your being packed off in disgrace, there is nothing you can do
for your brother that any other competent nurse can't. And
thanks to your brother, both Drumm and Kingsley managed
to escape, so that you are likely to be in considerable danger
in London. Your aunt agreed with me that you would be far
better off out of the way for the time being, and given her

preoccupation with your cousin Lydia at the moment, my mother seemed the obvious answer.''

He meant to defend himself, but everything he said merely confirmed the truth for her. He clearly could not conceive why she would wish to be with her brother at such a time, or that she might dread being forced on a total stranger. She said in a very low voice, ''You once told me you found it difficult to care. At the time I didn't believe it, but I do now. If I am impetuous and ill-bred, then I begin to think you are wholly without heart. And of the two of us, I think you are more to be pitied.''

There was a moment's silence. Then he said very quietly, ''In that case, Miss Ainsley, you should be happy to know that you have been revenged upon me. I had believed so too until you taught me otherwise.''

After that, silence reigned completely. For the next several miles she sat with head averted, having frequent recourse to the damp handkerchief crumpled in one hand and struggling to regain control over herself.

At last he spoke rather stiffly beside her. ''I'm sorry, Miss Ainsley, but we are coming into Dartford. I must change the horses there, for there's nothing after that until Chatham, and my grays will never last that long, I'm afraid.''

She had long since ceased the foolish tears and dried her eyes for the last time. She managed to say normally enough, ''You should not have delayed on my account. Pray stop where you will.'' She hesitated, in less control than she had believed, and added almost pitifully, ''Please—my brother—I beg you to set me down there so that I may catch a coach or the mail back to London. I promise not to do anything foolish, but I must be with my brother.''

''Yes,'' said her companion, ''I have long been aware that your brother has all your affection and loyalty. But I'm afraid he will have to survive without you for the moment. And don't think to try and escape me while my back is turned, for I have no intention of letting you out of my sight.''

She stiffened, and did not trust herself to make an answer. At the posting house she sat stiffly in her high seat, ignoring the bustle that went on around her. The Nonpareil and his grays were obviously well-known there, for the landlord himself hurried out to greet him and, though he eyed her with a little surprise, offered to fetch her a glass of lemonade, or anything else she might care for while she waited.

Phila declined this kind offer with what dignity she could muster, and hoped it would do the Nonpareil's reputation no good to be seen with her. She might have spared herself the effort, for the Nonpareil explained her presence easily by saying that she was a young friend of his mother's he was escorting on a visit.

The landlord's face cleared, and he inquired affectionately after Lady Annis. It seemed she didn't get about nearly as much as she was used to, for it had been a donkey's age since he'd seen her.

"Yes, my mother has become something of a recluse in late years," said the Nonpareil coolly. "She finds her comfort more important than the company of others. I'll be sure and remember you to her if you'd like. I know I can trust you with the grays."

"Aye, that you can!" said the landlord happily. "It seems like we don't see you as often as we used to, either, come to that, but I know those grays of yours well enough, sir. I'm surprised to see you without your groom, though."

"He was suddenly taken ill," said the Nonpareil rather shortly in reply. The change was completed then, and they were soon on their way again, the landlord waiting until they were out of sight before he turned and went in again.

After a moment Phila asked stiffly, "Is your groom really ill?"

"No. I thought you would prefer not to have a servant listening in," he said as stiffly.

She flushed scarlet and said no more.

By the second halt Phila was feeling all the effects of her sleepness night and all the emotional upheavals. He took one look at her face and went to procure her a glass of lemonade and a plate of sandwiches without asking her wishes.

She was too weary to refuse this time. She drank the lemonade gratefully, and even ate one of the sandwiches, and felt a little better for it.

He came himself to take the tray from her, and looked up at her for a moment, something like concern in his eyes. He started to say something, but she turned hastily away. After a moment he climbed back into the curricle without another word.

Sometime much later Phila returned to hazy consciousness, her cheek resting against something warm and hard, and wrapped in a cocoon of warmth. For a moment she imagined she was back safely in her own bed, but then the movement of a carriage penetrated her brain as it slowed and then turned off the road onto another, graveled one.

As memory returned she sat up with alarm, to discover she had fallen asleep against Mr. James's sleeve. The cocoon was a carriage rug that he had wrapped around her, and the quality of the sunlight told her that it was now late afternoon.

She flushed and said self-consciously, "I—I'm sorry. I must have fallen asleep. You should have wakened me."

"I should instead be shot for not seeing sooner that you are exhausted," he said, sounding more like himself than he had all day. "I may indeed be as heartless as you say, but I fear you are fast teaching me humility. I brought my curricle because I had no wish for you to be seen driving out of town in my traveling chaise, but you would have been far more comfortable in it, I fear."

She had been futilely trying to straighten her bonnet, which was lamentably askew, but at that she froze, his words reminding her of everything that had happened.

He shocked her even more by swearing under his breath, and then saying harshly, "Phila? What have I said now?"

She made herself finish retying the ribbons on her bonnet, though she only succeeded in making matters worse, for her bow was decidedly uneven. "N—nothing I—is your mother expecting me?"

After a moment he accepted the change of topic. "I sent her a note by special messenger this morning. Perhaps I should warn you about my mother, Miss Ainsley. I am quite fond of her, but even I must admit she has long passed the point of mere eccentricity. I believe I may once have told you she's a poet—quite a successful one, as it happens. But she uses that as an excuse, I'm afraid, to do exactly as she wishes, with little regard for either convention or other people's comfort. You can see that I came by my own consummate selfishness quite naturally," he added dryly. As she flushed up again, he finished still more dryly, "However that may be, I have hopes that you will like her, once you get to know her. I am certain she will like you."

Phila was by no means as certain, but once more he had left her with nothing to say. She occupied herself in inspecting the imposing private mansion coming into view as they turned a curve in the long drive. Nothing about it suggested that an eccentric might live there, for it was set in well-kept grounds, and looked peaceful and serene in the late afternoon sunlight.

Now that they were here she was aware of her heart beating a little irregularly in her bosom, and a dread of having the journey end, unpleasant as it had been, and being thrust among perfect strangers. If he had meant to reassure her about his mother, his words had had the exact opposite effect, for aside from being the Nonpareil's mother, her unwilling hostess now turned out to be a successful poetess, which was even more intimidating.

There was clearly no help for it, though, for already they were sweeping into the drive before the house, as a groom rushed out to go to the horses' heads. Phila straightened her spine, wondering what she must look like after a bout of weeping, and then falling asleep against a shoulder in an open carriage.

Then the doors were thrown open, and so fantastic a figure appeared on the porch, her arms opened wide, that Phila forgot every other consideration for the moment in wonderment.

30

Her son had said Lady Annis James was eccentric, but he seemed to have vastly understated the case. She was dressed in flowing robes of an exotic hue, and a turban covered her hair completely, so that Phila was at first uncertain whether the figure who had emerged to greet them was a man or a woman.

That mystery, at least, was soon solved as she embraced her son and then turned a pair of humorous gray eyes very like her son's on her uninvited guest. The eyes were set in a

weather-beaten complexion, and they began to twinkle even
more as they took in Phila's lopsided bonnet, untidy curls,
and general travel-stained condition. "And you must be the
child with that delicious name. I can't think what my son
meant by dragging you all this way in an open carriage, for
you are plainly exhausted, poor dear. Worse, I can see he
failed to prepare you for me. But no matter. We can straighten
it all out later. Come in! Why on earth are we standing on
the porch?"

"Because you haven't yet invited us in," complained her
son patiently. "And it is impossible to prepare anyone for
you, Mother. My mother," he explained to Phila, "once
traveled widely and now imagines herself an Arab Potentate."

"You are mistaken," protested Lady Annis without mal-
ice. "An Arab Potentate dresses far more ornately and uncomfortably than any European. I merely dress as I please in
my own home. Though I confess it has made me less and less
willing to abandon my comforts and return to civilization
in the form of London Society, if one can call that civilization. Why should I? At my age I care very little what people
think, anymore—I leave that to my children—and I can
surround myself with people who interest me, instead of
vapid fools."

"I hope you haven't invited anyone particularly interesting
at the moment," said her son dryly. "The last time I
came I remember you had some Eastern mystic who refused
to eat from a plate and sat meditating all day in the
library."

His mother laughed. "He said it was the only place where
the emanations were favorable. But I will admit he grew
rather tiresome in the end. I have nothing so exotic at the
moment. A rather bad writer, a philosopher whose ideas are
so advanced even I can't make head or tails of them, my
publisher, who is not interesting at all but is down here on
business, and Miles, of course."

The Nonpareil looked slightly relieved. "Is Miles here?
Good. I need not feel quite so much as if I am abandoning
Miss Ainsley in a den of lunatics. I should perhaps inform
you that Miss Ainsley has recently been ill, and is not yet
fully recovered."

"That settles it," said Lady Annis cheerfully. "She shall have supper on a tray and an early night, in that case. I won't expose her to the den of lunatics until the morning. Ah, Mrs. Turby! Just in time. Show Miss Ainsley to her room, and see that she is sent up a tray later. Mrs. Turby, my housekeeper, will see that you have everything you need, my dear. You will perhaps be relieved to know, by the way that my eccentricity does not extend to Eastern furnishings, which can be very uncomfortable, believe me, if you aren't accustomed to them. Good night, my dear. We can talk in the morning."

Phila had stood listening to this conversation stupidly, weariness and shock making her more tongue-tied even than usual. She tried to thank her kind hostess, but got so hopelessly muddled that in the end she was glad to escape and follow the surprisingly staid figure of the housekeeper up the stairs.

To her surprise she slept early and dreamlessly. By the time she had gotten upstairs, her few things had been unpacked for her and she did little justice to her supper before tumbling into the surprisingly comfortable bed.

When she woke, early the next norning, it was to discover the long rest had done her good physically, if it had done little to cure her spiritual ills. She dressed quickly, not knowing what was expected of her, and for all her hostess's kindness of the night before, dreading meeting her again and having to face the rest of her unusual household.

When she emerged from her room a uniformed maid was in the passage, carrying a pile of linen. She looked rather surprised to see Phila, but bobbed a curtsy and said, "Mornin', Miss! Her ladyship didn't expect you to wake this early, but she said if you did, you could come along and take breakfast with her. None of the rest of the guests is early risers, and her ladyship usually has hers in her rooms. They're at the end of the passage, there. I could show you if you'd like."

Phila declined this offer, having no trouble in picking out the rooms the maid pointed out. She felt a little as if she were going to an execution, for her heart was beating uncomfortably fast, but she smiled at the maid and turned toward Lady Annis's rooms.

Lady Annis had told the truth when she said her eccentricity did not extend past her own wardrobe, for the part of the house that Phila had seen so far was in keeping with its traditional exterior. Phila's own bedchamber had been charming, and apart from an occasional exotic screen or vase, she might have been in any wealthy Englishman's mansion. All of the servants Phila had seen so far seemed also to dress and conduct themselves normally, for which Phila could only be thankful.

She soon saw, when she rather timidly knocked on her ladyship's door and was bidden to enter, that Lady Annis, if she had restrained her impulses elsewhere in the house, had certainly not done so in her own rooms. Phila found herself in a large and airy sitting room draped in vibrant colors and filled with whatever exotic items Lady Annis had collected on her travels and had taken her fancy.

She gaped a little stupidly, and Lady Annis said in amusement, "Rather overwhelming, isn't it? My son cringes whenever he comes in here."

"No, I like it," said Phila with perfect truth. "It's—colorful and somehow cheerful."

Lady Annis laughed. She was seated at a small table set for two, her hair uncovered this morning to reveal soft silver curls that made her look both younger and a great deal more human. "Ah, tactful girl! I see you're an early riser like I am. Not even Miles emerges from his bedchamber before ten o'clock, and then he's grumpy until noon. I myself far prefer the day when it is all new and mysterious and as yet untouched by human hands. But I have discovered an increasing tendency in myself to rattle on, which I deplore! Come in and have some tea, and we can get properly acquainted. I must confess I have been longing to meet you."

Phila stared at her. "You have been longing to meet me?" she asked in astonishment.

"Yes, indeed, for I have heard a great deal about you. Does that surprise you? I may have withdrawn from Society out of choice, but I am not wholly cut off. I first learned of your existence from my daughter, who certainly managed to pique my interest, if not for the reasons she implied."

"Your daughter?" repeated Phila foolishly. "But—but I've never even met your daughter!"

"Haven't you? However that may be, she certainly knows about you," said Lady Annis cheerfully. "She, of course, knew nothing about your extraordinary adventures. My son tells me you're quite a heroine, and from what he was telling me last night, I agree. And to think I always had to go to the corners of the earth to find adventure, when all the time there were spies and intrigues to be found in London.''

Phila was so startled she spilled her tea. "He—*he* said that about me?''

"I was surprised as well," confirmed her ladyship with twinkling eyes. "My son is not usually one for hyperbole. He also said you were *gallant*, as I recall, which encourages me to think he is more imaginative than I had believed.''

But Phila had recovered herself. "He only s-said that so you would be kind to me. He thinks I'm outrageous and ill-bred and s-said that he thanks God he doesn't have the care of me!''

Her ladyship burst out laughing. "My dear, there may be hope for my son yet. Tell me all about it.''

Phila answered by bursting into tears.

Her ladyship allowed her to cry uninterrupted for some minutes, then said calmly, "My dear, go and pour that watery tea in some pot or other and allow me to pour you another cup, and then we can both abuse him to your heart's content. I would never have believed my son could behave so humanly. Tell me *everything*!''

That made Phila laugh, and after she had dried her eyes on her napkin since she had forgotten a clean handkerchief, and accepted a second cup of tea from Lady Annis, she surprised herself even more by complying.

It was perhaps not a very coherent tale, but Lady Annis seemed to possess her son's knack of understanding a great deal that was left unsaid. When Phila at last finished, and remembered to drink her by-now lukewarm tea, her ladyship said in her humorous way, "My dear, clearly I should make a habit of getting to London more often. I had no idea so much was going on there. And my daughter is a fool. Never mind that! Poor child, you are hardly in a position to perceive it now, but you have done me a very great favor, you know. You have somehow succeeded in forcing my son out of his well-bred, comfortable shell, and I am immensely grateful to you.''

"He wasn't!" said Phila, long past any pretense of tact.

Her ladyship laughed in her booming way. "No, of course he is not. After all, his life now is safe and ordered, pleasantly hedonistic, and wholly devoted to his own comfort without the necessity of considering anyone else but himself. Just the sort of life designed to make a mother shudder!"

That made Phila laugh again. "Naturally, you wish a life of danger and discomfort for him?"

"My dear, at least it would be living, not that cold, civilized existence he's created for himself! I don't know if you've seen it—yes, of course you have. For all your youth you're a very perceptive young woman. My son is charming, clever, urbane, considerate, conscious of the responsibilities of his wealth and rank—everything a mother is supposed to wish for in her son. He is also almost wholly unreachable. My daughter Lizzie believes he withdrew from the world after Caroline died, but I know that merely hastened a tendency already within him. My husband was just the same. He was a good and kind man, but he had a reserve that held him apart from the rest of humanity, and even from me and his children, all of his life. I have no desire to see my son follow in his footsteps."

She sat as if remembering for a moment, then shook her head briskly. "I'm sorry! It's not often my maternal instincts overtake me, but I must confess I've been more and more troubled lately. You've seen him as I could never hope to. Do you understand what I'm talking about?"

Phila blushed, but said slowly, "He says the same, that he finds it difficult to care, but I think that's not wholly true. He has been—more than kind to me, and my brother, and even a young cousin of mine, when he had no reason to be."

"Has he? I'm relieved to hear it, for it means things may not be quite as bad as I had feared. In fact, I am even more relieved to discover he has been *unkind* to you, for if he is capable of losing his temper and behaving badly, there may be hope for him yet. Yes, I know, I am a very unnatural mother. If fact, you may think I am the last person to talk about selfishness. But at least I have never run from life, as I suspect my son is doing. I *do* blame Caroline for *that*, for the accident, though completely her fault, of course, for she was spoiled and shallow with that sort of stubborn determination that only the truly self-centered can manage—but I digress, a failing of mine, you will have noticed. At any rate, her death laid Locke open to the censure of others at a time when he was no doubt blaming himself bitterly. As a result, he withdrew almost completely into himself. You know about Caroline, I suppose? No, I keep frogetting how many years ago that was now, of course.''

''You—you don't have to tell me,'' said Phila with difficulty.

''Nonsense! Since I've been this indiscreet, I can hardly stop now. They were to have been married, of course, though you may have guessed I was never particularly in favor of the match. Oh, she was lovely enough, but I always believed she would have made him the worst possible wife. She would have exaggerated all his own worst qualities, while having nothing to offer herself except a lovely face and a certain capacity for animal enjoyment. At any rate, a week before the wedding she took out a carriage and team he had forbidden her to drive, and broke her neck! I must confess I've always been secretly relieved. As for Tony—but perhaps I have been indiscreet enough for one day. Goodness, what a lot you have given me to think about.''

After a moment Phila managed to say politely, ''At any rate, I am sorry to have been thrust upon you this way.''

''My dear, think nothing of it! You will discover, when you know me better, that I never trouble myself about others. I hope you will manage to be comfortable with us. When my son returns—''

Then she saw Phila's face and said contritely, ''Oh, my dear, I'm sorry. Did you not know he left this morning? Well, never mind. I was charged to assure you your brother was in good hands and that he will forward your trunk immediately.''

Phila made some answer, thinking she had made enough of a fool of herself for one day than to reveal how very bereft she felt at the news.

32

If the Nonpareil was behaving in a way that warmed his mother's heart, that sentiment was not shared by his household, nor his sister.

His household had never seen him in such a mood, though in fact it saw very little of him at all. He returned from the country with a look that none of them had ever seen on his face before, not even those able to remember that terrible time years ago. Outwardly his manners had not changed, but his orders were brusque, and he seemed unconscious, most of the time, that there was anyone else in the room.

His servants drew their own conclusions, and two of his more privileged employees even dared to broach the subject, only to regret it. Mr. James's groom had his head bitten off for his pains, and even Mr. Shelby, when he asked him hesitantly one morning if something were wrong, could not help but feel that he had been snubbed and did not dare to bring the subject up again.

Lady Barbeaux, the Nonpareil's sister, was not so circumspect, or so easily snubbed. It was she who had been inveigled into nursing Derry, and though she had accepted the charge resignedly, if not willingly, given all her other responsibilities and a daughter's come-out to oversee, she certainly felt it entitled her to certain information, and did not hesitate to tell him so.

The Nonpareil had stopped by briefly to confer with his brother-in-law. He looked weary and out of sorts, which his loving sister also did not hesitate to point out to him, adding "And if you think you can foist a boy with a bullet wound on me and then disappear for days at a time, you are mistaken!"

"My dear," objected her husband mildly, filling his pipe, "we all have reason to be grateful to Locke. He has wasted neither time nor expense in an effort to track down those two villains. I myself believe them already escaped abroad, but we—er—naturally wish to take no chances."

Her ladyship did not wish to be distracted with facts. "He might at least spare a few minutes to reassure that absurd boy upstairs. He is convinced he has betrayed his country and you, and I am having trouble in determining which is worse in his mind, poor boy. It wouldn't hurt you to be kind to him."

"That poor boy upstairs," said the Nonpareil, "is to blame for allowing two traitors to escape."

"Oh, well! Have you ever discovered which one of them shot him?" asked Lady Barbeaux curiously.

"He claims it was an accident. I must presume he is still protecting his friend Kingsley. If you are in such sympathy with him, you might make an attempt to drag the truth from him."

"I will leave it to you men to play at intrigue," retorted his sister. "I must confess I am more concerned with a young and frightened boy. You thrust him on me, so now you must pay the consequences. In fact, I am beginning to suspect it is more your pride than your patriotism that has been pricked! They tried to interfere with your horse, and that is what you cannot forgive, if you ask me!"

"My dear," said her husband more sternly than he was wont, "you may quarrel with your brother as much as you want, but I cannot stand by and see you being unfair. Keep in mind that these men tried to ruin the young man you are so concerned with, and incidentally, to sell military secrets abroad at the same time."

"Oh, well!" she said with slightly less assurance. "I'm sure I didn't mean—and at any rate, however villainous they may be, I can't imagine why it should be Locke's responsibility to track them down!"

"It is my responsibility," said her brother evenly, "because it was I who allowed the thing to proceed, instead of putting a stop to it from the beginning. Ultimately, it is my fault that that young fool up there has a bullet in him, as his sister was not slow to point out. Nor, unlike Adrian, can I be so certain they have left the country. One of them already made an attempt to abduct Miss Ainsley. However selfish I may be, I have not quite reached the point of valuing my horses over humans, nor have I any desire to have that laid at my door as well!"

Lady Barbeaux stared at him for a moment, her mouth

slightly ajar. She had already heard from her mother of Miss Ainsley's visit, and though it had rather surprised her, the rest of her mother's highly interesting disclosures she had largely dismissed. Now she was shaken by a dreadful doubt, and searched his face more closely, the argument forgotten.

What she saw there made her heart twist in her breast, and made her suddenly curse herself for a fool. "Oh, oh—the devil!" she cried, blinking back sudden foolish tears. "If it means that much to you, why don't you marry the chit and be done with it?"

He stiffened visibly, and she had never seen him look quite like that, not even when Caroline had died. "However difficult it may be for you to believe this, Lizzie—I will confess it came as something of a blow to my own evidently exaggerated self-conceit—Miss Ainsley has made it clear that not even my rank and wealth could persuade her to have me. I had not known I had grown quite so insufferable until that moment. It was a salutary lesson for me, believe me!"

"Locke—oh, you *fool*!" cried his loving sister, searching for her handkerchief. "I cannot imagine what she said to give you that impression, but Mama, at least, is convinced the child is head over ears in love with you, and she's seldom wrong! She wrote me that you had quarreled, which I found hard to believe, but that she seemed to think it would be the making of you, but I had no notion—oh, Locke, are you *sure*? Her age—her background . . . ?"

But he had already gone, looking, she grumbled to her husband, as if he were half his age, and not set on ruining himself.

"And now I suppose I shall have to learn to love her!" she wailed. "And after all the *paragons* I've thrown in his way year after year!"

Sir Adrian patted her shoulder fondly. "Has it never occurred to you, my love, that he has never displayed more than the mildest interest in all those paragons you've been throwing in his way year after year?"

"But you can't deny he has shown more than a mild interest in Antonia Burke!" retorted his wife, fast recovering. "The whole world expected them to make a match of it. I can't think what he's thinking of to reject Tony for—for—oh, I can't bear even to think of it!" she wailed. "And how am I ever to face Tony again?"

"You had better bring yourself to think of it, unless you do wish to be estranged from your brother." He completely surprised her by adding thoughtfully, "As for Tony Burke, I have never been particularly in favor of that match, and nor has your mother, unless I'm completely mistaken."

She stared at him. "Good God, you never said anything! You know I had considered it a settled thing! And as for mother—she hasn't been to London in years! What does she know?"

"I have always considered your mother a particularly shrewd woman," said her husband of more than twenty years. "I fear I, too, must leave you, my love. I have an appointment with the Home Secretary in half an hour."

Lady Barbeaux blanched as a new thought struck her. "Oh, no. What on earth am I going to tell that absurd boy upstairs?"

After that unusual beginning, Phila found herself more at ease with her hostess than she had expected. Lady Annis, as she had said, was an indifferent hostess, leaving her guests to their own devices for most of the time, and only emerging from her rooms when her muse had deserted her. Sometimes she did not even appear for dinner, so that it must be supposed her particular muse was serving her once more. She was kind to Phila in her offhanded way, and her irregular household made it far easier than Phila had feared not to feel too much out of place.

Lord Beaverton, the Miles Phila had heard them mention, was even kinder. He was a distinguished older gentleman, as formal as his hostess was unconventional, and he took it upon himself to occupy Phila's time, strolling with her through the gardens, or taking her for gentle drives in the countryside. Phila gathered that his friendship with his hostess was long-standing, and she had not been there many days before she suspected it was much more than mere friendship, at least on Lord Beaverton's part. What Lady Annis's feelings on the subject were it was impossible to tell, but perhaps they had decided that their life-styles were so disparate a marriage between them would have been impossible. At any rate, it was obvious that Lord Beaverton was a frequent visitor, and was looked upon with such familiarity by her ladyship's staff that they frequently went to him instead of her ladyship with their problems. And since he would give them sensible answers instead of listening with only half an ear or refusing outright to be bothered at such a moment, as her ladyship was inclined to do, Phila soon saw their point.

Phila herself soon drifted into something like a routine there. The housekeeper, seeing that she was willing, and at something of a loss, allowed her to cut and arrange the flowers for most of the rooms in the mornings, and in the afternoons she would walk or drive with Lord Beaverton, who told her her presence had rescued him from excruciating boredom. That made her laugh, but she suspected it was true, for their fellow guests were far from conventional. Her ladyship's publisher had left the day after Phila arrived, and the bad writer and the advanced-thinking philosopher were far too engrossed in themselves to make very good company.

When Phila forgot herself and said as much to Lord Beaverton, it made *him* laugh a good deal, but he agreed with her. "Unfortunately, they both have all the temperament of an artist with none of the talent. You can see now why I am grateful for your presence, my dear. I hope you mean to take pity on me after dinner and give me another game of whist. Otherwise I fear I shall be drawn into another discussion of the rival merits of Eastern over Western philosophies. I hope I am not a Philistine, but at this time of my life I find I don't really care which is the oldest or the most likely to survive."

Phila laughed again and willingly enjoyed another lesson after dinner. He was teaching her whist and she had proved such an apt pupil that she occasionally even won large, if imaginary, sums from him. One evening Phila grew so excited at her string of luck, and Lord Beaverton so amused in watching her, that Lady Annis at last came down to see what all the animation was about. In the end she too stayed to coach Phila, so that by the end of the evening Phila had won a paper fortune from him.

Lady Annis laughed and rose. "You had best play him for something more tangible in future, my dear. Miles is lucky you are so easily satisfied."

Phila, still a little flushed from her winnings, said truthfully, "Oh, no, for then I wouldn't enjoy it nearly so much. This way I get all the excitement of winning with none of the fear of losing. I don't think I should enjoy gambling for real money nearly so much.''

This naive statement made her ladyship laugh again, but she soon returned to her work and Phila went upstairs to bed. But the next evening Lord Beaverton presented her with a pretty gold locket on a chain.

She blushed and tried to refuse it, fearing that he had misunderstood last night, but he insisted. "Nonsense! This has nothing to do with last night—although I am lucky to get off so easily. It is because you are a charming young lady who has taken the trouble to be kind to an old man. I could even embarrass you more by saying that if I had ever had a daughter, I would have wished her to have been just like you, but I won't. But I hope I am not so old I may not still buy a pretty girl a trinket now and again.''

So Phila allowed herself to be persuaded to accept it, and the days passed. She had received one letter from Priddy that came with her trunk the day after she arrived. In it she said that Lydia was being a perfect *worm* and lording it over all of them. Now that she was safely married, she had evidently decided to be gracious, for she was already talking of Letty's coming to live with her once they had found a house. Letty said what she meant of course was to have someone to fetch and carry for her, but it certainly wouldn't be her. She had no time for more, for the man was coming for the trunk any minute. Mama sent her love, and wondered if Phila remembered what had been done with the key to the storeroom, which had been unaccountably mislaid.

Phila wrote immediately to tell her, already feeling as if her life with the Coateses had been a very long time ago. Letty wrote back, thanking her, and adding that they were thinking of returning to Somerset soon. Aunt Chloe seemed to be satisfied, now that she had met Mr. Bevis, and there seemed little point in remaining in London. As for the other business, she hoped they were all not in too much disgrace, since she understood from Mr. Naseby that both suspects had managed to escape.

Neither Priddy nor Letty mentioned Phila's return. However unexpectedly pleasant her stay with Lady Annis might be, it was difficult not to feel as if she had been abandoned by everyone who mattered to her. She assumed that if Derry were seriously ill or in danger for his life that they must have contacted her, but other than that she did not even know how badly Derry had been wounded or where.

As for that last quarrel with Mr. James, it was still best not to think about it. She was unable, as his mother was, to be glad he had so far forgotten himself as to be unkind to her. As for the things she had said in return, well, she must just hope that they need not meet again. In fact, it was time she began being responsible for her own future, instead of relying on her brother or the Coateses, or Lady Annis, or even Mr. James. Lady Annis had made it clear that she might stay as long as she liked, but that was merely a temporary solution. As for her brother, she had long since decided that she must no longer stand in the way of his ambitions. If it were still possible, after all this, he must have his commission, and he must not have the weight of his younger sister's future on his conscience. She might return to the Coateses, though they did not seem overeager to have her returned to them. Or better yet, she might find employment somewhere. Lady Annis might be able to help her, and she at least would know herself no longer a burden on anyone. Under the circumstances, she had no reason to hope for anything more.

Then, a little more than a week after she had arrived, she received a message from her brother that knocked all such sensible planning out of her head.

33

Phila had been strolling in her ladyship's magnificent rose garden with Lord Beaverton when he was summoned to settle a domestic emergency. Lady Annis had locked herself in her rooms with strict orders not to be disturbed, and since she was giving a dinner party that evening for several of her neighbors, and the boy sent into the village had just returned with the distressing news that the delivery wagon had broken down and there was no fresh fish to be had, not anywhere between there and Chatham, the housekeeper requested instant advice, if his lordship would be so kind as to spare her a few minutes.

This was indeed an emergency, for Phila herself had spent all morning arranging the flowers for that evening, and knew that Lady Annis, though she claimed to be dreading the ordeal of entertaining a number of her more conventional, and frequently slightly scandalized neighbors, made it a point of remaining on good terms with the neighborhood. Lord Beaverton looked rueful. "Good God! What am I suppose to do, do you imagine, short of scouring the vicinity for fresh fish? Obviously, I had better go, however. I confess I wouldn't put it past our mutual hostess to have locked herself up just in case of such an emergency. Will you be all right here for a few minutes, or will you come back with me?"

Phila smiled and shook her head, promising to wait there for him. She had a slight headache from her hours indoors that morning, but perhaps more accurately she was suffering from a renewed attack of depression, never wholly absent however she tried to fight it. She had been in Kent nearly ten days, and had received no word from Derry, or an answer to her reply to either of her cousins. She did not expect to hear from Mr. James, but he might at least have written to tell her how her brother was, or what was happening.

She continued rather absently to stroll among the roses, though she was in little mood to enjoy them. The rose garden was out of sight of the house, but she was in truth not sorry to be left on her own for a little while, freed of the necessity of maintaining cheerful conversation.

Lord Beaverton had been gone only a very few minutes when a strange lad approached her and handed her a folded and rather grubby piece of paper.

She was surpised, and opened it quickly. Then, since she recognized the handwriting she looked up again, her eyes suddenly wide. "Where did you get this?" she demanded. "Who are you? You're not one of her ladyship's servants, are you?"

He was a sturdy, rather sullen lad, and had all the earmarks of living on one of the nearby farms. "No'm," he said, shuffling his feet and fingering his hat in an agony of shyness. "Man in the village give me a sow's baby to bring that to you and wait for an answer."

"A sow's baby? Oh, never mind! What man? What did he look like?"

He scratched his head, as if thrown by her question. "I dunno," he said at last. "A gem'man. Sort o' pale-like, with light hair. Said if I was to bring ma's trap, and bring you back with me, he'd give me another."

But Phila was already reading her brother's note. It was undated, and looked as if it had been written in some haste—or else by someone still very weak—for the pen had needed mending, and it began abruptly, with no other salutation than,

> Phila—
> Don't worry, I'm all right. I'm only writing to you because there's something I must do and it may be dangerous. I don't expect it to be, and anyway, I can take care of myself, but I just wanted you to know in case—well, just in case! At any rate, James is sure to be angry, so I wanted to warn you.
> I know you trusted him—James, I mean. Only I'm less and less convinced he cares for anything besides his own precious name. He cares more that Drumm tried to interfere with his entry in the Derby than that he tried to steal military secrets, and as for the rest—well, I didn't mean to go into all of this now, only that if he believes me so easily duped he'll soon discover his mistake!

On the second sheet his pen had deteriorated even further, so that Phila could scarcely read it.

> At any rate, I didn't mean to go into all that now, as I said. I can explain it all when I see you. I'm staying in the village, as the boy may have told you. He'll bring you to me if you can manage to slip away without anyone seeing you. I'd just as soon James not know what I'm up to since he'll try to stop me. I—well, I'm sorry to involve you, but I may need your help, and it's important that we stick together, now more than ever.
>
> > Derry

Phila at last looked up from the letter, very pale. She did not dare to speculate what this meant, except that Derry was bent on doing something foolish. Surely he could not mean to go after Drumm and Kingsley himself—or still believe Kingsley might not be as black as he was painted. He had been wounded once already.

"Oh, please!" she said desperately. "Take me to my— take me to the man who sent you."

Back at the house Lord Beaverton, returning from his errand, ran unexpectedly into a rather incongruous figure posing as a gardener.

"Eh, where's the lass?" he demanded sharply. "I thought she was with you?"

His lordship bore this unusual questioning in remarkably good part. "Yes, she was, but I was called unexpectedly into the house—" He broke off somewhat guiltily as he remembered, but Mr. Japes had already left him, heading off in a long lope toward the rose garden. After a moment Lord Beaverton followed, half concerned and half annoyed. "It's only been a few minutes, ten at the most! Good God, man. . ."

He might have spared his breath for all the notice Japes took of him. By the time his lordship reached the garden, long after the other, he was huffing a little, and said more testily than was his wont, "I tell you it's only been a few minutes! I daresay I shouldn't have left her, but . . ."

The garden was slightly sunken, and the whole of it was visible from where they stood. There was no sign of Phila, and he broke off once more. "I'm sure she merely got tired of waiting and went in. It is awfully hot, you know."

"Not in the last ten minutes, she didn't!" growled Mr. Japes, scarcely bothering to be respectful. "Done to a cow's turn again!" He was rapidly scanning the countryside even as he spoke, and then took off in that same deceptively slow, long lope that effectively ate up a great deal of territory, throwing over his shoulder, "Go up to the house and set a party to lookin' for her, but you won't find her! I ort to hang up me stampers and drink catlap afore the fire, is what I ort, to be so slumguzzled twicet! And if Mr. James don't have me head for *this* one, that's about all the use it'll be to me."

Poor Lord Beaverton stood staring after him for a moment, before turning and hurrying back to the house, still uncertain whether to be alarmed or annoyed.

*   *   *

Phila, scarcely able to control her impatience to reach her brother, sat rigidly beside the youth in a dilapidated gig. They were heading toward the village, but somewhat to her surprise the youth turned off the main road before they reached it, onto something that was little more than a track, heavily rutted and overgrown.

"Where are you taking me? Isn't my brother staying at the inn?" she asked anxiously.

The youth shrugged. "He said I was to bring you to ole Foncet's farm. Ain't nobody lived there for years, not since ole Foncet died." He obviously disavowed any responsibility for the vagaries of townfolk.

The idea of Derry's sleeping in an abandoned farmhouse instead of the nearby inn alarmed Phila even more, for it argued either a complete lack of money or the need to hide. She made no more objection, wishing that the gig would make faster progress over the wretched road. As it was, her teeth were nearly shaken out of her head before she at last glimpsed a shabby farmhouse, its chimney fallen and ivy overtaking its walls, so that it was scarcely visible any longer in the surrounding countryside.

The gig had not come to a complete halt before she was out of it, hurrying toward the farmhouse. At least most of the doors and windows were still intact, the door left standing wide to catch any hint of a breeze stirring on that hot afternoon. She noticed little else, except that the porch and doorway had been swept clean, and were thankfully free of cobwebs. She hurried in, her youthful escort already forgotten.

Once inside the door, she halted involuntarily, her eyes unaccustomed to the change from the brightness outside. "Derry?" she asked quickly, unable to see anyone in the gloom.

There was movement in one corner, and she was at last able to make out her brother's figure. He was bending over a sink, washing his hands, but at her voice he straightened quickly and turned.

She was so relieved to see him safe, and on his feet, instead of weak, or stretched out on a dirty mattress, as her vivid imagination had been picturing for some moments, that she started forward eagerly, her arms outstretched. "Oh, Derry!"

She found herself confronting Captain Kingsley, not her brother at all.

She halted, bewilderment mingling with an undeniable quiver of fear. "You—?" she managed. Then, "My brother! Where—what have you done with him?"

"Take it easy, Miss Ainsley," the captain said calmly, drying his hands on a towel. He was not in uniform, but he was as neatly dressed as if they had met in the city, and not in this dilapidated farmhouse. Certainly he did not look like the fugitive she knew him to be. "Your brother is perfectly safe."

She had backed a step or two before him. "Then w-where is he? Why did you trick me in this way?"

"I regret the necessity. The note *is* from your brother, Miss Ainsley. The only difference is that he is still too ill to come to you himself. He sent me to escort you to him."

She took another step backward. "I don't believe you! Where is my brother? What have you done with him?"

"Perhaps this will reassure you." He came toward her, but when she started backward in real alarm, held up his hands, then produced a folded piece of paper and held it out to her. "I am aware you have never liked me, Miss Ainsley," he said with his charming smile. "With some reason, I will confess. But your brother was right, you know. I was just as much Drumm's victim as he was meant to be."

She almost snatched the note from him and unfolded it quickly. It was once more in her brother's handwriting, with the same ill-mended pen.

Phila—

I'm sorry to have tricked you, but Jack will have explained the necessity by now. I was right all along about him. Drumm was blackmailing him as well—not that it seems to matter to anyone but me. James cares nothing if an innocent man is ruined, so long as he can get the goods on Drumm. He cares very little if I am, come to that, as I've discovered. In fact, I've discovered a great many things to the great man's discredit, but there's no point in going into all that now.

At any rate, it seems clear there's no future in the military for me now, after this scandal. Jack and I have made up our minds to go abroad as soon as possible. You can come with us if you want, for I'd just as soon break all ties with England, considering everything. But either way, I'd like to see you before we go. Jack will bring you to me. I'm sorry to involve you in all this, Phila, but there's no other way.

Derry

Phila continued to stare a little blindly at the letter long after she had finished reading it. She didn't want to believe it, especially the parts about Mr. James, but it sounded like Derry. Everything he said was consistent with what she herself had discovered, even with what the Nonpareil's mother herself had said about her son. He had not hesitated to remove her when she proved troublesome, and certainly he had reason enough to be angry with her brother as well.

She looked up then to see that Captain Kingsley was watching her with something very like sympathy in his eyes. "I'm sorry, Miss Ainsley. I was never the enemy you thought me, you know."

"How—how is my brother?" she managed stiffly.

He shrugged. "Not very well, I'm afraid. He shouldn't be traveling so soon, which is why I insisted he at least let me come for you. But he's right, I'm afraid. If your brother doesn't actually face arrest, as I do, he knows there's no future for him in the military now."

It was true, of course. She had been blind not to see it before. "Who was it shot my brother? No one ever told me."

"Drumm did, of course. Somehow he found out about our meeting. In fact, I wouldn't put it past James to have told him in order to trap him." He sounded bitter.

Phila felt physically ill, her headache returning to pound so painfully it was impossible to think. Nothing she had learned today should have surprised her. She had already known Mr. James had deliberately used her brother to bait his trap with little concern for his safety. And those dreadful things he had said to her. But then he himself had told her he had no heart.

She was aware that her first concern should be for Derry, but at the moment she seemed only able to think of herself. Once she would not have hesitated to go with Derry, but now a lifetime of exile abroad seemed unreal and frightening to her. How could he expect her to make such a decision now? Lady Annis would be worried. Even now Lord Beaverton might be looking for her. She was surprised to discover, now that she faced losing it, how much she had come to feel at home there, in so short a time.

That should not matter, of course, especially if everything her brother and Captain Kingsley said was true. But the thought of divorcing herself from everything she had ever known was far worse than any nightmare, even the pain of discovering Mr. James's betrayal. She could not explain it, even to herself, for she had clung to Derry before, dreading the day that he might be taken from her. Now that he needed her, she shrank from committing herself. She still loved him, of course, but somehow, without her knowing it, he had ceased to be the center of her universe any longer. She was even conscious of a faint irritation that he could place her in such a position.

But Captain Kingsley was waiting. She must make her decision. She looked again at his too-handsome face, and it was suddenly as if the painful fog in her head cleared a little. "No!" she said too violently. "I'm sorry you have had a wasted journey, but I can't go with you. Derry should never have asked! I can't just disappear—I should not have come now without letting someone know where I was going."

"And what am I to tell your brother, Miss Ainsley?" he inquired rather unkindly. "That you're enjoying yourself too much with your noble acquaintances to have any thought to spare for him?"

The fog seemed to clear a little more, so that she saw him as clearly as she had done before. She had always thought him too charming, and had never trusted him.

Her eyes grew huge as she realized the truth at last. "My brother didn't send you, did he?" she whispered. "He didn't write those letters. It was all a lie, wasn't it?"

"Bravo, my dear!" remarked a well-known voice directly behind her. "I should have known I might rely upon your good sense to see through him."

She whirled around with a little sob, unable to believe the Nonpareil was really there when she most needed him.

But her movement was never completed. Her arm was grabbed from behind, and she was jerked cruelly backward against Captain Kingsley's tall form. An arm was tight across her ribs, bruising her, uncaring how he hurt her, and she was held, helpless as a rag doll, her feet barely reaching the floor while something sickeningly cold and hard was pressed against her temple.

For a moment frozen out of time, the tableau spread before her. A Mr. James she had never seen before, looking grim-faced but determined, a leveled pistol in his own hand, standing in the doorway; another gentleman she half-remembered from that night in Derry's lodgings straddling the open window, looking frustrated, a pistol of his own wavering.

She felt vaguely foolish, for such drama did not happen to people like her. Except she knew instinctively that this was no dream, not even a nightmare, and that Captain Kingsley was extremely desperate, and would not hesitate to use the pistol whose barrel was pressed bruisingly against her temple.

"Let me get a shot at 'im!" begged the burly man in the window. "I know I can drop 'im."

"No!" said the Nonpareil sharply, his eyes never leaving their awkward figures. "It's too dangerous."

Behind her Phila felt Captain Kingsley laugh. "That's wise of you, James. I've a score to settle with this little bitch, and I'd as soon do it now as later. Drop those pistols, both of you!" All charm had disappeared from his voice.

"You'll never get away with it," said James calmly. "Let her go."

For answer Kingsley laughed again, and jabbed the muzzle ruthlessly against her soft skin. "Not a chance. She's going to see me safely out of England. Why do you think I bothered to come back for her? Unlike you and Drumm, my taste has never run to scared little virgins, especially when they've cost me as much as this one has. But you never know! I might discover her charm by the time our journey's over."

"Let her go," repeated the Nonpareil steadily. "If you do, I'll see you safely out of the country myself."

"You certainly will, if you expect to see her again. Does her brother know what you plan for her, by the way? But then, if he's wise he has little enough reason to complain. You have the reputation of being generous to your discarded mistresses, after all. A little complacency now could earn him far more than he can expect from a more permanent union."

Mr. Japes growled in his throat and started to haul his other leg over the sill, but was halted by Mr. James's snapped command. "Be still, you fool!"

Neither had as yet dropped their pistols, and Phila could feel the indecision in the room, and the tension. But at the moment none of it seemed real, for she was staring at the Nonpareil with new eyes after Kingsley's words.

She was allowed very little time in which to contemplate the possible truth of his statements, for the captain abruptly tightened his grip on her. "I'd advise you to listen to him," he said. "In fact, I'd advise neither of you to make any sudden moves, for I can hardly miss at this range. Now throw down those pistols, like I said, and get away from that door."

Phila saw the Nonpareil and Mr. Japes exchange glances, and knew that they had no choice but to obey. She acted instinctively, without thought to the danger, only knowing that Kingsley must not get away, and that anything was preferable to being forced to go with him.

She gave a low moan and made herself go completely limp in the captain's grip.

His arm tightened, and he made a desperate attempt to haul her up, but he had been distracted for a vital few seconds as he found himself with a sudden dead weight in his arms. Phila heard two deafening explosions almost simultaneously from opposite corners of the room, and then, almost as an afterthought, a thunderclap that seemed to fill her head with light and noise.

She seemed to be falling, weightless, through space. She felt no pain, it was as if she were watching her own body falling, tumbling, down and down and down into a great, bottomless blackness. She was grateful for the blackness against the searing light and noise.

When she struggled back to consciousness, she was still aware of no pain, only a curious lightheadedness, as if none of this were happening to her. She was partially lying on something extremely hard, but her head and shoulders were cradled in someone's arms, and it was that she thought was the cause of her sense of well-being.

When she lifted up her heavy eyelids, it was the Nonpareil who held her, as she had somehow known. She floated up an oddly weightless hand to disinterestedly touch the white cloth binding her brow. "Am I dead?" she inquired almost dreamily.

The Nonpareil's face cleared slightly. "By some miracle,

no. You foolish, brave child, whatever possessed you to take such a risk?''

"I couldn't go away with him," she answered as if that explained everything. "Is he dead?"

He hesitated, but only for a moment. "Yes, he's dead." His voice had hardened.

"I can't be sorry," she said, still dreamily. "I think now it was him all along who was most responsible, not Mr. Drumm."

"You're right, but then I have always known you to be wise beyond your years. At any rate, he need concern us no longer."

She felt so unlike herself that she had to ask. "Am I going to die?"

This time he smiled, and she thought she had never seen a more wonderful sight. "No, my poor darling. It's no more than a scratch, though I don't ever want to relive those few seconds before I reached you. But you've lost a little blood and are no doubt feeling lightheaded, aside from having a stupendous ringing in your ears. If you're up to it, I'll take you home now. No, don't try to move. I'm quite capable of carrying you."

He did so, and she made no protest, enjoying the feeling of being lifted high and weightless, and held safe in his arms. He had called her his darling, but very likely it meant nothing. There was something else she ought to remember, though, something that had been said earlier. But it was too much of an effort now to think of anything. She snuggled her cheek against his strong shoulder and surrendered once again to that comforting blackness.

35

When Phila next woke, it was to find herself in her own bed at Lady Annis's, and Priddy sitting in a hard chair beside her.

She blinked, thinking she must surely be dreaming. But when she opened her eyes again, Priddy was still there, looking unnaturally subdued.

"Oh, Priddy!" Phila said weakly. "I thought I must be dreaming. Oh, how glad I am to see you!"

Priddy rose quickly to hover over the bed, looking very unlike her usual contained self. "That's nothing to how glad we all were to see you," she said gruffly. "How are you feeling?"

"I don't know. My head aches, and it feels as if church bells were pealing all inside of it, but I think I'm all right."

Priddy looked relieved. "Mr. James said to expect that. It's from the pistol going off so close to your head," she explained, and shuddered a little. "I thought you must be dead when he brought you in, you looked so pale and limp. And there was blood everywhere!"

"Yes, but Priddy, what are you doing here?" persisted Phila weakly. "Is everything all right at home?"

"Yes, of course. Papa brought me." She grinned suddenly, looking more herself. "Though I'm afraid we arrived at a very awkward moment. You were missing and nobody seemed to know where you had gone. Lady Annis—you should have seen Papa's face, by the way, when he realized she was the mama of the Mr. James he had heard so much about! I like her!—insisted that you had merely gone off for a walk somewhere, but the other gentleman, Lord Beaverton, I think his name was, seemed more and more worried. Luckily, before Papa could decide that we had stumbled into Bedlam, Mr. James himself arrived, unexpectedly. It was easy to see that he was worried too, for he scarcely bothered to be polite. Then, before he and Papa could come to actual blows, or before poor Lord Beaverton could look any more guilty, *another* man came running in, all covered with dust, and said that you had been kidnapped. He seemed surprised and guilty to see Mr. James, too, but as soon as he recovered from the shock he almost fell on him in gratitude.

"After that, there was nothing but confusion. Papa was very red in the face by then—you know how he gets—and kept demanding to be told what the devil was going on. Mr. James was busy questioning the new man, and didn't appear even to hear him. Lady Annis was trying to calm everyone, without much success. It was just like a comedy, only we were all too scared to notice."

"Oh, Priddy!" said Phila in some awe. "Oh, I never meant to cause so much trouble!"

"You may not have meant to, but you certainly managed to," said Job's comforter, finally beginning to be able to see the humor in the situation. "Finally, Mr. James interrupted everyone by saying that the man knew where you were, and that he had every intention of bringing you back safely. Everyone began asking questions then, but he said there was no time, and he would explain everything later. That shut everyone up, of course, even Papa, though after they had gone, he began to fret that he should have gone with them. Lady Annis told him that he needn't worry; if anyone could bring you back safely, her son could. Then she actually smiled, and said that when her son could look like that, everything had to be all right, which only made Papa more convinced than ever that we had stumbled into a madhouse.

"After that, Papa paced the room, and Lord Beaverton tried to pretend to read a newspaper, though he too kept jumping at every sound. Only Lady Annis seemed calm, and read a book as if as convinced as she'd said that everything must be all right. It seemed forever before we really did hear the sound of a vehicle arriving, and then it was only to find you apparently dead in Mr. James's arms. He wouldn't stop, but carried you straight into the house and upstairs, saying only that it wasn't as bad as it looked, but to send for the doctor straightaway. Believe me, you were lucky you were unconscious. It was awful!"

"Oh, Priddy," said Phila again, weakly. "I've been such a fool! But I still don't understand what you're doing here. You're sure there's nothing wrong?"

"Of course not, silly," said Priddy, almost back to normal now that she could see for herself Phila was all right. "Papa came to London to settle matters with Lydia himself, and to escort us home. Which reminds me, you should have seen Lydia when she realized what he meant to do! At least I must admit her new husband behaved better than I expected him to. Even Papa said so." She shrugged her thin shoulders. "I still don't like it, but I don't care so much anymore, so long as Mama's not made unhappy. I don't doubt she'll end up proud of Lydia after all, especially when the grandchildren start arriving. But the important thing is that Papa wasn't at all happy about Mama's letting you go off like that. So after he took Mama and Letty home, he and I came here to get you."

Phila discovered she had to blink back sudden, weak tears. "I'd begun to think you had forgotten me, all of you," she admitted foolishly.

Priddy came close to gaping at her. "Forgotten you, when Mama wonders constantly how we ever got along without you before you came? If you want the truth, I think she misses you far more than Lydia. *I* certainly have. Even Letty says she never realized how much a part of the family you'd become. She's improved, by the way. She was never as bad as Lydia, of course, but—well, I guess the truth is, we've all become more of a family somehow, lately. And that's because of you. None of us cared anything for anyone else before you came."

"And I never knew how much you all meant to me until I left! But what's happening now? Downstairs, I mean?"

"Well, Papa's agreed to stay, at least until you're well enough to travel. Mr. James finally explained everything, after the doctor had been and said that you had suffered no more than a slight concussion. Papa was exceedingly shocked, and kept repeating 'Bless my soul!' He couldn't believe so much had been going on right under Mama's nose. He seemed to have a little trouble seeing you in the role of a heroine, too. I'm a little surprised myself," ended Priddy dryly. "You always seem to let everybody walk all over you."

For answer, Phila almost shuddered. "Oh, don't! I'm not a heroine, and I can hardly bear to talk about it. I didn't do anything except make foolish blunders and involve people who shouldn't have been involved. I hope I never, *ever* have any more excitement for as long as I live!"

Priddy grinned, but she recognized that this was probably delayed reaction to all that had happened that day, and belatedly remembered the existence of the medicine left by the doctor for when Phila awoke. She briskly administered it, saying pessimistically as she did so, "This is probably horrid! But the doctor said it would help your headache. I almost forgot to give it to you."

That made Phila laugh weakly, spilling some of the medicine on the bedclothes. But she obediently sipped at the bitter brew, wondering what was wrong with her that she should suddenly feel so dejected. Derry was safe, the plot had been prevented, even the Coateses had made it more than clear that they still wanted her. A short while ago she could have asked for nothing more. It was absurd that she should now feel so empty, as if none of it touched her anymore.

She moved her head restlessly on the pillow, trying to ease its aching, and Priddy, worried that she had overtired her patient, grew quiet, urging her to go back to sleep. Phila did not think she would be able to sleep, her head ached so, but Priddy's vile-tasting medicine must have been stronger than she had expected, for she dozed off and on the rest of the evening, vaguely aware when Lady James came to check on her, and when a tray for her supper arrived and was sent back to the kitchens untouched. Priddy remained with her, flatly refusing to allow anyone else to sit with the patient, and in the end Lady James consented and quietly had a trundle bed made up in the corner of the room for her.

Once Phila roused sufficiently to realize it must be very late, for all was quiet. A lantern had been left burning softly in the room, shuttered so that it would not shine in her eyes. When she saw Priddy, soundly asleep on the trundle bed, she smiled softly to herself and closed her eyes once more.

Whether because of the medicine, or merely due to her long sleep, by the morning she was feeling much more human, and was even able to consume some tea and toast for her breakfast. Priddy had just kindly restored some order to Phila's tumbled curls under the ridiculous bandage when there was a tap on the door.

Priddy put down her brush and went to open it, to reveal the Nonpareil standing outside, looking exactly as if he had just been strolling on Bond Street, and had not confronted a desperate spy with a pistol only the day before.

Phila blushed hotly. Priddy took one look at her and mumbled some excuse before slipping out the door, cravenly abandoning Phila.

The Nonpareil, as if unaware of the havoc he was causing, came to stand beside Phila's bed and look down at her. Since yesterday she had been longing to see him, but now that he was here she was absurdly shy. To her immense gratitude, however, he behaved normally, giving her time to recover.

"How are you feeling?" he asked gravely. "I'm glad to say you are looking a great deal better than when last I saw you."

She blushed again and put a hand up to the bandage adorning her curls. "I'm sure I look ridiculous. But thank you. I feel much better."

"So my mother reported. And you look—enchanting," he responded disconcertingly, and took Priddy's chair beside the bed.

Phila found she didn't know where to look. "I haven't thanked you yet for rescuing me once again," she said a little desperately.

"My role was very minor, I'm afraid. You were the real heroine of the piece."

He was being kind, but the memory of their last dreadful meeting stood between them. "No, for I should never have gone!" she blurted. "I never meant to cause so much trouble."

"You are mistaken," he corrected rather grimly. "Mine is the fault, not yours. I appear to have underestimated Kingsley, with near disastrous results." Abruptly his voice softened. "Don't look like that, my dear. Given your devotion to your brother, no one can blame you for responding to a note purportedly from him. It was, by the way, a clever piece of forgery. The first page was almost certainly written by your brother, I suspect on the night he was wounded. Kingsley merely added to it to play on your love and concern for your brother. He hoped to gain your cooperation voluntarily, since it would have made his escape a great deal easier."

She shivered, despite herself. "He nearly did," she whispered. "I can't be sorry he's dead. He was a terrible man."

"He was indeed," he said levelly. "Unfortunately, I won't soon forgive my own part in yesterday's affair. I strongly suspected an attempt would be made on you by one or the other of them, but I mistakenly flattered myself that you would be safe here."

But Phila had suddenly lost all interest in yesterday. "You—suspected I might be in danger?" she managed through suddenly stiff lips. "Is that why you brought me here?"

"Yes, of course. Keep in mind Drumm had already made one attempt against you. There was a chance they would not find you here, and if they did, I assured myself that the presence of my own man set to guard you, in addition to

Miles and any number of servants about the place, should have prevented your being hurt and terrified and my losing several years off my life from fright when I arrived to find you missing." Abruptly, he frowned. "Why did you imagine I had brought you here?"

"I thought—to punish me," Phila admitted in distress.

There was a little silence. "I deserve that, I suppose," he said at last. "I am aware that from the first I have appeared to you in the guise of a stern uncle."

"Not at first! It was only later—when I thought that you had come to despise me."

"Never that. I could never—despise you," he said, somewhat unsteadily for him.

But she was beyond hearing the odd note in his voice. "No, it was all true! Everything you said to me was true!" she cried bitterly. "I have behaved thoughtlessly—stupidly— even yesterday was all my fault, and I deserved far worse than I got! Only I never, *never* meant to involve other people, or make them worry. You must believe that."

Somehow she was in his arms, her aching head cradled against his coat front. "No, my sweet Phila, nothing that I said on that never-sufficiently-to-be-regretted day was true. I cannot excuse myself, except that I was operating under all the handicaps of a man seeing his whole life threatened, everything he had long since believed settled slipping away. You had succeeded in turning my world upside down, and I was struggling against it, convinced I was unable to change, or to tumble headlong into love, after all these years. And then, when you ripped up at me in that way, I was convinced I had lost you."

"Lost me?" cried Phila. "And I was convinced I had completely disgusted you by my behavior!"

His arms tightened. "My poor sweet darling, I am trying to remember that you are in no shape for this yet. But—are you sure? I have not your loving heart, I'm afraid. But I will try to be worthy of you, if you can find it in you to give me even some small part of your extraordinary capacity for love and loyalty. I find I am very poor without it."

"Yes, oh yes!" she cried passionately, flinging her arms about his neck. "You have had all my heart for so long I don't even know when it began."

"I think I began to realize that at last," he said unsteadily, "when you refused to go to your brother yesterday."

"And I thought you meant to marry Lady Antonia Burke."

"No, my darling. I might have been induced to one day, if you had not come along to show me how wrong that would have been. I needed you to turn my life upside down, and bring me to life again."

For answer she turned up her face fearlessly to his, ardently inviting his kiss.

He resisted only for a moment, trying to remember her weakened state. But it was clear Phila had forgotten it. She might be inexperienced, but she threw herself into this new experience with all the wholeheartedness she did everything else, and both were breathless when he at last remembered his conscience.

"My poor darling. I should not—!"

"Yes you should, for I have dreamed of what it would be like," said Phila. "Only I couldn't have dreamed anything like this."

He laughed, but could not resist kissing her again, a little roughly, forgetting both her inexperience and her invalid state. She returned the embrace with equal violence, making no objection to being roughly dragged onto his lap, or having her face covered with kisses.

When the storm had abated somewhat, and she sat once more in his lap, her slightly tear-wet cheek against the lapel of his coat and her curls tickling his chin, she said dreamily, "I still can't believe it. Are we to be married very soon? It will be so strange not to live with Aunt Chloe and Uncle Jos and my cousins."

"Yes, very soon! And I hope you will like it very much better. They are resigned to your loss, by the way. I had a long talk with your uncle last night, and I understand from Priddy that both your aunt and your cousin Letty have been expecting the news for some time now. My mother, incidentally, is very taken with young Priddy. She was impressed by her calm yesterday, and means to take her under her wing. Your aunt and uncle may be less prepared for that loss, especially since I am sure you will want to have her to stay frequently with us after we are married. But I hope they will consent to her visiting my mother now and then."

A new thought occurred to her, and made her pull partially out of his arms to turn an anxious face up to his. "Thank you! It is just what Priddy needs. I'll try not to plague you, but I can't bear to cut myself off completely from the Coateses!"

He dropped a swift kiss upon her curls. "I don't expect you to. Have them to visit as much as you like. Did you really believe me such a snob as to deny you your only relatives? I do draw the line at your cousin Lydia, however. I will not soon forgive her for her treatment of you."

"Poor Lydia," sighed Phila, resuming her former position. His hand came up to stroke her black curls and it felt so wonderful she closed her eyes. "I hope she won't be unhappy. And Derry. I had almost forgotten him. Is he really all right?"

The hand stopped for one moment, then resumed. "He is recovering rapidly, and developing a fast friendship with my oldest nephew. I think I first began to realize I was in danger of falling in love with you when I became aware that I was jealous of your extraordinary attachment to your brother."

She nursed his free hand to her cheek. "I don't know when I first realized I was in love with you, except that it was as if I had always known you, and every other man seemed to pale by comparison. Can Derry still have his regiment?"

"He not only can, I think the sooner he does so the better. I suspect that he is not going to be as amenable as your cousins to our marriage, and I *know* I will not rest easy knowing he is on the loose in London. A friend of mine is a major in the Light Bobs—*not* Kingsley's regiment, I hasten to add—and he has promised to keep an eye on your brother for us. Naturally we will have him to stay with us when he returns on leave, looking terribly dashing in his military whiskers."

She made no objection, and in fact, seemed almost asleep. He had almost concluded she was, when she surprised him by saying sleepily, "He will be so happy. But I had forgotten all about poor Letty. Do you suppose you could do something for Mr. Naseby as well? She is in love with him, but refuses to marry him so long as he allows his rich uncle to support him and won't help in his button factory. Perhaps if you could find him a position—what have I said that's so funny?"

He silenced her in the most effective way, his eyes alight with unholy love and laughter.

About the Author

Dawn Lindsey was born and grew up in Oklahoma, where her ancestors were early pioneers, so she came by her fascination with history naturally. After graduating from college she pursued several careers, the strangest and most interesting of which (aside from writing romance novels) was doing public relations for several zoos. She and her attorney husband now make their home in the San Francisco area.